Acknowledgements

In no particular order I would like to thank the following people: Ross Pirie, Paul Turner and Max Mc Nally, for reading the book and providing helpful feedback.

Freya Wilson for the painting seen on the front cover.

To my parents, for massively supporting this project through endless proof reading and enthusiasm!

To Magda, for being kind and laughing at the punchlines even when hearing them read aloud several nights in a row and convincing me it was worth publishing.

To Geri and all the characters in this book, for being interesting and amusing enough to bother writing about!

To my sister, Rowan, for chuckling so much when I told her the plot.

I'm sure I've forgotten other folk here but I relish all the company I keep, so please know you are appreciated! My friends all seek to support the democracy of creativity and the punk DT-DIY – dare to do it yourself - ethic, and I appreciate their support in various artistic projects regardless of one's level of talent!

Cheers, Andy

THE DOUBLE VISION OF GERI HAY

Introduction

'Listen to the hummingbird whose wings you cannot see, listen to the hummingbird, don't listen to me'

Leonard Cohen – Listen to the Hummingbird ₁

These tales are an irreverent mixture of truth, nonsense and are simply a celebration of characters too strange and special not to be preserved by pen and paper. These characters are friends who are both inspiring and terrifying as they crash their way through life without regard to its customs, niceties or norms. It is perhaps written partly as a wish to expose the good hearted and loyal nature of acquaintances often written off as day drinking fools. Folk whose philosophies are composed largely by themselves and not moulded out of society's dull dreams and demands.

Having had the privilege of growing up in an area of central Scotland where no private schools exist, my upbringing and group of friends were one of hugely mixed economic and social backgrounds. I socialised with people who had heroin dealers for parents and those who had millionaire bankers as their forbearers. The group of characters I describe in this book are and were so incredibly different to each other, yet we all put our enjoyment of each other's company before our differences and tended to laugh at each other's eccentricities instead of fearing them. To a certain extent we were all outcasts, void of the capitalist and academic ambition of the middle class, and the often, raw, macho culture of the underclass that surrounded us. We were freaks that enjoyed a drink and a tune and to be able to voice our meandering thoughts without fear of judgement. Some of us have fallen along the way and for whatever its worth, I wished to try and immortalise the dear oddballs I have the honour to call friends.

We learnt to speak 'proper' English in school as we were told it was necessary to find a 'proper' job, yet we spoke broad Scots at the pub and in the playground. I have a deep love for the richness and extravagance of both dialects and attempt to let them float alongside one another throughout these tales.

Finally, writing this was an attempt to consider my understandings of freedom and our conflicting paradigms for what this may mean and where this may lead us. The idea of a 'freedom from' the dull demands and expectations of where we grew up led to a notion of a 'freedom to' enjoy a wild and debaucherous lifestyle. While this was fun - and to a certain extent is celebrated throughout the first half of this book - it lead to deaths, divisions and a few chronic diseases within this group of friends. Now that some of us have reached an older if not wiser age it seemed prudent if not pertinent to reconsider what freedom may mean.

I hope anyone reading this may enjoy these characters and their exploits as much as I have.

Contents

Chapter 1 – The Double Vision of Geri Hay

Chapter 2 - Fleshlights, Dates and Kitchen Plates

Chapter 3 - A Christmas For Carol McNally

Chapter 4 – The Curse of Gout

Chapter 5 - Captain Ugly

Chapter 6 - Willie Shakespeare

Chapter 7 - The Royal Wedding

Chapter 8 - The Shindig

Chapter 9 - Absinthe Makes The Heart Grow Fonder

Chapter 10 - A Cornish Supper

Chapter 11 - The Theft of a Tree

Chapter 12 - The Pilgrimage Of Catholic Paul

Chapter 13 – A Visit to Edinburgh

Chapter 14 – The Brexit Blues

Chapter 15 – The Surprise Tattoo

Chapter 16 – The White Sands of Morar

Chapter 17 – The End of the New Beginning

Chapter 18 – A Walk by Blackness Bay

Chapter 1 - The Double Vision Of Geri Hay

'Who never gave the burning town a thought; To such a pitch of folly I am brought, Being caught between the pull, Of the dark moon and the full'

William Butler Yeats – The Double Vision of Michael Robertes [2]

The winter sun slouched over the horizon, assessed that the bare trees and thin clouds were too much of a nuisance to clamber over and so went back to bed, leaving the streets of Bedford in a pale half-light. Sensible men would take heed of winter's slovenly ways, but most men are not sensible, so the streets became crowded with pinched faces and hunched shoulders as the workers scurried hurriedly to places they'd rather not go. The buses steamed with the warm breath of the silent masses, who sat carefully avoiding eye contact whilst their fingers frantically conversed on the narcissist pit.

At a more appropriate hour, the sun decided to give the whole wretched thing another go, casting its golden light onto the world, and turning the dew drops into radiant pearls of mead. Like the freaks in the park, it cast an unwanted eye through a hole in the curtain, illuminating the copper beard of Geri Hay. He cursed in a language unknown, then stumbled to the window volleying further filth and threats towards Ra's rambunctious, golden fingers. The damage was however, already done. Ed, the cat, had woken and any dreams of crawling back under night's silent cloak, belonged to a fool. Geri Hay was many things, but a fool he was not, so he wrenched open the curtains, sending empty beer cans and glasses of ash crashing to the floor.

'Shut the fuck up!' came an irate voice from upstairs.

'Calm yersel!' Geri retorted, before stepping on Ed's tail and falling over.

'Fucking shut up, ya clown!' came the voice from upstairs again.

'Fucks sake, man, just trying to feed Ed, ya crabbit bastard' Geri shouted back. Glaring at the ceiling he steadied himself then marched in the direction of the kitchen. Above the fridge was a large bottle of port and several sachets of cat food. He took down both, giving the cat a generous breakfast then pouring himself a generous glass. The record player was still twitching from the night before, stuck in a groove between moving forward and back. Geri lifted the needle, which had stuck on "Streams of Whisky" by The Pogues and swaggered to the garden, cackling about 'waking the grumpy fucker up'.

The garden was a pitiful square of concrete and weeds and identical to all the others that lay behind the row of small, terraced houses. In the centre of it, a hammock was slung precariously between two poles and Geri flopped onto it, dressed in his boxer shorts and sun glasses. The blackbirds and robins chirped and laughed at his homemade tattoos and curling, yellow toenails but his neighbours did not. Having decided to forgive the sun's intrusion, he winked at the sky and toasted his elderly neighbour a fine day whilst rolling a cigarette. Puffing peacefully and humming to the music he lay back and began his day with a nap.

Awaking again a little while later, he realised that the daylight had seduced him with the empty promise of warmth, and that he was perhaps freezing to death. His cigarette had burnt out and left a trail down his chest like a sooty sort of Brazilian waxing; he stared at this a while, either lost in complete contemplation, or complete blindness caused by having forgotten to put his contact lenses in. Looking up he noticed his neighbour staring at him out of the window and attempted to give her a bow, whilst shivering an escape from the hammock. Upon reaching the back door he realised it must have blown shut and he was now trapped, nearly naked in a freezing garden. To make matters worse, he was being smirked at by some miserable old woman, who would no doubt piously, divulge the whole experience to the Daily Mail's letters page.

'Mighton, wake up!' he roared at the upstairs window.

A crushing silence was the only response, though he was sure he could faintly hear his bastard flatmate and best friend muffling a heinous chuckle. He roared again to no avail and decided that drastic measures were called for. This was a life threatening situation and what's more he had run out of cigarettes. There was nothing for it but to smash in the kitchen window. Next door, the old woman had come into her garden now and was pretending to examine her flowers whilst gleefully rubbing her hands. Maintaining a dignified posture he picked up a garden gnome and with the grim determination of a bullfighter, squared up to his glassy enemy. He swung his arm back and forth with smooth, circular motions that would have been the envy of Bedford's bowling team, and was about to lob Bashful through the window, when a furious voice shouted down,

'What the fuck are ye doing man?'

He hurled Bashful at the window, but the damnable creature ricocheted back and nearly hit his face.

'Mighton, ya fanny' shouted Geri back through chittering teeth, 'could you no hear me, ya swine, aye? I'm freezing my arse off oot here, let me in'.

'Christ oan a bike ah've just aboot had enough of you, break that windae and I'll break your legs'.

'And haw! Dinnae you look at me in that tone oh voice, ya auld crone.'

Mighton roared at the old woman next door who was shaking her head and hissing in their direction.

Sighing, Daire Mighton thumped his way down the stairs and opened the door. The old woman frowned at Geri's luck, and the sun smiled. It was not often Ra was granted the pleasure of shining his golden eyes over these two delinquents. He regularly strained an ear to hear the songs, stories, fights, falls and joyous squalor that emitted from their home, but rarely saw the culprits themselves. It was like reading a poem without knowing whose pen had marked the page. For alas, although both the scoundrels shared his golden mane, their freckled, northern skin could not long tolerate his warm gaze, and so it was that Ra had to make do with listening and chuckling from afar.

Inside the house - and after a few restorative brandies - the two friends had fallen happily into the flow of idle conversation, the likes of which is only available to those rare beasts, who converse for the sake of curiosity and conviviality, rather than to exhibit intellect or social graces. As such the conversation was light and easy and hopped merrily from topic to topic, like a lamb exploring both the flowers of the field and its own faeces without preference. The sacred appeared in the profane, the ordinary in the extraordinary, and mirth permeated the whole thing.

During this gentle ebb and flow, Geri noticed that they had received a parcel, stamped from Sweden and baring the unmistakeable scrawl of 'Paddy the Tink'. Inside it he found a 'bettering' book, on meditation and a long and largely illegible inscription by Paddy. In part, it appeared to affectionately point out that freedom was not synonymous with self-destruction, and to this the boys toasted, raising amber glasses of poison without a hint of irony or cynicism.

Around this time a flash of light and a vision, nay, two visions, appeared to Geri.

'Mighton, my dear man,' he cried. 'Most of the world recklessly pursue profits, and the others recklessly pursue prophets!'

'Very good, hen' Mighton replied, 'and what, pray, will you pursue?'

'I, Mighton dearest friend and Philistine, happen to hae found a fiver in ma troosers, and shall thus recklessly pursue profiteroles!'

With that, Geri donned his cap and swaggered to the door chuckling proudly.

Chapter 2 - Fleshlights, Dates and Kitchen Plates

'For me to love you now
Would be the sweetest thing
T'would make me sing
Ah, but I may as well try and catch the wind'

Donovan – Catch The Wind [3]

Christmas was fast approaching and the smell of mulled port permeated Geri and Mighton's tiny house. Decorations were sparse, limited to a string of silver tinsel adorning the record player and a selection of novelty, yule beers, which were already drunk and stacked in the windowsill in a Christmas tree- esque form.
The boys sat with their friend Kerry and the three sang along to Nat King Cole whilst devouring value priced, mince pies coated in a potent brandy butter. Geri interrupted the singing to say,

'Mighton go check the alcohols no evaporating its way fae that port tae where angels play.'

Mighton choked on a pie in rage, spluttering,

'Go check it yersel' ya lazy clown, I've checked the last three times, and I'm no gieing a shit anyway. Christ! If you have a bairn I'll dress it as a bottle oh port and you'll be sure tae take neurotic care oh it!'

This time the choking noises and flecks of pie were omitted from Geri's mouth. 'Preposterous!' he cried.

'I'll never hae a wain, but I'll rise and check on yon port as a civility to our guest'.

With that and a courteous nod to Kerry, Geri marched into the kitchen and served up what was admitted by all to be astoundingly good, mulled port.

The hours of the day past pleasantly and lazily and after the mulled port was finished, Kerry and Mighton braved the five minute walk to the local pub. Geri was left to his own devices, which at first he relished by making full use of the freedom of the remote control and Mighton's slippers, yet as evening drew in he became increasingly perturbed by the snagging realisation that he had no idea what to get Mighton for a Christmas present. This unease was heightened by hazy memories of Mighton proudly claiming he had finished his own Christmas shopping and the pointed stares he had seemed to direct towards Geri.

Geri stood, looking out of the window in the hope of inspiration. The sun was setting. Ed was unsuccessfully chasing birds. The old woman next door was glaring into space and somewhere a child was wailing. None of it offered any illumination or inspiration. 'Fuck it,' Geri said and slouched deep into the couch. As if on command that's exactly what his neighbours began doing noisily next door and simultaneously Geri was hit by a brainwave. If there was one thing Mighton enjoyed, it was sex. Having been crippled as a teenager by Gullain-Barre Syndrome and unable to use his body for two years, the lanky, ginger dandy now made up for it tenfold. As he said himself, he had no idea when or if his limbs would cease to function again, so he made sure to enjoy every perverse pleasure two or more consenting adults could enjoy. Somehow, he had a way with women and while Geri's shy recitals of poetry and pleasantries led to poor success rates, Mighton's forward and vulgar charm seemed to woo a surprising share of the female population. Mighton would often lecture Geri, spouting forth pious musings such as,

'There's nothing worse than boring sex, apart fae nae sex and you seem tae excel at both. Get oot there while yer sober an' young enough to raise a smile and go taste the wonders oh the day.'

Undoubtedly, if Mighton was anything, it was a committed pervert. Based on this lovingly drawn conclusion, Geri decided to purchase his friend a vibrating, rubber vagina for Christmas. Due to the speed and anonymity of the internet he was able to purchase the plastic fantastic with a few clicks of the mouse, and have it arrive –without embarrassment - in a matter of days. He wondered with mild amusement if his religious family who worked in the Grangemouth oil and plastics refinery could have inadvertently helped to make the monster.

'On the seventh day God made man and on the eighth man made rubber vaginas, a toast to these strange pre-apocalyptic times,' he said, raising the last of the mulled port and chuckling.

Time moved forwards - or at least it did so according to the distributors of tedious positivism – the Anglo Saxon tie wearers - a group famed for their tendency to reduce life's magic to numbers and pie charts, thus painting the world grey with their lack of imagination and insatiable rationalism. Leaves continued to fall from the trees, carol singers continued to sing out of tune and turkeys continued to curse their saviour's birthday. Proper pubs lit roaring fires and the young pretenders flashed their neon signs. Snow fell in Bedford Park and somehow everybody became united in either moaning about it or making snowmen. The boys awoke every morning for a week, to find some curious yellow snow outside the door; Mighton blamed Ed, but Geri set his suspicions on the old crone next door. Unfortunately though, it was impossible to rise at her ungodly hour to find out the truth.
In this manner the days were passed until soon enough it was but a week till Christmas.
On this day Geri waved the warehouse goodbye for a while and daundered home in a mood of elation and festive cheer. What a time to be alive! He rejoiced in being both released from the

dull drudgery of work, and in having the company of a young, Spanish woman to look forward to that night. He had recently met her at one of the parties at Joe Turner's house, though perhaps it would be more accurate to say 'the ongoing party' at Joe's house. As there had been an open-door policy for the five years that him and other tattooed waifs and strays had lived there. This resulted in a kind of perpetual celebration, with characters coming and going, some staying months on the floor and others barely lasting the night. In this regard, it had the format of a never-ending soap opera or perhaps was like waves taking temporary form out of an endless ocean of music and madness and beer. Anyhow, it was there, that through the noise of the fiddles and petty fights, Geri had first caught sight of his Latin love. He had been rather the worse for wear, having accidentally puffed on a crack pipe instead of a hash one, but nevertheless, although he could not remember her name, he could recall she had a generous bosom, and was almost certainly female.
He could also recall that she had agreed to come to the house based on the belief that he was a chef and would cook her some 'traditional British cuisine'. Unperturbed by the lie and the subsequent challenge, he stopped in at the butchers on his way home and bought as much goose fat, steak mince and corn fed chicken as his scratch card winnings would allow. These three ingredients, plus generous handfuls of pink sea salt and pungent garlic were the base flavours of his famed 'Cardiac-a-mince'. It was a dish which even pesky vegetarians like Paddy the Tink and pinch faced, cynics like Mighton, agreed was divine.

Upon arriving home the master chef went to work and soon the kitchen windows steamed up. Ed awoke from his slumber, salivating over the smell of succulent chicken roasting in goose fat and wild garlic. Fat, creamy potatoes were boiled for mash, and a potent gravy was spirited out of what remained in three old Buckfast bottles. The whole house smelt like a medieval feast by the time the meal was prepared. With half an hour to go and little left to do Geri borrowed the rum and cigarettes lying in Mighton's bedroom, and savoured them peacefully. He thanked the Gods that his friend was working a nightshift and thereby couldn't sabotage or witness his date evening. This was because the last time Geri had attempted to woo a young lady, with lies and poetry, Mighton had interrupted to ask her if she'd seen the curling, yellow talons on Geri's toes that he clipped yearly with meat scissors in the kitchen. Such comments had resulted in the only physical action of the night being a fist fight and a broken rib. The girl had left quietly in the midst of the altercation.

Geri polished off the last of Mighton's rum, and then sat daydreaming until his thoughts landed upon the rubber vagina. A vague intrigue welled up in him, and soon morphed into an insatiable curiosity. 'Surely Mighton would be grateful if someone first tested the product,' he thought to himself. 'He always tests any bottles of whisky he buys me, it's a courtesy if anything'.

After a few minutes of considering such justifications he fetched the quivering, rubber monster from under his bed and gave it a quick test. No sooner was he finished his hand to gland combat when remorse set in. It was a deep remorse accompanied by the special shame known only to those who have caught sight of themselves coupling with inanimate plastic objects in a mirror. Appalled and amused by his weak will, he returned to the kitchen and washed the rubber temptress in the sink, before cursing in the realisation that the cardiac-a-mince had turned from caramelized to cremate in his absence. Whilst salvaging any edible remains from the pan, the doorbell rang, breaking his volley of threats and shaking him into a panic.
 'Fuck! She's ten minutes early', he hissed, tripping over Ed and dropping some mashed potato on the floor. He scooped what he could back into the pan with his hand, picked out the worst of the cat hairs, and then sprang towards the front door, stopping only to spray some deodorant on top of his stained t-shirt. With much trepidation he opened it slowly, and was delighted to see

a buxom beauty standing outside. The euphoria was temporarily interrupted when he noted with some annoyance that she'd brought sparkling water instead of wine, and appeared to cast critical eyes over his stained t-shirt. Nonetheless, he hurried her in with excitement, and broke into an impromptu recital of a Wordsworth poem for her.
'I don't understand what you're talking about!' she said, her yellow, brown eyes glaring at him with intensity.
'Never mind never mind,' he said, ushering her through to the living room before dashing to the kitchen to fix them both a drink. She sat on the sofa and surveyed her surroundings like a soldier taking in the Somme. She observed all the empty cans, the scattered cat food, the multitude of broken instruments and the homemade bow and arrow on the wall. Then her eyes came to rest on the unusual appendage that proudly erected itself from a dinner plate on the table. Her stare evolved into a glare and then a look of righteous fury.

'What the fuck is that on that plate?' she shouted towards the kitchen.

'Ah! Don't worry about that I'm just drying a rubber vagina!' Geri cheerfully shouted back.
Silence followed, and assuming she was satisfied with this logical explanation, Geri whistled happily to himself, continuing to fix two generous glasses of 'old fashioned'. However, on taking them through to the living room he saw that nobody was there and that the front door had been left open. He gave his beard a puzzled scratch, slurped his cocktail and pondered the predicament. It was confusing, she had made no mention of being a vegetarian, and thus the rich aroma of roasting meats and garlic would surely awaken her primal, carnivorous cravings? What sort of strange and depraved creature walked away from cardiac-a-mince and cocktails? Who would deny themselves the chance to pet Ed or throw a dart at the picture of the prime minister on the wall?
Geri sat onto the couch, lost in a haze of bewilderment and contemplation. Sitting there with crossed legs and the last of

the evening light streaming in from the window behind him, he appeared to radiate fire from his ginger form, like a Celtic Buddha, lost at sea for a thousand years, only to be washed up upon the shore with a wicked grin and a lotus pose.
Meanwhile, the sun, who had been spying on the whole matter and biting its lips in nervous mirth, could take it no more. Like an over excited child, blurting out the answer in a game of charades, it thrust forward a finger of illumination onto the rubber contents on the plate. Clocks stopped and the moment transcended time and space and all crude symbols of linguistic understanding. Geri's glowing profile turned slowly to follow the beam of light. He knew the truth without needing words to acknowledge it. He also knew deeply that it didn't matter and that this was but a broken thread on the tapestry of eternity. He continued to sit in silent reverie, savouring whatever this was. Other men when touched by such moments of lucid and timeless clarity, feel the need to attach to it endless structures and symbols, rituals and rites or at least a lifetime of scientific investigation. But not Geri Hay, he just sat and enjoyed this formless elucidation.

All good things come to an end they say, and change is the nature of the game. So it was that Ed knocking over an empty can brought Geri back to life as we know it. He sighed, shrugged and then toasted the ghost of his lost Spanish love with a glass of porter.

'A lassie with nae humour is like a pub with nae beer. Come, Ed, tonight we dine on cardiac-a-mince my spoilt compadre!' With that the two friends strolled towards the kitchen and savoured the joys of culinary success and a life rich in wonders together.

Chapter 3 - A Christmas For Carol McNally

"The best portion of a good man's life: his little, nameless unremembered acts of kindness and love."

William Wordsworth 4.

It was two days before Christmas and Bedford lay under a fine dusting of snow. Children threw balls of ice and gravel and endowed snowmen with carrots for genitalia. Under the pines in the park, dog excrement lay frozen in stiff peaks, preserving itself with ungodly ambition, like Silicone Valley billionaires suspended in cryogen. Bakers could no longer meet the demand of mince pies, and the shopping mall Santa's could no longer bare to smile at every child. Everyone agreed that advent had been a long, expensive, repetitive month and that the holy day could not come quickly enough. Everyone that was, except for Geri and Mighton. For these two scoundrels, the broken record of the days sounded better with every repeat play. Fairytale of New York blasted tri-hourly from their record player, and whisky punch, served with sprigs of holly, continued to be embezzled without signs of fatigue. Mighton found endless joy and great energy in cursing every carol singer and Christmas tree in sight, while Geri found the season's peace through adopting an acute slovenliness that he reserved for the 'holy days of rest'.

So it was, that two days before Christmas, slumped on the couch in a daze of warm whisky and bad TV, Geri was startled from his idling by the door slamming and Mighton shouting, 'For fucks sakes man, whit kind oh a feckin' world is this?!' Geri felt a wave of guilt in response to this, but one that was promptly washed away by an even larger wave of laziness. It had been ten days since he'd washed the dishes and miscellaneous matter now lined the crockery. In his defence, he had already explained to Mighton, that this was the season of peace, and God's rest for merry gentlemen, yet the miser appeared to have no good will to give. Glancing at the kitchen, Geri felt another pang of guilt, yet again a stronger desire for an avoidance at all costs for the mountain of filth awaiting him therein. He decided to answer on the offensive, his friend liked arguing, and perhaps they could pleasantly pass the time doing that instead of the dishes.

'Mighton ya muckle nosed, carnapsious fool! I've telt ye i'll dae the dishes after Christmas. These are ma holidays and ah intend tae use them in the holiest of ways. If ye want them done afore then dae em yersel!'

Geri feigned a look of fury, but was secretly nervous he'd overdone it, fearing that if they came to blows Mighton might knock over the punch again.

Fortunately for him, Mighton looked more confused than angry and responded

'Aye yer a clarty bastard and we'll talk aboot they dishes soon enough, but that's no whits on ma mind. I just came fae chattin' wi wee Carol McNally doon the street, you work wi her felly eh?'

Geri, who had been too busy dreaming up excuses to listen, replied,

'Mighton, its clear ye cannae see the eczema I get when I wash dishes in winter. If there wis a skin fairy, no a tooth fairy then id be a rich man.'

Mighton looked perplexed,
'Geri stop blabberin' oan aboot the washin' i'm no talkin' aboot that. Ah says you work wi Carol McNally's felly eh?'

Geri looked up suspiciously and nodded to the affirmative.

'Right, coz I wis just gabbin' wi her the noo, and she telt us that thae swines ye work for sacked him four days afore Christmas. Didnae even hae the baws tae tell him, he just went tae the work an' couldnae swipe in.'

Geri sighed,
'Aye thats how they dae it right enough, they're layin' off a lot of folk this month so they dinnae have tae offer them permanent contracts. Feckin filth so they are!'

Mighton nodded,
'Aye but you've no heard the worst oh it. Wee Carol says it means they've no money for Christmas. Says they'll probably just hae a chippy fae their meal on the day'.

Geri rose from the sofa and gallantly if a little unsteadily, shook a fist in the air, and roared
'I'll no stand fer that, lets buy them the best oh ingredients fer a proper Christmas dinner!'

Mighton transcended the room, and slapped Geri on the back, crying,
'Thats a crackin' idea ma man, we'll make them a fine Christmas meal tae remember, and nae doot aboot it!'

The two of them stood proudly with arms around each other's shoulders, lost in a fantasy of long tables laden in opulent abundance, and undefeatable joy on the faces of the McNallys. Ed purred at their feet, and their sense of righteous pride appeared to filter through to every atom of the feline, via some unknown process of osmosis. He projected his whiskers like a gentleman's moustache, and thrust his tail heavenwards, with a great deal of pomp.

'Mon yersel' Ed!' Roared Geri encouragingly.
'We'll teach thae cunts at the work that we take care oh our own'.

His wild gesticulations caused him to lose balance and he grabbed at Mightons neck for support, bringing both of them crashing down, and knocking over both the table and the punch in the process. Despite this, they were still elated by their plans and hitherto unknown amounts of generosity, and both lay cackling on the floor. Ed, who never missed a spilt meal, lapped up the punch with gusto and soon afterwards fell into a deep and drunken sleep.

Geri and Mighton spent the afternoon watching Celtic highlights, and shouting at the television. After their fill of football, beers and quarrelling, they put on The Incredible String Band and devoted their attentions to writing a shopping list. Despite the impetuous speed with which they scribbled, the list was long and detailed and boasted a contumelious excess of dishes which would not have been out of place at the banquets of Epicures. Suckling piglets and corn-fed geese were among the less extravagant items that graced the pages. Venomous arguments surrounding the best kind of stuffing had broken out, so in the end they had opted to purchase four different kinds from the butchers and create two of their own, thus covering all bases. The alcohol list was a long and comprehensive affair, featuring vintages polarised enough to be found in both a wine merchant's cellar, and a wino's bathroom. Finally, the deserts, which were dedicated a page of their own, consisted of seven options, ranging from classic Christmas cakes to abstract absurdities such as sweet port soufflés.

They decided to procure all these delights at Marks and Spencer's, a shop they concluded to be of more esteem than the corner shop they frequented. They had never been to Marks and Spencer's before, so in order to meet the occasion Geri donned his funeral shirt and dress shoes, while Mighton wore his grandfather's velvet coat. These plus their tweed flat caps and badly patched trousers gave them a distinctly Dickensian air, as they marched down the street, and one which they stopped to admire in the reflection of every shop window they passed.

It is perhaps unnecessary to point out that Geri and Mighton were no saints, but it should be noted that if they felt somebody accepted them as they were, then they would likewise accept the person back with a rare friendship of an almost unconditional nature. Once this friendship was sealed, it could be terminated only by death or the most extreme of circumstances. The stealing of cars, borrowing of partners and breaking of instruments were all quickly forgiven as long as they were met with apology and the buying of a round. Within the bonds of such friendship, self and other blurred and to help each other out appeared as natural and needless of thanks as the left hand helping the right. So it was, as a simple act of friendship and one void of pious or a sense of duty that the boys stormed into Marks and Spencer's.

Inside the shop the aspiring, middle classes were annoyed to see these two reprobates appearing where they did not belong. Surely it proved that the labour exchange was too generous, or the minimum wage too high, if these uncouth specimens could afford to shop in the same place as themselves? Aghast by the potential lack of distinction between yours truly and these red headed wastrels, the shoppers made a mental note to visit Waitrose next time, and helpfully nodded Geri's direction to the nearest security guard. They appeased themselves, with the thought that the pair were likely as not common thieves, and certainly not fellow shoppers. This was a place for lawyers with stomach ulcers and second home aspirations, not for wine-scented scamps, the likes of which audaciously dared to take more than one of each free, cheese sample.

Geri and Mighton were however oblivious to the stares that met them. Their attention was taken up by the fact that although they had prepared a list lacking naught, they had not prepared for the price of it. Great munificence they may have wished to bestow, but they could never hope to pay to for it. They considered Robin Hood tactics of wealth redistribution, but catching the stern gaze of the security guard, swiftly ruled them out. Alas, with great lament they scored off the more lavish items from the list and returned to the free cheese samples to muster cheer.
Utilising both their overdrafts and Mighton's busking funds, they purchased a large turkey, roasting potatoes, two kinds of stuffing, a trifle, a brandy pudding, a bottle of Advocaat, and a crate of Belgian beer. They had enough additional change left over to visit the corner shop and buy Mr McNally some Buckfast and rolling tobacco as a stocking filler. Mighton

bought himself a bottle of Irn Bru there - as he did every day - and complained that the price was double the one written on the bottle - as he did everyday – and the owner of the shop told him to, 'Piss off and get someone else to import it' , as he did every day.
Both the shop owner and Mighton enjoyed the sour exchange of words, and parted with satisfied smiles, as they did every day. Finally finished their fatiguing expedition, the two friends hurried home with lusty anticipation for the rust flavoured, soft drink of Scotland.

Geri petulantly agreed to wash two glasses, fearing deeply that this could undermine his stance on the crockery. Sitting back on the sofa, each toasted the other with a glass of the radioactive, orange bubblegum, and 'Fairytale of NewYork' was played once more for good measure.

Christmas Eve came and snow began to fall thicker and thicker. The betting office odds favoured a white Christmas, and the corner shop began to offer deals on sledges and snow shovels. Geri and Mighton met their merry crew at Esquires bar and enjoyed an eve of jollification before heading home and planning the delivery of the McNally's meal.
An icy wind whipped their faces and reddened their cheeks as they wound their way homewards. The malice of winter was of no concern to the boys though. They were too busy being lost in thoughts of tomorrow and a tuneless renditions of 'The Road To The Isles' to notice. The street lamps winked them on their way, and before long all things were silent, except for their two mouths, that snored in tandem.

The ringing of church bells awoke the day, and what a day it was! A truly white Christmas, with every surface pristine and virginal. Such a morning hinted the presence of some greater force at work. Whether this was the hand of God, granting the world a new page, or the nose of the devil sneezing Columbia's purest over the rooftops, some unseen force was at play in the making of so white a day.

Children gaped out of windows in delight, parents tried to remember where they hid presents, and everybody was glad that the wait was over and Christmas could begin.
Mighton and Geri gave Ed a festive breakfast of fresh sardines and a bowl of cream. They then sat down to enjoy their own meal of scrambled eggs and reduced-price smoked salmon. These festive delights were washed down with a kind of celtic

bucks-fizz, this being a blend of Buckfast, Irn-Bru and crushed ice.

'Whit a fine day it is, let's take the scran round tae the McNallys soon, so they've time tae cook it' said Geri through a mouthful of egg. Mighton agreed and they got to work repacking the food into numerous bags. Mr McNally's proposed stocking gifts - of Buckfast and tobacco - were found to be a lacking a stocking to put them in. Geri suggested that Mighton might have some kind of stocking in his room as he no doubt enjoyed cross dressing once in a while, to which Mighton responded,
'Yer gettin' carnapsious ya wee clown. I dinnae wear stockings, and it's no thae kinda stockings anyway ya eejit!'
Geri conceded the point and suggested offering the gifts in his work helmet. They tried this, but then decided it was perhaps an unwanted reminder of a place bound to be far from fondly thought of by Mr McNally. Eventually they decided to wrap the gifts in a bath-towel, which was warmed in the oven to remove all traces of the mornings shower.

With great excitement they collected all the gifts and tripped out the house with them. In their hands were plastic bags filled with turkey, pigs in blankets, fresh vegetables and a trifle. Held tightly in their armpits were boxes of crackers and crates of beers. Balanced between Mighton's chest and chin was a Christmas pudding and a can of haggis, and under Geri's neck was the Buckfast and tobacco wrapped in the towel. The McNally's home was only five doors down the road, yet the journey could have been to the Antarctic, so long it took and so fraught with hazards it seemed to be. Each uneven paving stone and stretch of ice brought with it wicked possibilities of dropped trifles and broken bottles. Still, the boys persevered admirably, and neither would have dreamt of admitting to the other that they had bitten of more than they could chew. Instead, they 'encouraged' each other with a litany of tips and idle threats, filling the street with a sing-song of violent poetry. This mad dance of juggling their wares, cursing each other, and grinning wildly, ended in them eventually reaching the McNally's door without any casualties. The journey felt like it had been an eternity and they both trembled and sweated.

Mr McNally was quick to answer the door, and shook Geri's hand, before welcoming them both in gladly, as if he'd been expecting them. He was a tall man with a kindly face. His shoulders were stooped and his huge hands, hung awkwardly like prime steaks by his sides. He showed the boys into the living room, gave them both an ale and introduced them to his children. Mrs McNally soon came into the room and Mr McNally presented her to Geri, saying
'This is me work mate Geri and his mate we've met before at the pub quiz, they've just come round to...'
Here he stopped a minute, scratched his chin and said
'Well I'm sure I don't mean to be rude, and any neighbour and enemy of the warehouse is welcome here, but why did you come round?'
Geri and Mighton both felt a sudden twinge of embarrassment, they did not wish to patronise the couple, and struggled to find the right words. Mighton, who was less used to such feelings and any concerns for social graces, spoke up.

'Well, ken, we heard aboot they swines giein' you the sack and aw, and Carol here says it meant use were broke fer Christmas and wid be eatin' a chippy. And well, we ken how it is tae be broke an' that, an' the way we see it is whoevers got the money buys the beers an' whoever disnae, disnae. It always kinda works oot, so anyways this is fir use, hope use enjoy it!'

Geri nodded in agreement and the boys handed over their great excess of carrier bags.

The McNallys looked confused for a few seconds and then both of them burst out laughing.

Mrs McNally hugged Mighton and Mr McNally slapped Geri on the back, saying,

'This is the nicest, oddest thing anyone's done for us in years boys. You've cheered me right up, I'll get out the good whisky and posh glasses and we'll have a Christmas toast in your honour! Not sure what the wet tobacco in the burnt towels for though?'

He left the room chuckling and looking a lot happier than when they'd come in. The two young children rummaged through the bags and began whispering in their mother's ear. Presently, Mrs McNally turned to Geri and Mighton and said,

'Listen, I couldn't be more grateful or heart-warmed but I'll be honest with you. It's a family tradition of ours to have a chippy every Christmas, we're proper skint this year no doubt about it, but that's not why we're having a chippy! Its lovely of you to bring all this but these fussy little bleeders won't touch it' she said nodding her head to her children.

'Why don't you two stay for lunch and I'll cook this up for you both and we can have our chippy, and then we can all eat your deserts together?'

Geri and Mighton looked at each other, a little crestfallen and disappointed. Then Geri began hissing with laughter and cried,

'Aye why no?! It's gonna be a fine scran and it'd be a pleasure to share the day wi use'

The children and Mrs McNally departed excitedly for the China Star takeaway, it was not known for its fish and chips, but it was Bedford's only chance of chips upon Christmas day. Mighton and Geri made themselves comfortable and Mr McNally returned from the loft, with his 'special occasions' bottle of Lagavulin. He poured them both a generous measure, and then beamed at them, toasting,

'Merry Christmas one and all!'

The day was indeed merry, and filled with laughter, good will and all the joys of the season. Geri and Mighton devoured a turkey designed for six and ate their fair share of trifle and brandy pudding. The children were deeply satisfied with their chippy and soon returned their attentions to bickering over which Christmas cartoons to watch. Mr and Mrs McNally were endowed with magnificent smiles for the rest of the day, and any lines of worry that their faces had told of, softened and faded with the telling of jokes and the drinking of drams. Eventually Geri – now a little rosy in the cheeks and soft between the ears - told the whole family his rubber vagina story, slapping his knee and roaring with mirth in the process. It appeared he had misjudged the appetite of his audience for such debaucherous tales, and poor Mrs McNally blushed in Catholic decency as her children began asking what rubber vaginas were. Recognising it was time for a speedy exit and some sobering winter air, Geri and Mighton, gave their thanks for the day and bid a fond farewell to their hosts. The McNally's gave them enough parting hugs and kind words to turn their ears red, and gently insisted they should take the burnt towel and the Buckfast wine home with them.

The boys took the long way home via Bedford Park, and sat a while on a bench beneath the pines. The icy breeze would have petrified most men's marrow, but such fears were not countenanced by Mighton and Geri. Indeed, they were of bold northern stock, and wore whisky jackets besides.
They sat on the bench, sipping Buckfast and watching families navigate sledges through the excrement, obstacle course.
In silence, they reflected on the day's success and savoured the smiling faces of the McNallys. Finally, Mighton turned to Geri, and toasted him with the bottle, singing,
'God bless you Geri mental man let nothing you dismay. For wine is our saviour and was shared on Christmas Day'.
With that the two friends shared a laugh, and a merry Christmas was had by all.

Chapter 4 – The Curse of Gout

'Curl up in the window-seat behind an enormous book, setting the drug of dreams against the pain of living'

Robert Sencourt on TS Elliot 5.

At the back of Geri and Mighton's tiny house was an even tinier bathroom. It had been added as an afterthought in the 1970s and jutted out into the garden, a poky cupboard made of rotting wood. It was however Geri's favourite room in the whole house as it was the only place he could sit and enjoy a cigarette without Ed pestering him for food, or Mighton pestering him to return his cigarettes. It was also an excellent place to read a book in peace and quiet, and having been banned from all public libraries, it was the closest Geri came to a calming room of literary intent. An array of Oor Wullie annuals carpeted the floor, alongside Behan, Steinbeck and a multitude of empty cans and old toilet roll tubes. Using a damp towel to cushion the cold lid of the toilet seat, Geri could pass many hours on his porcelain throne, smoking and reading to his heart's content.

He had given up on wading his way through Walter Scott's Waverley and now alternated between some Stevenson and Woolf. He chuckled at the humour of the former and began rolling a cigarette from his pilfered tobacco when an almighty ruckus occurred in the kitchen. He could not make out the words but he could hear Mighton yelling at someone with ever increasing volume and fury. Not to worry he thought, his friend would soon tire himself out and then he could continue his leisurely read in peace again. He smoked his cigarette and then threw the butt in the sink, straining his ears to hear the minute hissing noise as it was extinguished by the drip of the tap. This entertainment was soon over and he returned to waiting for the shouting to subside. It did not, Mighton continued to yell at somebody, and he appeared to be squealing in pain between his yells. Geri rolled another cigarette and tried to ignore these interferences and get back to his reading. It was of no use, the pitch and intonation of his friend's West Lothian brogue cut like a knife through his concentration.

'Jesus wept! Whit the fecks the problem oot there?' muttered Geri to himself as he rose to his feet.

With great irritation he placed both his books on the mouldy floor and made his way to the kitchen to try and placate his noisy acquaintance. As he entered the room Mighton threw down his phone and then yelped in pain again, rubbing pityingly at his knees.

'Whit the hells goin' oan in here man? Louder than seven hells by Christ!' said Geri.

Mighton glared at him

'An so might you be if ye'd caught the gout man!'

'Whit ye oan aboot?' said Geri, genuinely curious now.

'Ma granda's got gout an a seen him when ah wis last hame an noo the doctor says av got it an' ma knees are killin' me! I wis oan the phone tae him there tae let him ken whit ah think oh him spreadin' it tae me!'

Geri face lit up with mirth and shook his head happily.

'Mighton ya damnable fool! Ye cannae catch gout man. Christ you're unlucky, whit is it wi' you collecting weird medieval illnesses, it'll be the Plague next!'

'Feck you man ma knees are in agony! Where dae you think ah caught it fae if no ma granda? Old boy called me an eejit when ah blamed him!'

Geri took out his mobile telephone and searched for information regarding the causes of gout. One article suggested that it could be hereditary, but he chose to ignore that, preferring the sound of another article which posited a rich diet and alcohol as the cause.

'Says here its yer ain fault Mighton. Says that port, cigars and an indulgence oh rich foods such as cheese can lead tae it.'

Mighton snatched the phone off him and read the article himself.

'Whit a load ah pish! Ye cannae trust whit ye read oan the internet ya fanny, every cunt there thinks Elvis is still alive and that the moons made oh cheese! Besides ah dinnae drink port, smoke cigars or eat much in the way oh cheese, so it must hae came fae ma granda.'

Geri chuckled, and pointed at the contents on the table beside them.

'Aye maybe so, but ye do drink yon tonic wine, smoke roll ups and eat a fair few chippies, its just a poor man's version oh the same thing.'

Mighton refused to concede to this logic but he made a mental note to phone his grandfather later in the day and apologise. He wagged a finger at Geri and said,

'Load ah pish man, totally different things! I'm away noo tae buy some painkillers and some mair tonic tae take the edge oaf this agony, so clean thae feckin' dishes in ma absence and dinnae you go raiding ma rollin' baccy again.'

Geri nodded subserviently, waited till his friend had limped out the house and then made his way back to the bathroom. It should now be possible to finish his books in peace and quiet and enjoy the last of Mighton's tobacco without being caught he thought. As he sat down again upon the damp towel he began laughing out loud at his friend's idiocy.

'Catchin' Gout, whit an eejit! Well I'm like Florence feckin' Nightingale, saving him from Gout with every one oh his cigarettes I smoke', he said to himself as he took Mighton's tobacco from his pocket and began rolling another smoke.

Chapter 5 - Captain Ugly

'The first man to compare the cheeks of a young woman to a rose was obviously a poet, the first to repeat it was possibly an idiot'

Salvador Dali [6]

Spring brought a vernal freshness to Bedford, blessing its parks and meadows with blooming bouquets and an unreasonable pollen count. Like clusters of custard, great swathes of daffodils danced in the breeze and flirted unashamedly with the bees. Even the sparse patches of plants which had failed to survive in the tower block's concrete entrance, showed signs of re-birth, with daisies and dandelions cautiously emerging from their subterranean refuge.

It was past five in the eve and the counted down hours were over for the masses, who now walked homewards gaily and without jackets for the first time in many a month. Even those who habitually marched home with a military two step, slowed their gait and let the sun sink in. Minds that tended to be trapped by the dull stresses of the desk long after leaving it behind, were thrust into an awareness of nature in all her abundant glory. For all their power, habitual worries could not compete for attention against the scent of mowed lawns and the chirp of sparrow songs that radiated from a world in bloom. This sensory overload evoked childhood memories and a forgotten sense of possibility. Old Mother Nature and coy Miss Spring had offered man a new beginning, a chance to forgive and forget culture's ugly atrocities and move forwards together, but would man return the favour? Well, as happenstance would have it, one such chap was ready to give it a good old whirl at any rate. Indeed, sitting down by the embankment, Geri Hay sipped a cool beer and toasted the day around him. He dipped his feet in the rivers flow and gazed up at the endless blue above. However, his reverie was temporarily shattered by a woman shrieking as a duck shat from point blank range onto her head. The feathered fiend quacked in glee before landing smoothly on the water and bobbing away with the current. Geri attempted to smother his mirth and selflessly offered the woman one of his nearby socks to mop up the mess. Lamentably this appeared to cause further offence and the woman marched away in palpable fury. Geri hissed with laughter and observed the feathered, river pirate with respect and envy. How fine it looked to float down the stream with such idle pace and mocking grace. It seemed man could not compete with this fine creature. Indeed, the only humans on the river were college students, who competitively paddled punts, and bloated old men aboard floating ostentations, tokens of success that had generally cost thirty years of slavery and a triple heart bypass. The river scene ticked the two boxes of modern life's dull demands; to be standardised and sanitised. It seemed to be crying out to be reimagined with magic and revelry and it was at that moment Geri Hay decided to buy and captain a freak-filled pirate boat. Satisfied with all aspects of this daydream – apart from the minor detail of financing it - he dipped his feet deep into the water and watched the world go by.

Later that day Geri reconvened with a few of Bedford's other waifs and strays in the beer garden of a public house called, The Bear. Mighton had recently finished a twenty-four-hour shift at the care home he worked at and was tired, tipsy and more than a little irritable. Therefore, when Geri offered him a unique opportunity to co-own a boat, he greeted the suggestion with a string of cynical expletives, quipping that Geri could 'barely master the fucking bathtub, let alone a boat.'

Geri snorted derisively at this and called the man a fool, countering that he had purchased a second-hand, Scout's book on nautical matters and now had a rudimentary knowledge of knots, port and starboard and more importantly he already enjoyed rum. Mighton retorted that the only port Geri knew about came in a value price bottle, and that nobody had ever learnt anything of worth from reading a book. This was a sensitive issue for Mighton, for although he could recite countless poems and ballads, he was heavily dyslexic and had virtually never read a book, learning all that he knew from oral recitals. He was often heard to say that 'words that cannae talk are aw the use oh legs that cannae walk, as lame and crippled as ah wis.'

Mighton had been an insufferable invalid, filled with fury every time someone pitied him, when for the first two months he had been paralysed from the neck down and spent his days and nights in the neurology ward. In his words he had been 'left wi' the crazies' and thought he was close to his end several times. One time a naked, demented woman had leaped onto him in the night, slapping him and demanding he made love to her. The worst thing about this he claimed, was not that he could not move to press a panic button, but that his nether regions could not move to oblige the good lady. Another time, he had been left alone in a bath and slowly slid down the tub until the water submerged all of him apart from his – fortunately rather large - nose. When the nurse returned, she laughingly scolded him and asked what he was doing down there, to which he had replied, 'having a feckin' picnic hen, whits it look like?'

Refusing to shy away from confrontation with all that life could bring he demanded his friends mistreated him every bit as much as each other. They honoured this religiously, feeding him value price whisky through a straw and sending him constantly flying from of his wheelchair, whenever they crashed it against a curb. One Halloween, when seeing his comrades being attacked by local delinquents, he had propped himself against a lamppost and joined the affray, jabbing with his health service crutches and laughing wildly to himself. He might have won the scrap too if he had not been knocked out by a Teletubbie brandishing a knuckleduster. Upon being one of the very few to recover from his condition, he chose to live his life with vigorous zeal, relishing both folk music and cursing loudly above all things. He empathised more than most with the nature of suffering and split his time between hedonistic chaos and caring for others. His relationship with Geri fitted crudely into both these categories.

Back at The Bear, a pleasant thought occurred to Geri. If Mighton did not co-own the boat then when aboard it he would have to succumb to the title of cabin wench, while the honourable Geri Hay would be the captain astride its mighty bower. Inspired, he hurried away to spread the offer of shared boat ownership through the rest of the beer garden's potential crew.

Two weeks later, having goaded the affable Rob Carter with the proposition, the two of them set off to the north to view a boat. Geri boasted to all his friends and warehouse colleagues of the great, masted warship he would return with and merrily whistled sea shanties the entire journey. The drive went smoothly despite the car's lack of MOT and tank of illegal, 'red' diesel. An amicable time was spent and the two squabbled only briefly over captainship and Geri's ceaseless whistling of the same shanty. After following an infinitude of winding roads through the Yorkshire Dales they finally found the barn where a man called 'Big Jim' was selling boats. Big Jim was a blonde haired giant and looked like a cross between a Viking raider and a second-hand car salesman. After several minutes of attempting to oblige with Big Jim's complicated and incomprehensible security system – which consisted of Jim roaring out passwords through a hatch for them to repeat back into a broken entry system - he decided to let them in and swung open the doors to a huge, gloomy barn. Whether or not Jim had any ownership or entitlement to all the wares within it was hard to say but what was clear was that the man had no shortage of boats, or indeed motorbikes, fake spirits and stuffed animals. Big Jim explained jovially that he was having to 'disappear for a year or two' and thus all contents of the barn and the barn itself, were for sale and negotiable in price. 'Right orf the back of some great big lorries these boys'

Geri's spirits lifted at the possibility of negotiating an affordable price for a speed boat that sat gleaming beside a badly stuffed badger.

'I like the cut of yer jib ma man! How much for yon speed boat' he enquired.

'For you me lad, fifteen G's' cried big Jim, slapping his hands together as if to seal the deal.

Geri looked a little crestfallen, but persevered valiantly,

'We have three hundred and twenty two pound atween us, and a ten litres of red diesel, what wid ye cry us fer that?'

'For you me lad, seeing as how you caught me on such a generous mood and all, I says you can have this here gallant little wave rider'

Jim gestured at a deflated dinghy that lay in a heap next to a rusting outboard motor. Catching the look of disappointment in the boy's eyes, Jim quickly countered.

'And of course I would throw in two bottles of Old Bagpiper, the finest whisky to ever fall orf of a lorry'

Without waiting to consult Rob, Geri thrust a hand forward and shook Jim's,

'It's a deal, perfect to christen her maiden voyage'

Rob shrugged, examined the engine a little, before saying,

'Fuck it why not!'

Jim helped them put the dinghy in the car, explaining hurriedly that he was expecting an imminent visit. With everything packed away, he offered them a final chance to own a stuffed rabbit, reduced in price due to its missing an ear. Had Geri's wallet not been empty he would have considered purchasing the poor creature for a figure head, but as it was, he was forced to decline. Jim waved them off, glancing furtively over his shoulders and then slamming the huge doors shut.

'Where dae ye think he's off tae for the next year or two?' asked Geri innocently as him and Rob sped off.

'Her majesty's pleasure I reckon, and us too if we don't get moving' said Rob with a nervous smile.

The journey back to Bedford dragged and every police car posed a threat to their illicit cargo and red-diesel, stained engine. However, they encountered no problems and by the time midnight came around, they were sitting in the glow of the conflagrant jars of diesel which flickered a constellation around Rob's garden. They shared the first bottle of Old Bagpiper and toasted their future nautical adventures together.

'This tastes a tad like diesel' said Geri sleepily sipping his glass.

'Wouldn't worry bout that, it'll help ya float' replied Rob calmingly.

The next day, the sun - keen to witness this maiden voyage - beat eagerly down upon Bedford. The boys rose unhurriedly, and Geri decided that to phone in sick to the warehouse where he was already supposed to be, was perhaps magnanimous and in fitting with the decorum of a launch. They collected Mighton from the house and left Ed the cat in the care of Sean, a young homeless chap they had allowed to sleep on their sofa.

Weeping willows graced the riverbank and water voles peaked out curiously at these copper bearded pirates who cursed venomously at an old instruction manual. It was near the lunching hour and the smell of a BBQ drifted over in plumes of delectable smoke. The rich aroma awoke many insatiable appetites along the river; and swallows swooped for flies, herons wrestled fish and Geri's sandwiches came to a premature end. Fortunately for these virginal pioneers, Rob was a heaven taught mechanic. Though he neither needed nor wanted any pieces of paper to prove it, Rob could turn his hand to anything technical and the engine soon hummed agreeably as he spoke to it in tongues.

The dingy had a rough, dilapidated charm that suited its crew wonderfully. It was perilously shapeless, due to Geri forgetting the pump and insisting that Rob and Mighton should inflate her manually, excusing himself from this duty on account of his childhood asthma. Despite custom, it was of mutual decree that to christen the vessel by breaking a bottle over her rubber sides was both unwise and unlikely to attract luck. So, after hauling a treasure trove of tonic wine, tin whistles and discount snacks aboard, the three sailors hopped on, and Geri gave a long winded speech, hailing the beauty of the boat and so forth, until Mighton threatened to throw him overboard if he didn't soon navigate her onwards. They chartered a course east towards Danish Camp and the river laughed merrily to see these scurvy souls floating by, lost in songs and alcohol. It lapped and splashed as high as it could, cackling wickedly at the curses that came tumbling from Mighton's mouth every time it soaked his jeans. The vessel bobbed down this blue ribbon at a respectable speed, and Mighton gave up on keeping dry and instead concentrated his efforts on rather rousing renditions of 'Over The Sea To Skye' and 'The Loch Tay Boat Song'. Geri joined the choruses with inarticulate fervour, and Rob lay back enjoying the melody of the engine and the heat of the day. They left Bedford town behind and sailed past meadows, cows and endless hedgerows, where once wandering tramps had slept under stars. Onwards they journeyed, taking in the area where all the local hippies lived in huts and barges. Old women smiled and children laughed as the boys came sailing by. Bountiful vegetable gardens graced the riverbanks there and benches were placed around them, upon which outcasts sat enjoying the even tenor of the summer days. Rob explained that this community would soon be evicted due to planning laws and the proposed building of apartments. Mighton shook his head at this and Geri spat contemptuously in the water as though it housed the makers of mad laws.

It was a perfect day of the quintessentially English sort, a kind of Wind in the Willows remixed on speed. The only flaw was that the further they travelled the more inebriated they became, which made it harder to lift the boat onto the banking with every lock they encountered. Those on board the bigger boats had paid for keys and so sailed smugly through the locks without hindrance. Mighton asked in his best attempt at Queen's English if one of them could 'do us a favour and leave the gate open for us?'

The man on the boat disdainfully replied, 'It costs money to have a key and one must be prepared to work hard in order to achieve said money'.

Mighton spluttered furiously about being a care worker and 'what kind of creepy cunt wears white troosers an' a blazer anyways?' But the boat had already roared proudly away. With no other choice, the boys were again forced again to carry their own vessel around the lock. Geri attempted to give captains orders as to how to do this, to which Mighton responded, 'I'd rather take orders fae Captain Pugwash than you, Captain Ugly, so shuttit!'

'Silence starbolin, and hand me the scuttlebutt,' Geri shouted, secretly wishing that his book of nautical terms had come equipped with a guide to pronunciation.

'Haw! I'll scuttle your butt if ye dinnae shut yer trap, ya great clown,' roared Mighton, as he jabbed a bony pinkie in the direction of Geri's eye.

Fortunately, any optical intrusions were avoided, as Mighton lost his balance and landed rump to rowlock with a bump and a howl.

Rubbing his posterior, the lanky Scotsman glared in fury at the rowlocks.

'Ha! That'll teach ye for yer vile and mutinous ways, Seaman Stains, me old matey!' chuckled Geri, as he wobbled unstably onto the land with a tin of beer in each tattooed hand.

Rob separated the engine and carried its heavy weight easily around the lock, while Mighton and Geri attempted to lift the vessel above their heads. This task was hampered by the prohibitive height difference between the boys. Being a head taller than Geri meant that Mighton shouldered the bulk of the boats weight upon his head and neck. The pair hobbled along, shouting unwanted advice at each other. Geri informed Mighton that he had legs like a pair of baguettes, lacking the required physical strength to carry the boat at a respectable pace. Then adding insult to injury, Geri hissed through a fit of drunken giggles,

'Naw naw! In fact ye look like yon crippled, baby giraffe we saw mincin' aboot in that documentary'.

Mighton swung round, brandishing a long finger and informed Geri that he wouldn't be seeing much more after he'd 'poked him in his nasty wee squint eyes'.

Finally, they made it round the lock to the water. Rob was already at the riverbank enjoying a smoke, and appeared not to have broken any sweat, despite carrying the engine some thirty metres. Emasculated and embarrassed, Geri and Mighton replaced their squabbling with a steely silence and glared at each whilst sipping a fortification. Rob broke the impasse with the news that they were now close to a river side pub and could tie up the boat and enjoy a cool beer or two. The atmosphere improved tangibly and all three eagerly worked together to get the vessel reassembled as quickly as possible.

Within twenty minutes they had arrived at a jetty, above which lay a vast lawn leading to a promising looking country pub. With a hand painted sign above the door and squint, oak beams holding up its head of thatch, Geri assessed that it would be a surprise if it was one of the tax-dodging chain bars he despised so much. However, on seeing the Jaguars and BMWs parked to the side of it they silently acknowledged that this place presented a different irritation to those of the tasteless pints and tuneless corners of the chain pubs. Instead, such an establishment as this – while undoubtedly home to rich, real ales – would also be home to rich, and real little England

Tories. None of the boys cared so much how others chose to vote but they were aware that such pundits tended to look unfavourably on tattooed Scotsmen - the likes of which were foreign to the Etonian pastures of their youth - and occasionally denied them access to 'their' pubs and clubs.

The boys entered with trepidation, but the barman caught their eyes and offered a subtle yet welcoming grin towards them. He was secretly enthralled to receive boating customers that potentially could converse in a language other than that of mortgage rates and index pensions.

As the boys ordered their beverages he nodded courteously and gifted them free snacks and another uncustomary smile. Elated from having finally acquired a cold glass of beer, the boys thanked the barman and wandered outside to lay on the grass and watch the swans. Geri mumbled something incomprehensible and then marched back to the bar, returning with a whisky for each of them, assuring them 'the best way to raise yer spirits is wi a hand tae yer mooth!'

The whiskies warmed their throats and keen to give the squawking swans a run for their money the boys began to sing some Celtic tunes in acapella. The volume increased as they competed for the attentions of a busty women, already surrounded by a salivating pack of well-dressed suiters. She looked their way wistfully for a second and shone them a smile of unfettered affection, then sighed and returned to finding a 'suitable' suitor.

As the lads burst into an explicit version of 'Seven Drunken Nights', the barman – who had ventured outside under the pretext of collecting glasses - enjoyed another lift of the corners of his mouth, as he observed the irritation on the faces of his usual clientel. He became gregarious and more generous with every measure of amber that he poured, and the boys drank them up gladly. As far as the river was concerned, it had seldom had better company. All day it had been blessed by a presence beyond the standard and monotonous, and it gurgled to itself in frothy contentment.

The busty woman eventually left with a wealthy man and bats began to dance as the growing dusk hailed the end of the day. As twilight descended the boys decided to return to the boat and they wobbled and fell as they attempted to cross the vast lawn. After a few tumbles they made it to the vessel and charted their way homewards. Silhouettes of willows wept above them and a cold mist crept in. All of them regretted having no warm clothes as their beer jackets began to wear off. About two miles from Bedford, the engine started to cough and splutter. Eventually it puttered off into a deathly silence.

'Start it Rob?' Geri demanded, shaking with cold and cursing the biting mists.

'No can do mate, its gone run outta fuel. Best bets to store the dinghy behind that hedge and we can come back for it tomorrow'

'The engines alright tae leave, but some swine will steal the boat it's no so heavy. Mighton mark my words, it'll be a sabotage of this cabotage if ye dinnae help me get it hame!' pleaded Geri.

'Naw, it'll be sabotage of a simple cabbage, that's whit! Am no dragging this muckle brute hame. You're the captain, Captain Ugly, so deal wi it, I'm walking hame its freezin'!'

Mighton smirked and leapt out the boat, shivering and hugging his freezing torso as he waited for Rob. Rob shrugged at Geri saying,

'Sorry mate, but it's no use to drag it back, it'll be fine, c'mon lets go'

'Mutinous feckin' wenches and jessies!' cried Geri, 'I am a captain by God and a captain stays wi his ship'.

'Geri ye've mair alcohol in ye than a guid bottle eh Scotch, mon noo and we'll get it in the morn, it's a good three mile tae go' coaxed Mighton.

'Aff ye'se go jessie feckers, i'm standin' by ma tub,' roared Geri passionately.

The lads needed no further encouragement and staggered off, rubbing their icy hands together and stumbling into the night.

Geri watched until they had disappeared, and a wave of pride washed over him. Here he was, alone by the water, the fearless captain of a fine vessel. Whistling what he thought might be a sea shanty he half carried, half dragged the deflated dingy slowly along the riverbank in a pious fashion. The fact that the sharp sticks and stones tore holes in its deflated sides bothered him not a jot. He had proved his worth to the river and the seven seas and that was enough for him.

Under the milky moonlight all that could be seen was the vague silhouette of Bedford's last pirate as he shuffled along.

Chapter 6 - Willie Shakespeare

"Come, gentlemen, I hope we shall drink down all unkindness"

Shakespeare - The Merry Wives of Windsor 7.

Geri and Mighton sat in front of their television in a state of irritation and despair. They had just finished watching Celtic lose their final match of the season and having nobody nearby to blame but the screen they both looked for a source to vent their frustrations upon.
Mighton was the first to break the silence.

'That wis feckin' shite man eh? I wis very dissimpressed there'

Geri turned his head abruptly and addressed his friend with a critical and withering stare.

'Dissimpressed were ye aye? That's no even a feckin' word ya clown ye'

Now it was Mighton's turn to look angry and he wagged a finger at Geri crying out,

'Dissimpressed's a word if I say it's a word an' noo am disimpressed wi you ya carnapcious cunt!'

Geri revelled in seeing his friend so wound up and in having found an outlet to direct his frustrations towards.

'Of course it's no a feckin' word if you say it's a word! Who the fuck dae ye think ye are man? Willie Shakespeare? Ye dinnae get tae go roond makin' up words unless yer a poet laureate or the likes.'

'A poet whit?? Am a poet L'Oréal…coz am feckin' worth it and dinnae ye go forgetting it sonny Jim!'

Geri shook his head and tutted as he feigned shock over his friend's misuse of the English language. In truth he couldn't care less but he was enjoying watching a prominent vein on Mighton's forehead pulsate and it was nice to know someone else was feeling even more irritated than himself.

'Poet laureate I said ya fool! Shakespeare contributed tae the rich tapestry oh oor language and that gie's him the right tae add in a word or tae. The only thing av seen you leave oan a tapestry wis vomit on that embroidery at yer gran's hoose!'

Mighton waved a fist. He did not like to be reminded of this incident and furthermore he had always deferred the blame to Geri for it, as Geri had on that day offered him Bushmill's whisky without first telling him what it was. Mighton had always claimed that it wasn't the quantity of whisky he had drank that had caused him to projectile vomit over his grandmother's handwork, but the Protestant nature of the whisky in question.

'Dinnae bring that up again! Ye ken fine it wis you sneakin' me proddy whisky whit done that, and av contributed just fine tae oor language, as ye call it ya wee sassenach, av written fine words an' set them tae tunes wi both The Romany Rogues and The Dirty Tales.'

Geri loved both of his friend's shambolic bands and was forced to grudgingly acknowledge this point.

'Aye fair play. Feck the queen and her dugs, was a fine line ye came up wi!'

'Aye! Thank you. So dissimpressed is noo a word and ye can use it if ye like.'

Geri let the word sound a few times in his head. It had a good ring to it, maybe he would use it sometime he thought.

'Alright then wordsmith, you win, noo lets sing some songs and forget that awful feckin' game oh fitbaw!'

Mighton grabbed his guitar from the floor and began to sing a ballad called Lazy Eyed Jane, that he had written together with Paddy. Geri raised a glass and joined in tunelessly and loudly.

'I thought of you darling the day before last
I'm not good at love songs but I'll give it a bash
Just saying if you come back I'll buy my own beer and all that
Hell I'll que for you at the bar, you mind how we were with a jar.

The hangover hits fore the last round is bought
I'm a fuck up I know it but you sure love the lost
Nothings for free and I guess I'm the cost

Come back to me lazy eyed Jane
What's loves perfume without pain

Well life seems too slow and death seems too fast
I exist in between them, but I know it can't last
You're a rock of salvation I spied from the mast
In truth you're my only friend
Coz the beers just leave me in the end

Do you do the love thing
I want to know
I more do the beer thing and sometimes the snow
But I'm open to love hell I'll give it a go

So come back to me lazy eyed Jane
What's loves perfume without pain'

As Mighton finished his rendition Geri applauded wildly.

'Great effort man! Ye can make up aw the words ye damn well like, yer ma Willie Shakespeare!'

Chapter 7 - The Royal Wedding

'Pardon My Sanity In A World Insane'

Emily Dickinson [8].

Union Jack bunting lined the estate, in migraines of red, white and blue. The reptilian heads of royals and those tenuously connected to them filled the front covers of every tabloid in the land, and conveniently relegated changes in fracking policy to the back pages. Great masses of people had queued on the streets outside Buckingham Palace, waiting for days on end to catch a glimpse of the God's of tabloid mythology. Apart from in the army, this was the only time when the underclasses and upper classes stood in the same place, with a common cause. However, unlike in the army, here the upper classes stayed, shoulder to shoulder, all the way to the frontline with the underclasses.

Corner shop owners filled their shelves with gossip magazines, their glossy cover's promising salacious secrets of 'our' Royal Wedding and 'day of pride'. Yet, despite the corner shops' lavish displays of deference and devotion to Britain's rightful rulers, their owners still became uneasy at the sight of every flag-clad, white skinhead who entered their premises.

Every non-white school child knew that the boots of the skinheads stomped a little closer to their 'foreign' heads at events of collective patriotism such as a royal wedding. During these times, the 'non-whites' right to live and work in Britain proved to be a painful reminder - to skinheads and gentry alike - of colonies and domination long lost. Worse still, the gods these 'foreigners' revered were not always the same as the one who had supposedly elected the Hanover's to the throne.
Such tensions were running high, when Daire Mighton entered the Bedford corner shop. He held the door open for a wiry man

sporting a notably gigantic, Union Jack ring. Its sharp edges were perfectly proportioned to leave a royal seal stamped on the noses of infidels.

It was a Saturday, and as Mighton always did on the rare weekends he was free from work, he had begun his day with a trip to the shop for cigarettes and samosas.
Having purchased his hereditary heart attack, he smiled, comforted by the knowledge that with every oily mouthful there should be less need to worry about his non-existent pension plan and old age.
However, this nihilistic satisfaction was interrupted as his eyes became bombarded by a barrage of royalist headlines that leapt at him from the shelves.

'Christ oan a bike! Is there really wankers that buy this patriotic pish Salem?!'

The shop keeper glanced nervously at the floor and began muttering something, but before he could answer, the man with the Union Jack ring snorted, and bellowed,

'You wot?!'

The shopkeeper gave an inwards groan and the Union Jack ring seemed to gleam red in bloody anticipation, yet Mighton continued with blind indifference.

'Whit dae ye mean *I wot*? Just whit I says wee man. It's patriotic pish, unelected powers, granted by God, tae rich cunts. I'm nae foolin' maself intae thinkin' im part oh this weddin' even if ma taxes sponsored it'.

The little man's eyes bulged and he massaged the monstrous ring with a pulsing palm.

'The taxes of some commi, pleb cunt like you don't compare to the money wot they bring in to us. It's a fact that nearly two billion a year is wot they bring in to our economy, so wot you got to say to that eh Jock?'

'I'd say slavery wis good fer yer British economy and yet we wrote aff that ootdated practice, all the while wi squeaks oh protest fae yon royals an aw yer ruling classes toffs!'

The man looked more astonished than furious now, and with a bewildered tone he cried out,

'You bloody wot?! You can't compare slavery to our queen!'

'Ma man are ye deaf?!' said Mighton. 'I just did and fir the sake oh yer blocked up lugs ah'll say it again. Baith things are guid fir the economy, but whae gies a fuck? They're baith morally apprehensible and based oan grim hierarchies. Yon German queenie's family got tae a throne through blood shed and oppression, and made plenty money fae slavery, no through the will oh God! Nae wonder baith Hitler and the Mail held them in high esteem, feckin' blue blooded fascism! But hoot toot! That's just ma opinion, dinnae let me spoil it aw for ye.'

The man's head appeared to emit steam, like a dumpling prematurely plucked from hot broth. All disbelief and surprise had now transformed into a trembling kind of rage, and through clenched teeth his words jammed and scraped, before shooting out spasmodic, rusty bullets.

'Listen...you...cunting faggot...four generations of my family...have fought and...died for our...queen'

'Well then, its high time she fights and dies for use' said Mighton, neatly side stepping back and exiting the shop with a wink at the owner.

Outside the summer's heat hit him, and whether the clouds had been deliberately dispelled by chemical gasses, good luck or a patriotic God, it was hard to say, but it certainly was a beautiful day for a wedding. The hot air seemed to be trapped between the small rows of brick houses and Mighton sweated profusely as he walked homewards through the narrow lanes. Every Sky television dish was dressed in British bunting, almost as though Murdoch himself was there dancing on the estate walls. Smells of barbecue coals being lit early in countless gardens, caused his stomach to grumble and he began to nibble the corners of the second samosa that he'd bought for Geri. By the time he'd reached their faded front door, there was less than half of the greasy triangle left.

As he kicked the door open, Ed leapt up to great him and then sprang out into the street in great haste. Mighton tutted and made his way to the living room skilfully navigating a course past all the empty cans that covered the floor.

Geri was reclining upon the couch, gazing at the television and smoking a hand rolled cigarette. Dressed only in a tattered pair of boxer shorts, a straw hat and Mighton's silk dressing gown, he looked like a cross between an 19th century gent and a mentally ill gigolo. He waved a hand of acknowledgement at Mighton, and in doing so dropped a large amount of ash down the silk robe.

'Christ Geri! Ma misses bought me that, its ma shaggin' robe!'

Geri swung his head down and stared at the sleeve.

'Jesus! Is that whit that stain is? Ah thought I'd dropped ma breakfast yoghurt.'

Mighton began chuckling, but stopped abruptly, crying,

'You dinnae hae any scran in the fridge ya cheeky wee shite! Hae you been stealin' ma caramel yoghurts an oatmeal again?'

Geri was in the process of racking his brains for plausible excuses, when Mighton interjected with a horrified yelp.

'Geri sir! Dinnae tell me yer watchin' the royal weddin' are ye? Nae wonder Ed bolted oot! Whit the hells wrang wi ye man?'

Geri wheezed clumsily on his cigarette, dropping more ash on the robe, before wiping it in with a dirty hand, and replying.

'That's a fine an' fair question ye pose, nae doot aboot it.'

Here he stopped to further ponder the question and scratched absentmindedly at an itch in his nether regions. Mighton began to speak but Geri cut him off with a wave of his cigarette and another shimmering cloud of ash.

'Truth is, ah came tae yon wedding by mistake, it wis the first thing oan the telly. But ye ken how we agreed we love tae watch the Huns getting pumped even mair than watchin' the boys in green win? Aw fir the thrill oh gettin' unco wound up an' hurlin' drunken abuse at the screen?'

Mighton nodded suspiciously and so Geri continued.

'Well it's kinda like that. I've been enjoyin' a good rattlin', roarin' volley oh abuse at the screen all morn, an' a must say ah feel a new man! Better oot than in eh?'

Just then the costs and designs of the bridesmaid's dresses were announced on the television and delighted claps could be heard from the old woman next door. Mighton hurled the remainder of the samosa at the screen and unleashed a string of curses. Geri nodded encouragingly whilst crawling over to the TV to pick up the samosa, which he cleaned with Mighton's robe before popping it in his mouth and returning to his seat. Mighton joined Geri there, and was soon roaring again at the TV and the idiocy of the presenters and public.
Geri raised a clenched fist screaming,

'Mon yersel' Mittens, gie them hell!'

Mighton continued to roar and Geri dashed into the kitchen, reappearing with a bottle of ginger wine and two cracked mugs.

'Good for the throat, longevity oh the vocal cords an' aw that!'

Mighton accepted the mug graciously and the pair spent an enjoyable afternoon screaming at the screen.

Outside in the terraced gardens, barbecues sizzled, and flasks of fake champagne popped. Fireworks went off and racists raised righteous hands in salutes to a long dead empire. The old woman next door – being somewhat deaf - heard only muffled shouts and cries above the blaring of a TV and forgave the unruly boys for some of their sins, relieved to learn that they were at least British enough to be so excited about the royal wedding. So, yet another divided evening was passed in the United Kingdom, one of celebrations for some, commiserations for others and yet too much alcohol for nearly all.

When the next day came, Mighton got up before Geri. His throat was hoarse and raw from shouting, yet he was grateful to his friend for the suggestion of such riotous entertainment. He decided to treat Geri and wandered to the corner shop to buy them both samosas and Irn-Bru.

The street was covered in broken glass and the omnipresent bunting hung a little more tired and drooping than the day before. Besides for the birds in the trees, the day was dead, with the British public either nursing celebration hangovers, or still hiding at home, cursing skinheads, and a silly tax system.

As Mighton struggled down the road, he recognised a man leaving the shop as being the angry man he'd met there the day before.
Before the man could say a word, Mighton tipped his hat and croaked,

'Mate I owe ye an apology. Yon wedding wis mair fun than any footbaw match in the world. Aw the best tae ye sir, aw the best.'

The man glared, then seeing Mighton to be serious, embraced him in a sinewy hug, patriotic tears glistening in his eyes.

'It wos a great day for a great nation. Welcome home to Great Britain my son, best fuckin' country in the world!'

The shopkeeper gazed out of his window in astonishment at these two men hugging. How volatile and erratic these white Englishmen are, he thought as he shook his head. He comforted himself that hopefully there would be no more royal weddings anytime soon and whistled as he began to take down his bunting.

Chapter 8 - The Shindig

'There can be nothing more frequent than an occasional drink'

Oscar Wilde [9].

A party tended to be unplanned at Mighton and Geri's house and was rather something which grew quickly like malignant cells multiplying at a terrifying speed. At such times the craic became a ceilidh, the sesh a shindig and a party would spawn into being. Their door was perpetually open to all, and after pubs shut and parks grew cold, a delightful and diverse collection of beings could be found behind its crooked frame. Due to their proximity to a gay bar on one side and the Jamaican area on the other, it was not uncommon to find drag queens and young Jamaican military men conversing and taking the proverbial piss out of each other in the small hours of a Monday morning. Likewise, bohemian atheists chinked glasses with young Catholic mothers while kebab shop employees and Polish labourers danced up and down the stairs. The only *sine qua non* of the night was to live and let live, and apart from Mighton and Geri's inevitable squabbling, this rule was generally adhered to. Imaginations were unchained and most folk managed to rid their minds of a lifetime of cultural colonisation.

This Friday, however, was to be one of those rare and wonderful eves known in the dwelling as a 'real' party. The finer points, distinguishing a 'real' party from a customary eve, were somewhat hazy, but specific to the 'real' version, was Mighton and Geri's prior acknowledgement and acceptance, that; the event would be loud, shambolic and that without intention they would probably break each other's possessions. The event worthy of such honour was Mighton's birthday. After the past two years of venturing to Benidorm for such festivities, the boys had had enough of 'scum in the sun' as they dubbed it and decided to celebrate this one on *tera mater*. This decision was in no small part due to the last holiday's range of minor mishaps, including floating towards Africa, passed out on a lilo, and subsequently dealing with angry coast guards, aggressive sunburn, and other such incommodious vexations.

Every odd ball in Bedford was invited to the party, and many more from the 'old country', as Geri wistfully called Caledonia, in his absence. A ripple of excitement pulsed through the hearts of the invited freaks and unsavouries all over the world. This was to be a night of heathenry fit to match old Tam O'Shanters tale's and with whisky enough to sate Finnegan's Wake. It was destined to become an event, for bards and Buckfast tramps to sing of for all eternity to come, and fortunately for all future souls, there was to be plenty of bards and tramps attending all ready to transpose the night's happenings to lyric. Geri's number of invitations were extravagant and beyond an extensive list of friends, all the local check out girls, and old Indian news agents were encouraged to, 'fire on roond for a craic and a can an' what-not'.

It seemed people were to be arriving from all over the world. Paddy-the-Tink, Linlithgow's lanky poet and lapsed Buddhist was hitchhiking there from somewhere or other and Ivor Ryder-Jones, Welsh barbarian, bard, and banjo picker, had promised to take sick leave from a new job in London to join. The news of Ivor having a job troubled Geri, he had never known Ivor to have a job beyond busking and begging, and he was concerned by this ill-fitting life choice yet at the same time relieved to see it was not a choice taken too seriously and one that could be happily ditched in favour of a party. As word of all the attendees trickled in, Geri and Mighton began to feel excited, it seemed life's most unusual chess pieces were on the move to the same corner of the board, ready for of a gargantuan evening of merriment and decadence.

Geri could not get either the day of the party or the day after it off work as a holiday. He had tried seducing his boss with flattering lies and fluttering eyes, but his lies and his eyes were shaky and didn't reap the desired results. Insulted, he muttered that his boss must be the only man alive who could have no homosexual tendencies when concerning such a dashing young man as himself. However, he managed to swap a shift and get the Friday of the party itself off work, albeit not the deadly day after.

After an agonizing wait, the Friday in question came and Geri decided to get his blood circulating by playing a spot of football in the park. Joined by a bunch of waifs, he sprang hither and tither round Bedford Park, chasing after the ball with zealous enthusiasm. There were nearby females to impress, and he envisioned himself as a slight gazelle, speeding over the African plains. The summer sun was warm, and his face became as red and contorted as his beating heart, which pounded an erratic and dangerous rhythm against his ribs. The rules of the match were simple; a can of lager was to be held in each hand, and every possible hack and foul should be immediately undertaken. All was going swimmingly for Geri's sporting prowess until the boot of a two tonne Scot slid and smashed into his lower leg. There was a sickening, crunching sound and Geri passed out. 'Big clumsy Johnny' – the large Scot -looked moderately concerned and he sat patiently by Geri's side waiting for him to awake. The stocky fellow passed the time unperturbed by sipping from the can he had commandeered from his unconscious friend. Returning to the lucid world a few minutes later, Geri howled in pain and demanded strong alcohol and a doctor.

'Dinnae be a fanny', said Mighton.

'It's just a wee scratch, an' it's a Friday, if ye go tae the quacks noo, ye'll be there aw night and ye'll miss the shindig. Just get a drink in ye hen and rest the leg'.

Geri accepted the idea of a cure through alcohol and allowed himself to be supported home by a couple of the female football players. However, by the time they got back his foot had swollen to twice its usual size and turned the colour of a rotten peach. Sitting on the doorstep to greet his miseries was Ivor who had somehow arrived from London with only one shoe on and was strumming a banjo while idly picking his nose.

'Alright boyos, how you all doing' shouted Ivor in his resounding Welsh brogue.

'No bad. You've got egg or summit on yer beard' replied Mighton as he hugged the hulk of a man.

'So I av, could be kebab from yesterday, got a free one, I was jammin' with this awesome Kurdish guy in the kebab shop. Jeesus!! What you done to your foot Geri?' said Ivor.

'It's a sporting injury', answered Geri, 'feels like it feckin' well needs amputated. I ought tae get tae the doctors'.

'Doctors?!' asked Ivor, a little confused. 'No need for that dude, I've got some mead I found'.

With that Ivor produced a bottle that both looked and smelt like urea and shared it round the merry throng.

Despite Geris complaints, the day progressed smoothly, and the sun projected affection with feverish intensity. Bedraggled outlaws, tattooed orphans, and nervous neighbours made their way to the house. Ed the cat was torn between proudly meeting guests at the front door and stealing sausages off the enormous BBQ that Rob had welded out of an old gas canister. Meanwhile Ivor and his banjo were helping to raise the spirits and volume of the party with an ear-splitting version of 'Cannae Shove Yer Granny Off A Bus'. Mighton, who had given up on trying to play with him, shook his head with a grin. Like most musicians who attempted to join in with the Welsh giant he was befuddled by Ivor's unique sense of rhythm, whilst simultaneously in awe of his rich, booming voice. On anyone else it would have sounded cacophonous, yet Ivor Ryder-Jones mastered his deep vocal cords and sang like the voice of a mountain, an ancient God of stone from some bygone era. The party cheered and sang, the uninvited neighbours hissed and cautioned, and Ed continued to dash between sausages and door greetings.

At a certain point in the evening, the sun reluctantly sank from the sky and the moon graced the night's stage, encouraging lunacy and reckless kisses under her soft, and charming glow. Shooting stars winked at her slender creamy curve and Orion danced madly in a bid to win her favour. Countless miles beneath, equally mad dances were transformed into stop motion silhouettes by the moonlight appearing and disappearing behind the clouds. These courting rituals and ceilidh freestyles were performed by various revellers in Geri's back garden. However heavy work makes for thirsty mouths and the guests reached a consensus that it would be prudent to send a search party into the night to locate, purchase and/or purloin ales in great number just in case they should run out. Geri and Ivor were greatly sympathetic to the cause and so offered their services freely and headed into the town. Geri's foot and ankle were now purple and pulsating, so he threw an arm round Ivor's huge shoulders and together they stumbled and tumbled along, singing old rebel songs and Hamish Henderson poems as they tripped over one another.

A little lost in their search for a purveyor of cooking lager they found themselves pressed against a modern, glass cube that labelled itself as an RnB club. The music that blared out was both egregious and commercially crass, and within its confines swayed beautiful people back and forth, stealthily glancing at the window and fixing their hair in its reflection.

'That's one fuckin' depressing glass coffin. Jeez I've seen more animated corpses at a wake.' said Geri, sounding genuinely despairing.

Ivor produced a dirty, plastic comb from his shirt pocket and ran it through his thick beard and thinning curls. He licked a hand, slicked his remaining locks back, then turned to Geri and said, 'that's as may be but I'm in the mood to talk to a beautiful woman in a dress, and seeing as most of the beautiful women at yours are trannies and I'm not that pisky enough to be so inclined yet, I'm going in here! Oh and I'll buy a whisky or two if there be a man brave enough to follow me in?'

Geri stood for a moment shaking his head morosely, then shrugged and hobbled after Ivor, sacrificing his principles for the promise of some of God's own fiery water.

At the party, Paddy and Mighton passed a bottle of Buckfast back and forth and made promises to make life changes and busk round the world one day.

Mighton laughed, 'I ayewis think it's a wee bit ironic that we toast tae tomorrow wi poison! Och ah ken I should drink less man, but I wanna kick the erse oot it while ah still can'.

Paddy pondered this a while and said, 'Nah man, this is good. I've seen it when creative folk calm down an' accept reality for what its prescribed tae be. I dinnae think destruction oh yer body is a necessary part of freedom, but it keeps life's party going and it's a hell of a lot better than destruction oh yer soul.'

Mighton chuckled, replying, 'Paddy yer words are always pretty but I can assure you I aint got nae soul'.

Paddy replied at breakneck speed in his muttered, machine gun brogue. Every word shot was fired out after its predecessor, as if in a race to reach the listeners' ear.

'Aye well, hmmm, that's as may be ma man, but the point remains. Point, yes, aye. That use work enough to get by, but it's not the focus of yer lives. No! No! No! Use get it oot the way. Done! A necessary evil oh oor corrupted times, pay it nae mind, then it's gone and use play music, sing songs, meet folk every night. In this age oh isolation use are part oh something communal in a rough and ready sort of caring way. I've been on the periphery of the other side brother. I've seen good folks caring about shitey, pointless jobs just coz they pay a bit and give some intellectual kudos. Darwin would be proud of use. Humanity's pinnacle, perhaps. No stressed, no slaves! Aye yer livers could be better, but other than that, hmm aye!'

Mighton interjected, 'I'm no lazy, ya clown! I've worked hard aw ma life, an I care aboot ma job man, ah like helping folk there, but I just dinnae want it tae be my life, I need time for music, an merriment and taking in aw the mad magic of it aw afore ah drop aff ma perch.'

'Exactly!' Shouted a now animated Paddy, waving his hands round in crazed gesticulations.

'Most folk dinnae have or make time to take any of it in beyond the monotonous and mundane, hmm hmm hmm, yes, aye, that's whit kills the soul, or yer rock n roll or yer joojoo as Ivor calls it! Folk aw stressed up, living at their work long after they've left it, or worse still they get intae it, enjoying the empty, egoistic reward it brings. Taking it seriously, talking about it endlessly like it mattered and demanding others dae the same. They end up wi' money but nae time or imagination, evenings watching TV, boasting oh their day's success tae a bored partner and trying tae kick the shadow of doubt oot their minds. We're aw prisoners oh an inherently amoral system, but at least use dinnae invest in it and take it seriously, use live aroond it, and fill this world wi' colourful, creative chaos. That freedoms worth more than aw the 'best' jobs we were groomed fir as the young office fodder of this imperial abomination. Or worse still we were tae sign up to get shot at for minimum wage in the pursuit oh her majesty's black gold in foreign lands. Ah purposelessness, dreams, music, oneness, kindness, aw that clichéd but wondrous stuff! Shit the memories we hae brother, they gigs in the Bathgate Working Men's clubs we done with Ally and all the rest oh the revolving line up oh the Romany Rogues. True rock n roll, without an ounce of hope for a pay check or fame! Fer hearts no charts!'

Mighton snorted and responded, 'ah Paddy, I love ye, but you dinnae half talk shite, two 'fans' came to those gigs an' baith for the free sausage rolls on a Wednesday night. But aye whit a band eh, at least we enjoyed it! Big in ma heart if no in the charts!'

The pair laughed and raised yet another glass to the moon who was also half full.

Inside the house, the party raged on, and the floor shook as a mass of feet jumped up and down to 'In The Rare Old Times'. A girl in the corner, induced in psychedelic rapture tried to paint the ecstasy of the evening, using cigarette ash on a chip shop newspaper to create an abstract work of genius understood only by herself. Upstairs a couple fornicated on Geri's filthy sheets, and in the landing, Ed toyed with a burnt sausage.

Meanwhile, in the RnB club a young lady approached Ivor and Geri and much to Ivor's irritation, began to talk to Geri. Having overheard he was Scottish, she enquired as to the difference between Edinburgh and Glasgow. She had, she told him, been accepted to study law at both places and heard, on the good authority of past alumni, that Edinburgh was a delightful place, while Glasgow was perhaps somewhat less salubrious, and had a penchant for violence? She batted her eyes, and awaited his reply, keen to be shocked by accounts of the crimes both physical and cultural, committed by the heathens of the west coast. As Geri pondered over an answer, she waved her hand in front of his face, demanding details with the impatient force of someone used to getting their own way. Geri coughed patiently, closed his eyes, and cleared his throat with all the professionalism of the best pub story tellers. The girl sighed, and surveyed the redness of Geri's face and hair and eyes with a mixture of intrigue and repugnance. She had known that the Scot's cows and squirrels were red but hadn't thought the same applied to their populace. Ivor, who didn't care for silence in front of dames, cleared his own throat and was about to commence upon some heroic tales of his own bar room brawls and dragon slaying, when Geri finally spoke,

'Well hen, Edinburgh is a beautiful place, it's like a dream wrapped in winter, but like most pretty things it has a tendency tae be somewhat vacuous and precious. Glesgy oan the other hand is mair like the broken toothed smile of a tramp, naebody could say its stunning, but it's got personality and its hard no tae crack a smile back in return.'

The girl looked confused and a little annoyed by the lack of gore in this explanation, so Geri further ruminated and then offered a different explanation.

'I'll gie ye a wee example tae paint the picture. If ye go tae a gig in Edinburgh, every cunt will stand still an nod an scrutinise, and compose a wanky review in their head as if they were being expected to critique it fir The Times. It's no aboot soul or emotional impulse, its aboot intellect and provin' the worth oh yer ain evaluation. Noo, go tae the same gig in Glesgy, hell any gig there, an every cunt will be oot with one objective, tae have a good time and enjoy themselves. They'll be up jiving, an' grinning and getting' the drinks in for the shitest busker in toon. Ken whit I mean?'

The girl blinked at him with an irritated lack of comprehension. She began to wonder if the creature in front of her was one penny short of a pound. Geri, assuming the same about her, tried one final time to give a simpler explanation.

'Weegies will chib ye hen, aye, but it'll be the friendliest chibbing ye've had in aw yer puff, an' im even telt that cunts ring ye a joe baxi after. So it's no all bad eh?'

Deeply satisfied with the simple conciseness of his words, Geri crossed his arms and smiled. Sadly, any such genius was lost upon the young lady, who informed Geri in no uncertain terms that she was not aware of the verb 'to chib' and disliked the 'C word' and then flounced off. Ivor glared at Geri for losing the dame and tried to persuade him that if they ceilidh danced hard enough it would display their Celtic roots and doubtlessly begin conversations with other elusive beauties. Geri snorted and made his way to the bar. Unperturbed, Ivor jigged and whirled on his tiptoes in an astonishing display that resembled and smelt much like a billy-goat breakdancing. The crowd parted around him, and ubiquitous clouds of designer perfumes became punctured by the pungent smell of burnt sausages and molten testosterone. Geri returned and nobly joined his friend, swaying, and limping whilst glancing nervously down at his throbbing foot. Ivor glared at him and gave him an encouraging punch to dance harder. The jab floored Geri and a large bouncer marched over and grabbed Ivor. Ivor seemed to think this was a competitive display of affection and tried to win over the bouncer by engulfing him in a manic bear hug. The two men became locked in a battle of wills and strength. Seeing the dancing stop and the clubbers staring at him, Ivor was hit with a fear that the world had again misjudged his intentions and shouted.

'I just wanna hug everyone, you are all sound folk see, no problems?'

He dropped the bouncer and ran over to hug a well-groomed man on the dancefloor. At this point several other bouncers joined the affray, pinning Ivor to the floor and phoning the police. Ivor protested loudly, but he couldn't move, and Geri had no chance to help him. The police soon arrived, and Ivor was allowed to his feet to explain himself. As soon as he stood up, he immediately attempted to hug a policeman in order to explain his benevolent intentions. He was immediately pounced upon and locked in the back of the police van, where Geri generously hobbled in to join him. The constables wagged their fingers, sighed, and tried not to show smiles as Ivor recounted his version of the events. Fortunately for Ivor the police had no space for a loud, singing drunk in the cells and so drove the boys home. When at the door of Geri's house, one of the policemen produced a piece of paper and explained that it was notification of a strict ban from Bedford town centre for twenty-four hours. The boys hastily agreed to such terms and the police bade them farewell.

'Ivor you fool' Geri lamented, 'we cannae go in tae buy bevvie noo'.

Ivor nodded apologetically saying, 'don't worry about it lover, Mighton can go, it's his birthday, and besides there's more of me mead in me banjo case'.

Geri gave a relieved smile and limped towards the house, dragging his injured foot like a dead body behind him.

Inside the house the party was still raging on, and Ed was very proud to play host to such a wild extravaganza. He swanned up and down, nodding his furry features to the guests and flashing his anus to the fairest amongst them. However, despite the good vibes and bad dancing, the beer situation was becoming critical. Some fared better than others in the search for hidden cans and bottles. Those few with surplus tins hid their remaining stashes in the garden hedge, but this came with the problem of finding them again amongst the tangle of bramble thorns that covered the bush. Their yelps as they thrust furtive hands into the hedge caused the other revellers much mirth. Ivor downed the warm dregs of two already opened cans of beer he found in the bathroom and was immediately hit by the suspicion that one of them perhaps contained urine. In his tired and tipsy state, he was unsure how to handle such information and decided it was best processed after a snooze on the floor. It was a wise decision for as soon as he settled his head on the cold linoleum, he became rewarded by the auspicious sight of an unopened Tennents sitting under the bath. He opened it hurriedly and the warm beer replaced the essence of urine from his delicate palate. Rejuvenated and amazed by the unpredictability of the world he sighed with joy and gave a silent thanks for his luck.

Mighton and Paddy could handle the impending demise of beer no more, and with pride and arrogance decided that if a job was worth doing, it was worth doing properly, and that they and they alone could handle the responsibility and challenge of making it to the off licence and back again. The only hitch was that Geri and Ivor had spent most of the collected beer funds on whiskies in the RnB club, leaving the coffers near empty. Paddy decided that the solution was to take a guitar and a mandolin and try and busk their way to beer riches. The timing was opportune - albeit dangerous - for it was nearly the fighting hour, when the clubs and pubs turfed out their clients onto the streets, thus giving buskers an increased probability of earning cash but also a bloody nose. The boys were drunk enough to brave such risks and wandered to the town centre where they unsheathed their instruments and broke into a version of 'The Dundee Weaver'. The pub round the corner had just closed its doors for the night and a small crowd of red eyed wastrels, looking to party or to fight began to gather round them and dance. Coins rained into the guitar case and Paddy and Mighton bowed for their public and began a version of Paddy's song, 'The Tory Blues'. The trickle of stranded drunks converged into a swelling sea of bodies that swayed in front of the boys. The crowd became loud and ecstatic as they screamed the choruses back at the buskers and clapped their hands. Angry young men found a voice for their political frustrations and an electric tension filled the air. Tonight, there would be blood, but who's and where? The moon beamed down and encouraged lunacy by her simple act of presence. A woman shouted out of an upstairs window that this was not the time for protests, and that the council provided forms on how and when to have them, ideally quietly on workday afternoons. The crowd roared at her to shut up, but she shouted back that she had phoned the police and wouldn't stand by and let 'a bunch of bloody commies destroy Britannia!'

The constabulary arrived moments later and sighed at the sight of yet more trouble causing Celts.

'Better than armed robberies' sighed one of them, and they duly attempted to terminate the street party. Mighton and Paddy were warned that if they did not immediately cease to sing then they would be charged with instigating a riot. This appeared to vex the already riled crowd. A shouts erupted from there midsts,

'Don't pay no notice to the coppers man, fuckin' pigs, we is filmin' you innit, they touch you and they'll be done for, you aint doing no harm man!'

Mighton and Paddy were perplexed, on one hand this was the most rousing performance that they'd ever played, and a previously unknown energy pulsated anxiously and ecstatically through them like electricity in their veins. Yet, on the other hand, an increasing number of 'boys in blue' were turning up and the idea of spending a weekend locked in the cells instead of at a party was less than appealing. Fortunately, they were saved from having to choose between convictions or comfort when a member of the crowd invited everyone back to their house to continue the party there instead of the street. The mob, enticed by the promise of more alcohol, dissipated, sneering at the police as they swarmed by. Mighton and Paddy quickly concluded that their return to their own party could wait a while longer, and with an apologetic smile towards the policemen, they too turned and followed the direction of beer and the unknown.

As they sped to catch up with the mob, pangs of shame at having failed to return triumphantly with alcohol to their own party stabbed in their chests.

'Spontaneity should ayewis be savoured, and every adventure taken, and every thirsty guest at yer pairty surely kens that?' questioned Paddy desperately.

'Och aye, an' we'll be back soon enough' replied Mighton in earnest. They grabbed their instruments and ran after the crowd.

However, despite their good intentions, Mighton did not return to his party until the next day. That said, it would be unfair to the guests there, not to mention that the party carried on most nobly despite his absence. Indeed, it had taken on a life of its own. A heathen and immortal force, like a hurricane dancing into the limitless depths of insanity. Eventually though the festivities had reached a zenith and exhausted by this storm, the guests found floors to dream upon and beds to share. Only the hardy and mentally deranged remained awake. This ever-dwindling group had sat peacefully sipping dregs and telling stories of long ago, with their heads lolling and eyes rolling. The last to bed were Ivor and a fair maid whom he had simultaneously wooed and deafened with booming Welsh lullabies. Eventually all had turned quiet, save for the snores of drunks and purring dreams of a cat.

The next morning the sun rose early, keen to see all remnants of the night's revelry. The old woman next door also got up early. So dizzy was she in her eagerness to be disgusted by the contents of her neighbour's garden, that she completely forgot to read her morning copy of the Daily Mail. She scanned the mass of limbs and blankets, aching to see evidence of drugs and ring the police. None could be seen though and despite her pointed coughing nobody awoke, and the party slept on. Upstairs, Geri's nautical dreams were shredded by the piercing ring of an alarm. He was hit first with pride that he had remembered to set an alarm, and then with irritation, that it had ended his cosy slumber upon the floor. Looking up he made out the hazy shape of Ivor and a female in his bed. He smirked and fumbled across to the windowsill trying to find his contact lenses and bring the world into clarity. He found the Guinness glass he had left them in, but the saline solution and lenses appeared to have vanished.

'Fucks sake, I need tae get tae work, where the hells ma lenses?' shouted Geri accusingly at the glass. He then began to panic and wondered if he had slept with them in and had blinded himself as his concerned optician had predicted. He rubbed his eyes hard and stared but could still only just make out the outline of Ivor's forested back, while the details of its thickets, moles and tattooed creatures evaded him.

'Ivor! Wake up ya rancid beast, where are ma contacts? They're ma last pair an' I sat oan my glesses! I'm sure ah left them in yon glass.'

Ivor replied groggily, loud syllables separated by agonising delays, 'calm down dude… it's early… and if you mean… that pint of salty water…. then I drank it when…. I came in'.

Geri turned an unhealthy shade of purple and then sighed, calmed down and resigned himself to the fact that he was not fated to go to work today and would probably soon be looking for a new job. His attention then turned to his foot, which, even with his current lack of vision he could easily tell was neither the colour nor shape a foot should be. He crawled down the stairs and found a few folk now awake. They too shared his concerns that his foot looked not as a foot ought and offered to escort him to the nearest accident and emergency department. Geri began to enjoy the attention and suggested he would need a stretcher. His ever-resourceful friends sat him on an oversized sofa cushion and dragged it towards the door. Ed, still keen to play master to all ceremonies, rushed over to give Geri's toes a farewell lick. Having done so he nodded his consent for the cripple to be dragged out onto the street. It made for a peculiar sight, and more than one passer by wondered if Geri was a homeless king being dragged to some cardboard castle by his serfs. He sat astride the velvet cushion, bellowing orders, and waving graciously at strangers, his purple foot erect in the air. However, the day was hot and it made for fairly insufferable work to drag Geri all the way to the local hospital, so when a pub came into sight, Geri's servants revolted and went inside for a cold drink. Geri was incensed and roared of his injustices and inability to continue alone. Nobody responded or returned, so eventually he got up from the gutter, dusted down the cushion, and continued his journey with it clutched to his breast.

On entering the hospital waiting room, Geri was met by a barrage of stares and funny glances towards his foot and cushion. However, he merely smirked, put the cushion on the floor and sat on it, gazing mockingly at all the other poor fools perched on hard plastic seats.

After waiting an hour and dozing on his dusty cushion, he was received by a doctor, who fitted him with a plaster cast and told him that his foot and ankle were both broken and he was advised not to work, walk and especially not dance upon it for at least two months. The thought of being bed bound for a period delighted Geri and he made a list of all the books he would read as soon as had acquired new lenses.

After a stop at the pub and having a reproachful word with his servants, both man and cushion returned to the house, where Ivor, Paddy and most of the guests had skulked off without aiding the much necessary clean up. The newly returned Mighton laughed at his foot, then pointed him to the couch and offered him the remains of a large breakfast funded by the previous night's busking escapades.

The day passed quietly, and the only reminders of the party were the ghosts of empty bottles that lay scattered across the floor. The boys congratulated themselves and agreed that the night had been a success, and Geri suggested,

'If madness is liberation, then we saw freedoms baws first hand'.

Mighton poked his foot and told him to 'stop talking shite'. In the late afternoon, the boys received a phone call from Ivor, letting them know that he had made it to his work on good time but had then fallen asleep in the bathroom there for four hours, having gone there to check himself for pubic lice using his boss's antique magnifying glasses. His boss, alarmed that Ivor's snores could be the sounds of an epileptic fit, had finally kicked open the cubicle door, and been confronted by the sight of Ivor devoid of trousers, and clutching his prized artefact. He had thereby sternly explained to the Welshman that while disappearances were sometimes excusable, the manhandling of prized, Victorian artefacts was most certainly not.

The boys cracked up.

'Does that mean yer oot eh a job an' aw then Ivor, just like Geri?!' asked Mighton.

'Fraid so lover. Is it alright I crash the couch a couple weeks? Don't think me mam or missus will be too chuffed'

Geri and Mighton invited him for an elongated stay and revelled in the fact that the modern world still spawned such unusual and delightful creatures as Ivor. With cups of tea, they toasted God and thanked him for mental illness while playing on the Brian Jonestown record of that very title. Peace entered the valley and Mighton donated his and Paddy's remaining busking proceeds to Geri to help with his impending unemployment. Through eyes stoned by prescribed pain killers, Geri smiled up at the ceiling and thanked it that he no longer had to work yet could still afford to eat and more importantly, drink for a whole week. Perhaps he truly was the genius of the tavern!

Chapter 9 – Absinthe makes the heart grow fonder.

'I sit at my door, smoking a cigarette and sipping my absinthe, and I enjoy every day'

Paul Gauguin [10].

It was a few weeks after the party and Geri, Mighton, Paddy and Bedford's own Joe Turner were sitting in the park drinking beers and watching a charismatic religious gathering from a safe distance. All four of them were wearing matching, white plastic sunglasses to hide the fact that they were very stoned. They didn't tend to smoke with any great regularity but having found a bag of marijuana lying on the floor after the party they had unanimously deemed it wasteful not to smoke it to its natural conclusion and besides, as Paddy had pointed out, it was not like they could put up posters around Bedford enquiring after its rightful owner. They had decided to wait for a sunny Sunday and enjoy sampling it in the park while listening to the fantastic harmonies and incomprehensible lessons on morality that a local gospel group offered there throughout the summer months. The sunglasses, they hoped, would avoid any 'red eye' being noted by Bedford town's constabulary and do-gooding pensioners. They had been purchased for a pound a pair at a local pub from a man that wanted to be rid of them in a hurry. Mighton had unstintingly coughed up for four pairs, stating sagely that what they lacked in UV protection, they made up for in Kurt Cobain-esque chique. The others were less convinced but were happy enough to err on the side of caution when being high in public.

So, there they sat there, enjoying the high and the bombastic choruses, whilst mulling lazily over the debatable morals that the gospel choir emitted. Throughout this haze they relaxed, knowing that their altered state of mind was discreetly concealed behind shields of cheap, white plastic. They had smoked all of the bag's contents before leaving Geri and Mighton's house and this also steadied their nerves, as they now had nothing on their person that could count towards a possession charge. They were thus free to enjoy the music and the sating of their dry throats via a steady stream of cold lager and this they did.

Eventually the choir finished their performance and began packing away the folding chairs and makeshift pulpit before leaving the park. This caused the boys to awake from their collective daze and notice that they sat in deathly silence. Now silence and Scots make poor bedfellows at the best of times so Joe attempted to pre-emptively strike down any paranoia or unease that could arise from the quiet by posing a question.

'Hey Geri! That Ivor mate of yours from the party the other day is a funny fucker I'nt he? Where did you lot pick him up from then?'

Geri tugged at his beard, rolling his eyes back as if to search for a memory in the depths of his skull, and then turned slowly to Mighton saying,

'You knew him from when The Romany Rogues started out did ye no? First time I seen him was when he turned up with you, Paddy, Ally and Catholic Paul tae one of yer concerts at that shit hole place in Bathgate use used tae gig at. He wis trying tae play a moothie and chow down some sausage rolls he nicked fae the bar at the same time, it wis fuckin' hilarious. He choked and coughed them all up over some radge, local! I reckon the guy would have chibbed him too if Ally hadn't had the foresight tae knock him oot first!'

Mighton and Paddy burst into peels of inebriated laughter.

'Fuck me! That's right ah mind that' cried Mighton, tears of mirth now visibly appearing from below his sunglasses.

'But it wisnae me that foond the beast, I just met him at wan oh oor gigs, I think he only turned up tae play on the possibility oh free beer and hot chav lassies in the audience. Cunt had never even heard the tunes afore, just turned up and jammed, but he ayewis played well!'

Joe raised an eyebrow.

'Someone must surely have invited him to play with you boys right?'

It became Paddy's turn to leave the void of the silent high and return to being his syllabic self again.

'I can tell ye how it went Joe. Me and Ally kent him first man, noo it's a good story I reckon but it's no short, a man like that needs a good introduction eh. Are use in the mood to hear a yarm lads?'

His friends nodded a lukewarm consent and lay down upon the grass, keen to hear where one might hunt for a creature like Ivor Ryder-Jones. Paddy flashed a crooked grin, which displayed several chipped teeth all of them casued by falling on Buckfast bottles over the years. He downed the rest of his can, cracked his knuckles, and then began.

'Afore I can explain how it wis that I stumbled upon Ivor late one night I need tae introduce at least you Joe tae a couple of other characters fae up oor way that have nae made it doon tae Bedford yet.'

Joe nodded accommodatingly and Paddy returned to his tale.

'They are Ally MacLeod and Lachlan Cassady. Ally I'm sure ye'll meet some day, he likes a pairty and a jam sesh and seeing as use dae plenty oh both here I'm sure he'll wind his way doon at some point. He's a top lad like, despite being a loyal Hun and at least on paper an Orange Order man, an' a crackin' guitarist, comedian and a lot more benevolent of nature than his inherited interests and scarred knuckles may suggest.'

Geri interjected, 'Aye the mans a one off Hun if ye ask me like, introduced me tae The Pogues and Behan's novels, the mad fucker loves them both, he's no a bigot just ended up in thae funny clubs, mostly for the sesh I guess!'

Mighton glared at Geri, 'Here! Baw jaws! Is it Paddy tellin' the story or you?'

Geri threw up his hands theatrically and then waved at Paddy to continue.

'Well anyways, Ally wis a founding member oh The Rogues along wi me and Mighton and it just so happens that he's one of the wittiest fuckers on the planet. Folk take to him real quick and any fears they hae aboot his reputation for scrapping melt away as soon as they meet him. I knew him fae school, he used tae shop lift Christmas presents for anyone that wanted, but only fae the supermarket like not fae the wee local shops, the man's got a code eh! He'd sell whatever you wanted tae you for a quarter oh the retail price. I bought my folks gifts fae him fae years, my ma found out later, and she still loves him!

Anyhow, I'd started workin' at a function centre in Edinburgh, in the cafe like washing dishes and that, and I'd met this new guy Lachlan there. All the other folk in the kitchen listened tae happy hardcore pish but he'd ayewis hae the Velvets on, so we got chatting a bit aboot music and that. He was training tae be a rugby teacher at that time, so I was suspicious at first, coz I'd never met a rugby player that wisnae a cunt, but he wisnae and that's for sure. I soon realised he was mair of a freak than he let on, he looked dead normal like, then one day he came intae work in his usual sports gear but with a pair oh bright blue cowboy boots on. Feckin' things had spurs and everything! So anyway, I worked out there was more tae him than met the eye, and I wis right. One day after the boss took away oor breaks and stole oor tips again, we decided that Lachlan would hold watch while I filled up a two litre cola bottle with different spirits fae the bar there. We got pished together in a nearby park and cemented oor friendship. The cunt had loads tae tell, he'd travelled a lot, was living with thirteen Spaniards in a three bedroom flat and hinted without boast that he'd met a fair few women from a fair few countries during his time on this mortal coil. That was something I came to find out aboot him later, that he never boasted about anything, just let you talk, but the man was like a magnet for exotic lassies. Every other cunt would be fighting tae outdo each other in front of them, like peacocks at a pairty and big Lachlan Cassady would make nae effort, feck off to bed early and while everyone else was still fighting and shouting the lassies would excuse themselves and just kinda naturally gravitate to his bedroom. I mind me and Ivor discussing it, he reckoned its coz he looked really Celtic with these bright blue eyes and freckles and all but I'm fecked if I can tell you his secret. All I know is that the summer when the Rogues had first started, me and Ally stayed at his hoose almost every night and partied with the Spaniards and most every night we'd end up sleeping in the hall waiting for him tae finish shagging some beautiful lassie that the rest oh us had failed miserably with! It was a hell oh a summer, Ally had some money coming in coz he'd already started oan the rigs then, so he stood for the beers, and all the Spaniards loved that, so we were welcome to pairty and crash there most nights.'

Paddy stopped his story and looked intently at Joe before continuing.

'It's maybe hard for ye tae grasp having grown up in Bedford and all, but we came fae West Lothian where being Irish was exotic! Aye back then before the Poles came it was the most monotonous, mono-cultural place on God's green earth. So, imagine how excited me and Ally wis to be at parties filled with mad Spanish cunts speaking a language we couldn't understand and trying to teach us flamenco guitar and that. And by Christ the women, they were fiery motherfuckers, a passionate and political lot as likely to punch you as kiss you, och aye it wis a good time there.

Geri interrupted him again,

'Paddy your no meant to be recounting an odyssey of every odd cunt in Edinburgh, your meant tae be telling us how a man meets a freak like big Ivor!'

Joe glared at Geri,

'Shuttup man! You ain't got no respect for a storyline innit? You need to set the scene and all, but you just wanna go straight to the punch line. Jeez its dick'eds like you directing porn that have ruined the industry, no bleedin' plots just straight to pumping! Ignore him Padwise son, on you go!'

Paddy smiled and nodded.

'Well as I say Ally and I had started crashing most nights at Lachlan's, and one night from somewhere Ally had procured this mad absinthe shit. I mean ah ken its ayewis strong, but this shit wis lethal. It hit yer feet afore yer heid and fore ye kent it ye'd be were fawin' erse over tit. Anyways, we'd been knocking it back and then we'd gone tae that rock bar Opium doon the Cowgate in Auld Reekie. We were having a great time and Ally wis on fire wi' the jokes an' as I mind it we were making good progress wi' some punk lassies. Well Ally offered tae buy everybody a roond so me and Lachlan volunteered tae wait at the bar and leave him entertaining the girls. It wis a busy night so we were waiting quite a while and the room was fair spinning aroond us coz of this vile absinthe shite. Suddenly we hear a commotion and turn roond tae see Ally with his face aw bleedin', being flung oot oh the bar by a big bouncer. Well, we ran over and asked whit wis going on, we just assumed he had gravitated towards a scrap like. Ken he's one of they cunts that loves tae stick up for the underdog, fists first if ye ken whit I mean! The bouncer told us tae take him hame and look after him, says he was clearly deranged as he'd just headbutted and smashed a huge mirror on the wall. We got a wee bitty concerned coz Allys no the attention seeking or jumpin' aff the Forth Bridge type, so we headed oot tae see what was going on. Ally was sitting on the pavement rolling back and forth and laughing hysterically, his face wis a mess and there was a fuck tonne eh blood pishin' oot his forehead intae his eyes. I kinda freaked oot but Lachlan was used to patching up rugby wounds ken, so he produced a tissue fae somewhere and mopped Ally up. With the worst oh the blood wiped away it turned oot no tae be that big eh a cut just a hell of a bleeder. But aw the while that mad cunt Ally wis just pissing himself laughin' and we couldnae get an explanation oot eh him. Eventually though he calmed doon and Lachlan coaxed oot the story. Apparently all the while we'd been at the bar, Ally in his wasted and para state had been noticing a guy glaring at him. Well, the guy wouldnae look away and Ally just knew the guy was gonna punch him or square up. He also knew the first law of street fighting, the only chance of winning against a big hard cunt is to surprise them and let them think you're a madder fucker than them. So, it always helps tae throw the first punch.'

Paddy became momentarily distracted from his story and muttered, 'not in the eyes of the law though, or in my case, I ken fine I'm bleeder no a fighter, but anyway that was Ally's way tae see things. So aye as I was saying, this radge cunt at the bar was eyeing Ally something awfy and Ally knew he was too pissed tae hope tae stand a chance in a scrap, so he thought tae throw the first blow and hopefully scare the fecker aff. So, bang! Ally cracks his forehead as hard as he can at the cunt, only to realize he's just heid-butted and smashed a huge mirror on the wall! He was that pissed he hadnae noticed he'd been glaring at himself! He found it hilarious but sadly the bouncers didnae. Noo it wis oor turn tae start laughing and laugh we did at the poor bastard! We knew fine we'd no get intae another pub wi' Ally looking the way he did, so Lachlan suggested we walk off the absinthe and head back to his place where he had superglue to seal up the cut. Sounded fucking brutal I thought but he assured us it was a fail-safe rugby technique. So, we started on the long walk back tae his flat, but the night air turned the absinthe drunk into a horrible dizziness and by the time we had reached the meadows we were half walking half crawling along. We lay down by the crossroads in the middle of the park there to regain oor breath and there must have been a haar coming off the sea coz you couldnae see fuck all. Then suddenly in the midsts of the mists we heard this mental noise, some Welsh cunt spouting obscene poetry and attempts of flattery to female passers-by. It was the strangest and funniest monologue I've ever heard. Ally and I began pissing ourselves, when Lachlan shouts into the night, 'Ivor is that you?'

Well out the fog springs big Ivor he was even bigger then too coz he was into lifting weights in those days. There he was this broad-shouldered giant with a mad afro and a Zappa beard. He looked proper mental coz he was trying to impress the birds by no wearing a t-shirt, showing off his hairy barrel of a chest, while squeezed over his shoulders wis this tiny, tight Japanese school boy's blazer. I just assumed he'd been at a fetish night, but it turned oot that he had ended up at a school exchange for a year in Japan all paid for coz his grandad had been a prisoner of war there. Anyway, none of the uniforms there had fitted his frame, and he reckoned that was manly as fuck, so he'd kept on wearing it! Cunt can speak Japanese by the way!

Well, Lachlan gets chatting tae him, and it turned out that they knew each other from when they had worked together at a bar sometime, and had encountered a shared interest in rugby and Captain Beefheart. He introduced Ally and I to Ivor as fellow musicians and Ivor nodded respectfully at that and told us that he was 'fair to fluent on the banjo, harmonica and fiddle'. He asked us why we were lying down at the crossroads and Ally jokingly says 'tae meet the devil and and swap oor souls tae play the guitar better'. Well Ivor loved that, and he made load roaring noises and nodded manically.

'We'll see about that boyo!' he laughed, and we all went back together tae a party at the Spaniards. I mind nothing mair aboot that night, the Spanish parties at Lachlan's were ayewis intense and colourful and I wish I could recall mair details, but I dare say I passed out in an absinthe coma.

The next morn I woke up with nae memory of meeting Ivor or of Ally heid-butting a mirror, the only thing I was aware of was I needed tae donate my guts tae the nearest lavvy pronto. So, there I was spewing doon the pan, when I look up to see a man dressed only in greying y-fronts, pulling out his cock and pissing neatly past the side of my face and down into the bog beside me. I had no time tae complain coz the stench of the piss got me hurling again immediately. When I finally looked up, there was Ivor smiling at me, and he said something along the lines of,

'Sorry but when yer gotta go yer gotta go, dont fret luvver I'm a good aim! And Lachlan says I mustn't use the sink again. Not fer peeing nor for me vicker's baths'

I was stunned into silence, but I must have been staring at they awful greying y-fronts, coz next thing I knew he'd reached down into them and pulled out a harmonica.

'Har! Har! I wasn't standing to attention if you were worrying, just helps to look like you can deliver a nice, nine incher when you're out on the town if you know what I mean matey!' he said, and then he started playing the harmonica there and then in the bog at whatever ungodly hour it was. Well despite, my thumping head and lurching guts I could respect right away that Ivor knew how to play some mean blues on a moothie, so I invited him to jam wi us at the next Rogues gig, that one at the Forest Cafe if ye mind it Mighton?'

'I mind that gig alright', cried Mighton.

'You organised it with all they hippies there, and they promised to pay us in magic beans, which we naturally enough understood tae mean swedgers. But Christ no! It was just a free dinner of some awful, middle class baked beans withoot the sauce that we got fir oor efforts!'

'Haha! Aye that's the one, aye!' said Paddy.

'Well, anyway, that's where you meet a monster like Ivor, in a park at night, screaming obscene poems at female passers-by. The kind ah man yer warned tae phone the police if ye should meet, until oh course ye realize he's a warm-hearted, misunderstood fucker. Well, ah loved Ivor right away and him Ally hit it off like a house on fire coz they both liked boxing, and blues, and he loved Ally's tale aboot heid-butting the mirror! So, the day after we met him he became an honorary Rogue and that's ma story!'

The boys gave Paddy a slow, stoned round of applause and then lapsed once more into silence. They became lost in thoughts as to what kind of social conditioning and happenstance created a man like Ivor Ryder-Jones, but such things are a story for another day.

Chapter 10 - A Cornish Supper

'One cannot think well, love well, sleep well, if one has not dined well.'

Virginia Woolf [11].

High waves crashed upon the Cornish cliffs with brutal force and a terrifying noise. Gulls screamed and a mordacious wind whipped the salty grass into submission. The night was clear with a full moon, and turbulent waters danced under her dazzling command. Despite the gale, one could faintly hear the distant ringing of a village clock striking midnight. It was holiday season, and though the hour was not so late most of the nearby world lay sleeping. London stockbrokers had gone to bed early, ready to rise early for what they firmly assured their families would be a better day, one full of sunny surfing and Waitrose picnics. Twitching in their beds they dreamt furiously of a time when man could buy better weather and where modernity would finally triumph over that obstreperous imp that was nature.

Despite the majorities' contempt for the weather, down on the stormy sands a few souls void of culture's condemning grip, celebrated nature's anarchistic and unpredictable temperament. Astonishingly underdressed for the gale, they hopped up and down using their lifted shirts as kites, and flew along the blustery beach. Bottles denoted 'Half price Pigswill and Genuine Scrumpy' were passed around and joyful encouragements were roared towards the night's fury. It seemed reminiscent of an ancient time as this crew, with their homemade tattoos, fake gold earrings, and drunken poetry, explored the Cornish coves by moonlight. The moon herself blinked and had to look twice before giving a sad sigh and accepted dolefully that she was still gazing at the 21st century. The innocents that she looked down upon, reminded her of an eon ago, when man was a child of nature, adventuring for adventuring's sake, not to conquer in culture's dull name. Well, there was promise found amongst the purposelessness of these folk anyway, and with that in mind she winked at the sea, and orchestrated a splendid display of rips and swells.

The crew was comprised of Geri Hay and an assortment of his companions all of whom had agreed to go camping for as long as they could afford, to celebrate his birthday. They had heard that Cornwall was every bit as fond of Celtic heathenry and salacious shanties as Caledonia, and had thus ventured to the most southern tip of Old Blighty's coast, for a scrumpy fuelled jolly. Ivor Ryder-Jones was there and proudly wearing his grandfather's tiger claw cufflinks as an earring, in a bid to attract lady pirates and mermaids. He sat on a rock by the sea, swinging his thick legs in time to 'Barratt's Privateers', which he attempted to roar over the sound of the screeching seagulls. They taunted him and circled closer and closer, glaring with beady yellow eyes, and squawking in fury. Ivor glowered back, and strummed harder and louder on the banjo, spraying it with flecks of blood as the tight, steel strings bit into his fingers. Eventually the seagulls recognised that this was a fight unlikely to be won by mortal creatures, and so gave in and flew off to defecate on expensive, tourist cars. Kerry Baxter – the only girl willing to join these fools - applauded Ivor's commitment, and toasted his success before passing him the bottle of warm scrumpy.

The crew had decided that as it was no night for setting up tents, it was better to explore the coastline, and worry about beds later. Everyone was overjoyed to escape the sweltering confines of Mighton's pokey car. Indeed, the radiator had broken, thus requiring the heater to be on, for the full duration of the journey. This combined with the clammy warmth that had come before the storm, and the windows not being able to open had made for a rather wretched drive, or as Mighton put it, 'a foul cunt oh a trip, and yin made all the worse by Ivor's sweaty, commando arse, drippin' under yon kilt fae cheak tae seat'.

Geri felt he had done his best to placate Mighton and elevate his mood, telling him 'if ye stop being such a miserable cunt, ye might enjoy yersel'.

Mighton had responded that Geri could add the cost of his car being cleaned to the belated petrol money he was due in that case, and added, 'dinnae get full oh yersel just coz its yer birthday ya wee gobshite'.

In this way the journey had continued, and eventually they had made it all the way from Bedford to Cornwall's windswept coast. There, they reconvened with those fortunate enough to be smoothly driven in Rob Carter's air-conditioned vehicle and despite storm warnings, made their way immediately from the scrumpy shop to the seaside.

The winds continued to howl, the waves to crash and mad cats laughed and prowled under the moon. Geri and the gang danced and drank and drank and danced until there was no more dancing or drinking to be done. At this point they realised they were cold and lost and that their heads would soon collide with the stomping heels of a scrumpy hangover. Utilising his 'army cadet leadership skills' Ivor took charge over the impending situation. Like an obverse Pied Piper, he sang sweet and mesmerizing melodies coaxing the inebriated fools to follow him, up the cliffs and away from the raging sea. For a giant man, he had dainty feet, and upon these horned hooves he skipped and hopped up the hill like a mountain goat, while the others tripped along behind him.

The moon was solicitous and illuminated the ground with benevolent beams, till soon the carpark was reached. It was agreed that it was a fool's errand to pitch tents in what could well be a tornado, so, armed with nightcaps and sleeping sacks, the friends passed the remainder of the small hours in a comatose-car-repose. Geri, who was the last to enter Mighton's minute vehicle, slept soundly upon the handbrake, his legs raised high, parallel to the windscreen, with his toes touching his beard. The gearstick protruded proudly from between his thighs, and he looked like a Yogic virility statue. All bodies were crushed between the two cars, except for the one labelled Ivor Ryder-Jones. This one lay prostate on the floor of a nearby public toilet. Cloaked in an old blanket he breathed heavily, and lay clutching a pepperoni sausage. Snails, escaping the wrath of the night, crawled over the slumbering giant and his sausage, leaving behind a slimy trail of liquid pearls upon his shirt and snack.

The next morning the sun rose and beat hard upon the Southern coast. This delighted the gentrified tourists, but any such delight disappeared as they walked past Mighton's car. For them there was more likeness between Geri's dozing form and a flexible pervert attempting self-fellatio than to that of a Yogic statue. Two particularly zealous bankers knocked on the car window, and demanded the friends swift removal from the car park. For one of the bankers, it was the most spine tingling encounters he had had for years. So thrilling was his gallant act of public service that Mother Nature called rather urgently, and he was forced to rush to the nearest lavatory. Springing inside, he stepped on a scantily clad Welshman, who was crawling around on all fours and mumbling about finding a 'perfectly good sausage'. Squeaking in fear lest he had encountered the inhabitant of his nightmares, the poor banker turned and ran before this deviant could utter another word. He grabbed his wife, telling her they would not be returning to Cornwall, as it was a place full of 'funny people and queer sorts'.

As both the temperature and the amount of eyes that glared at them began to increase, the gang tumbled out of Mighton's car and made their way down to the beach for a breakfast BBQ. Upon realising that nobody had remembered a BBQ they attempted to build a little fire on the sands, but the wood was still sodden and refused to cooperate. Instead, they dined on bread rolls and beer and began a merry singsong. Geri attempted to instigate a rendition of 'Happy Birthday' twice but was curtly reminded by everyone that it wasn't his birthday until the following day.

The waves continued to break hard on the shore, but the sky relented from further tormenting tourists with rain, and the clouds had well and truly released the sun from captivity. Kerry, warmed by wine and these first rays, suggested a swim. The boys looked at each other aghast, for all the sky was now repainted as a summer blue, the wind was still cold and the waves looked cruel. Geri, a self-proclaimed, and self-tattooed 'sea farer' felt too ashamed to speak of his feelings and looked at Mighton pleadingly. Mighton, however, was painfully aware that he had oft bragged of January swims in the North Sea and felt that he could not refuse the challenge. The rest of the crew silently looked at their feet and prayed someone would refuse. 'Terrific idea, Kerry me love' cried Ivor, and began to undress with one hand, quaffing scrumpy all the while with the other. The boys glared at him but he was impervious to such unkindness.

The giant man was soon naked, save for the thick coat of fur that covered his body and an uncomfortably snug pair of saltire underpants. He jogged down to the waves still holding the scrumpy.
'Jeez! It's like Baywatch on bad acid! Where did you buy those pants, Ivor?' shouted Rob after him.

'Found them in the women's underwear section at a second hand shop in Glesgy. Real men wear thongs!' cried Ivor, leaping into the waves.

Kerry followed his lead and the men, not wanting to be outdone, and Geri not wanting Ivor to drop the scrumpy, ran after them.

The sea was warmer than expected and booze and adrenaline numbed the gang to its colder currents. As they swam out, local fisherman laughed at their screams and shouts, and wealthy tourists watched from the cliffs, morbidly excited to finally witness the complete extinction of the working classes from the area. Paddy and Mighton, who weighed much the same as upon the day they were born, were the first to feel the chill, their teeth chattering and their lips turning blue.

Paddy lamented that he deserved a milder fate than to die in the ocean, and cried out,

'Pass me that scrumpy Geri, if I'm tae die in these waves, let me at least be jaked enough to enjoy it!'

Geri swigged the cider before swimming over with it, proclaiming,

'Tis a fine fate auld Davy Jones' locker, Paddy ma lad, a noble way to die for a sailin' man like me upon the days oh my ain birth!'

'Geri ye talk mair shit than yon fish's tit! 'Days oh yer birth', ya only get yin, yer no our German Queenie! Hurry up an' pass me that scrumpy next am freezin ma baws aff!' roared Mighton with the satisfied chuckle he made every time he insulted the British monarch.

Gulls screeched overhead sometimes swooping close enough for the friends to hear the beat of their wings as they fought with the wind. All the heavens rang with their clamour and the air reeked of salt and fish.
The acquaintances continued swimming and drinking, until Paddy and Mighton began to cramp and struggle, and Geri convinced himself he had seen a shark. Hurling themselves out of the water they dried their bodies frantically with their socks and tried not to shiver too obviously. They agreed that swift motion would remediate against the cold and decided to walk along the clifftops to a renowned folk pub some miles away. Shortly into their promenade the wind dropped and the day became ripe with warm sunshine and goodness. The lush, green

countryside sparkled in verdurous charm and little stone cottages sat picture perfect with thatched roofs and lobster pots gracing the walls. The clifftops sported bristling, green, crew-cuts, these trademarked coiffures maintained by both sea air and the mouths of the sheep that dominated the fields. To the south, ocean views extended as far as the eye could see, while to the west the Asparagus Isles erupted from the water. As the path wound its way inland, thick brambles and tall oaks hugged its sides, providing homes for small birds that chattered gaily. The friends walked with a lazy gait and stopped often for ice creams and idling. Paddy attempted to walk and play a version of The Romany Rogue's 'Patriotic Fools' on the tin whistle and the rest sang along, using its lazy rhythm to set their pace. Through the rolling countryside they went, over stiles and under fences until they eventually made it to Cadgwith. This tiny hamlet was comprised of around forty or so whitewashed cottages which jostled with one another for space by the harbour. The sun shone on the sea there lighting it up a luminous turquoise and in the nearby yard lay colourful, old boats, lazily decomposing in their retirement home. The place clung on to the looks and smells of a traditional fishing harbour and had more or less staved off gentrification and death by glass gables. Smelling the warm tar and hearing the sounds of Cornish accents on passers-by, the friends were filled with a sense of relief that they had perhaps stumbled upon a place that was not entirely forced to prostitute itself to tourists.

Here they began busking by the shore, which seemed to soften the London gentry's resolve towards them. Indeed, the 'Sky Boat Song' and 'Heart In The Highlands' brought in enough coins to buy fish and chips and another flagon of scrumpy. The sun now beat down, and Mighton and Geri, who freckled under lightbulbs, began to savagely fry. Due to its strength and price, homemade scrumpy was all that any of them considered to be a plausible cure for dehydration and they drowned themselves in it. A continuous supply of the lethal liquid was dealt to them by a local teenager who had parted company with his teeth and therefore the ability to articulate constantans. He had an endless stash of bottles which he procured from behind various bins and lobster pots in exchange for money or cigarettes. At one point when he disappeared to urinate, the friends tried their luck at finding his hidden bottles themselves, but found not one. Yet upon reappearing the toothless man plucked one out of exactly the same place. It was mysterious and an excellent sales trick, causing the friends to purchase more than was perhaps sensible. Needless to say that by the time the Inn opened they were all more than a little wobbly on their feet.

The Cadgwith Cove Inn was a cozy little fishing shack, boasting a wide collection of ales and a fine beer garden full of sea air and sea views. Its walls were stone, its décor scruffy and its prices inclusive and conclusive to merriment. It lived up to its reputation and could have given the great bastions of its tradition a run for their money. So great was it that Geri and Mighton, who were connoisseurs of public houses, proclaimed generously that it took rank alongside The Royal Oak in Edinburgh and Madden's Bar in Belfast. They cried it to be a, 'Stalwart to its kind and one of a rare and disappearing breed'.

Folk songs were passed in a friendly circle, and anyone who wanted could choose a tune and lead its rendition, encouraging all the patrons to join in. There were two fiddles, a tin whistle, three mandolins, a horn pipe, endless chair and foot percussion and uncountable rowdy voices. The lads brought out their instruments, and Geri stood in the middle, waving his arms like a mad conductor and lost in a joyous trance. Those not involved in the singing of every sailing song with relish, busied themselves in providing applause and drinks, and Geri secured a few whiskies on account of his 'birth-days celebrations'.
The entire evening was passed in joy and not a single discordant word was uttered throughout. Time seemed to run away with itself, and as the hours became smaller and the tales taller, the time bell finally rang. An old man stood everyone a nightcap and soon afterwards the pub began its noisy exodus. On the street more scrumpy appeared from hedges, hands were

shaken and promises of eternal friendships assured. Reflecting the spirit of this hive of congeniality, the gang were offered a ride back to their tents in the back of a fish van.

'The drivers pished as fuck! It's a death trap' warned Geri.

'Aye so's they cliffs in the dark, and if I'm goin' tae ma death am no walkin' tae it!' replied Mighton.

'Feck it! A fish vans a fine enough death for a sailor' cried Geri gallantly, and his friends laughed and piled in taking a bumpy journey to their beds.

The following day the sunlight spread warm and soft over the horizon. The tyranny of the waves was reduced to a gentle lapping and all across the sands strode young families. Parents walked briskly, watching the sky with warning eyes, waiting for the weather to change. Children marched by their sides with solemn determination, propelled onwards by promises of ice cream and other such bribes. It would have been a wonderful morn to celebrate the day of one's own birth and the unfathomable miracle of being, but Geri Hay lay fast asleep till well beyond the noon. When he eventually woke, it was with aches and groans and without recollection that his birthday had finally arrived. Whether the perpetrator of this indisposition was scrumpy or the previous day's long walk and overzealous exercise would be ungentlemanly to proliferate over, but he blamed the latter.

His tent was damp with humid heat, and his only thoughts were to escape its sticky confines and drink a gallon of iced water. Such ambitions were thwarted by the entrance zip being jammed shut and refusing to cooperate. Being in no mood to bargain with it, he kicked hard with his clawed, yellow toenails and ripped his way out. He tumbled groaning into the world and blinked in the bright sunshine at the tattered remains of his red tent.

'Happy Birthday, ya cunt!' smiled Mighton pleasantly, adding,

'Is that you re-enacting clawing yer way oot yer ma's hole?'

Geri was too tired to revile this and gesticulated helplessly towards a water bottle.

Mighton tossed it his way and the rest of the gang, who had been celebrating Geri's birthday without him, sang happy birthday.

The water was far from fresh or cool, but it sated his thirst and dampened the blows of the hammers in his head. Upon hydration he became aware that 'his day' had come, and began to notice the birthday singing and attempted to reanimate his spirits by joining in.
Kerry made a debonair affair of mixing an Alka-Seltzer with some scrumpy and other dubious 'remedies' and enquired what he was receiving from his father for his birthday. Geri replied that he had the need for nought so had asked his father for specifically nothing at all. This irked Paddy, who was permanently penurious and a professional free-loader. The lanky poet ran his hand through his curly mop, and greased it back in a manner he felt was professional and salesman like. Shining a wry smile and a cunning green eye on Geri he began his pitch,

'Geri, your old mans not skint right?'

Geri tensed, aware that a game of intellectual chess had begun and that he wasn't yet sure of its rules or prize. He consented with a shrug and Paddy continued,

'Well we've spent every penny we've got at the pub last night, you reckon he'd wire us the money tae indulge you an' yer pals in a birthday lunch?'

This plan was met by a meadow of smiles and all eyes turned to Geri. The proposition seemed harmless, and in fact inspired, so he clapped his hands in a histrionic outburst and saluted his lanky acquaintance. It had long been his dream to be a benevolent dandy, and he became immediately lost in dreams of his possible titles and legacy. A 'donator of sherry to the mouths of the needy'. A 'benefactor of fine wines and *la bella vita* upon fellow waifs and strays'! Indeed, he had long wished to bestow generous profusion to his friends and perhaps he would have been unstoppable in this pursuit if it was not for the fact that he was generally broke and confined to minimum wages. Yet now another could pay the way while he enjoyed the rewards and congratulations.

'A fine plan, Paddy ma man, braw indeed! Ma old man's an excellent sort and would'nae begrudge ma pals and I a birthday feast. We'll have a lobster each!' exclaimed Geri wildly.

Everybody cheered and Geri rang his father, who generously and easily agreed. The rest of the afternoon went by in great cheer, and the friends researched Cornwall's best lobster restaurant. None of them had dined on such a delicacy before and excitement ran high. After much discussion a suitable restaurant was located, it was one that offered panoramic ocean views and whole, local lobsters, albeit at an undisclosed price. Geri dismissed any anxieties concerning cost as 'trivial matters' not fit for a day of such import as his own birthday. The only worry he had was that the restaurant seemed to demand the wearing of ties.
'We all stink oh campfire smoke and we've no one eh they rotten, rags roond our necks atween us' he lamented.
The group debated this predicament for a time, until the ever resourceful Kerry came up with the solution of fashioning colourful cravats out of her spare, summer frock. Ivor and Paddy helped her and soon some garish neck wears were produced. They looked less like ties than like foppish

handkerchiefs, yet nevertheless they could be tied around ones neck. The remaining portion of the afternoon was spent washing smoky hair in the ocean and polishing trainers on the grassy slopes. Rah beamed generously as they strutted up and down the beach admiring each other's clothes. Upon the hour of five, the friends swaggered their way through fields of cornflowers and made their way to the restaurant. Despite walking slowly, the day's heat caused them to work up a sour sweat on the surprisingly long journey, yet they paid such trifling matters no mind. Each individual was clad in splendid accoutrement, seagull feathers adorned flat caps, and all clothes though washed of smoke, now hosted white stains from salt water rinsing. Paddy and Ivor had their kilts with them and their highland colours shone in the sun as they descended the hilly path. Geri led his ragged army of friends through the restaurant doors, and like an ostentation of peacocks they descended upon the dining room.

What a dining room it was, huge oak beams held up a cathedral like ceiling, while plush pink carpets covered the floors and huge bay windows boasted unparalleled views of the nearby ocean. Their choice of eatery had no doubt been astute.

The waiter twitched hysterically as they entered, whether with mirth or perhaps with nerves it was hard to say, but motivated by the fore given promise of lobster purchases, he begrudgingly showed them to a table.
'Fuck me! What a view!' whistled Rob, as he surveyed the endless ocean.

The three other tables - all occupied by guests dining with the silent reserve of those who have trained to be unexcited by life - tutted and whispered amongst themselves, hoping their children wouldn't meet plebs like these at the schools they paid for.
Undeterred, the friends continued to converse loudly and crudely, laughing at the likeness between the cliental and the stuffed animals that stared haughtily from the walls. The

whisky collection was discussed with animation and Geri concluded that there was not a distillery he could think of that was not present there. The holy trinity, Lagavulin, Ardmore and Ardbeg were all there. Smaller and larger distilleries had all found their place, older, newer, sweeter, and stronger malts were all present and a good few smoky bruisers besides. He rubbed his hands in uncontained glee and cast his eyes around the rest of the room. The seats were carved ebony, with crushed velvet cushions upon them. Crystal chandeliers decorated the ceiling and the napkins were cut from finer cloth than most men's wedding kilts. It was, all in all, a place most suitable for such a birthday.

He magnanimously invited his friends to spare no thought to cost and to drink and dine upon whatever they wished.

'Jeez Geri! Your old man must be doing alright eh?' questioned Kerry, surprised.

'Aye, ah guess he does man, he worked his way up fae nothing at a bank over a number oh years. We live different lives but I'm proud oh him, he did whit he wanted wi his life an I dae whit a want wie mines' replied Geri.

'Why don't you get him to sort ya a good job mate and we'll munch lobster more often?!' asked Rob.

'Coz much as ah respect whit he's done, it's no whit I want tae do, an' I know first-hand that golden handcuffs are the hardest tae take off!' said Geri with a laugh.

'Well, we're just lucky he parts with his money, they often don't' said Ivor, adding 'I mean that old men dont. Jeez I wish old men would part with their money as easily as they part with their advice, busking would sure be a delight!'

Geri laughed and raised a glass, about to give another birthday toast when the waiter came over to take their order. The waiter's continued disdain for their presence was embodied by a collection of physical twitches as he served them. He wrinkled his nose in repulsion over their various grammatical felonies yet all the while he responded with perfect manners albeit ones served with ice. Each of the friends ordered a minimum of three courses and four whole lobsters were commissioned as an amuse-bouche. The food was prepared slowly and lovingly, and took its time to arrive. The group made use of this by playing cards and devouring some of the older delights from the wine list. Bottles of ruby reds and crisp whites appeared at the table, and even though nobody drank them, several rosés were ordered to help fulfil the excess of the occasion. Geri sat in a blissful state, and stared out of the window watching the last of the sun sink over the ocean and vanish behind the gentle waves. The lapping waters played a lullaby upon the cliffs underneath and he was transcended to a high place.

Eventually the meal arrived, and the table was painted by its bold colours and textures like a summertime Picasso. There were fat, pink prawns swimming in butter, juicy steaks, sautéed potatoes, warm-smoked, sides of salmon and four enormous lobsters cooked in wine and garlic. Even the vegetarian options of cheese soufflés looked decadent enough to wet the most carnivorous of mouths present. Geri gave a grace, saying '1,2,3 go!' and the friends turned from admiring the meal to furiously attacking it. It was tackled with much passion and spontaneous outbursts of poetic acclamation of its glory. Even the waiter struggled not to smile, as he saw the joy on the faces of the gorging philistines.

As folk like to say about such occasions, 'all good things must come to an end', and so it was that the food eventually came to an end, or at least a new stage of its perpetual reincarnation. It was with some surprise that the friends found themselves finishing the food, rather than it finishing them. The waiter

cleared the plates and Geri grabbed his sleeve and whispered in his ear that he'd like to order a birthday cake, or at least some kind of desert with a candle in it. Being curtly informed that this was neither appropriate nor possible, Geri sighed, and said, 'In that case I would be obliged if ye would bring us a fifteen year old bottle of Lagavulin, the great chieftain oh its race!' The waiter blinked a little incredulously but maintained his cool composure and said not a thing. The whisky was brought alongside several crystal glasses and a small jug of water. Geri inhaled deeply from the bottle, orating a heartfelt panegyric of the pleasures of the malt to the guests in the room.
The gang took a glass each and gave Geri what he thought was a long overdue toast. They then burst into singing happy birthday in a loud slur as the waiter winced in the corner, and blinked apologetically at the other guests.

The dram was consumed at a pace far faster than the one it had been created at, and before they knew it the whisky had vanished, the other guests had disappeared and it was time to pay and leave.
The bill was brought in an appropriately discreet, leather booklet and Geri coughed nervously and inhaled sharply as he opened it and saw the figure. He came under a volley of questions regarding the sum, but he refused to disclose the amount. Geri walked to the bar and casually rang his father and uttering the sum in a low whisper and demanded his credit card details. The call appeared somewhat frayed, and Geri returned looking a tad flushed.
'Seems the auld man was mair under the impression we were going oot for fish an' chips!' he whispered.

'Whit fanny gave the man that impression then?' gawked Mighton.

Geri glared at him and his friends offered to do a whip round, collecting from already empty overdrafts to attempt to make up the difference. Geri shook his head gallantly, crying

'If a gentleman can't treat his friends oan his ain birthday then when can he?!'

Filled with the spirit of the Blitz and a sense of noble pride, he paid the cheque, thus sacrificing his rent money, and two new credit cards. The waiter impatiently accepted the payment from the multitude of Geri's credit cards, but looked happy for the first time when Geri slid him a handsome tip.

'Buy yersel' an ice cream' Geri said to him, lost in the drunken ecstasy of generosity.

They left the establishment, and began the long and painful walk back to the tent, each person supporting a belly as full as an egg.

Later when lying on their beds of grass, every one of them suffered the most excruciating gastric aches, and tossed and turned, vowing never to indulge in such gluttony again. They cursed Geri for his kindness and vowed a return to the plainer pleasures of pot noodles and crisps.
Only Geri slept well, a born Epicurean, too dandy for his knees ever to dare to swell with gout, he lay contentedly, dreaming the satisfied dreams reserved for philanthropic gentlemen.

They left Cornwall the next day, and despite pleads and threats, Geri never did disclose the price of his birthday meal, though it is known that he had to rely on Mighton to pay his rent for two months after the event.

Chapter 11 - The Theft of a Tree
'This land is your land, This land is my land,
This land is made for you and me'
Woodie Guthrie [12].

A fallen ash lay dead on the ground. Geri and Paddy sized up the trunk in silence. It would be hard to lift, there was no doubt about that. However, it was also perfect for the purpose they had in mind, and there was no doubt about that either.

Paddy was spending some time living back at his parent's house in West Lothian and had decided to use his time there to build a gypsy caravan with his father. His father was one of the few people that still built traditional, horse drawn caravans for the itinerant travelling community in Scotland. The wagons were carved of wood, with a canvas stretched over the top, and decorated lavishly with ornamental scrolls, lucky symbols and an extravagance of gold leaf. Paddy himself had spent some of his own upbringing growing up in one such caravan in West Lothian, where his hippy parents had renovated a ruined cottage and raised a few sheep. At the time he had found this wooden home to lack comforts and was mortified to be the only child at the local school to be collected in a horse drawn cart. However, while he had not enjoyed being easily distinguishable as a child, he grew to enjoy it in his teenage years and began to find his parents' alternative lifestyle and living arrangements something to be proud of. They were, he felt, a splash of colourful rebellion amongst the grey scale of the ex-mining area he had grown up in.

The select group of freaks that he called his friends had enjoyed coming to visit and camp out beneath the stars on his parent's tiny plot of land. They would soon relax into these foreign surroundings, filling their imaginations readily with the Scottish folk tales his family would tell, and their bellies with delectables, chargrilled to perfection over an open fire.

Geri had been one of this group and he had long suggested that Paddy should learn from his father and build a gypsy wagon. Paddy had for an equally long time shunned such suggestions, not wishing to become a mere mirror image of his parents. But age often brings folk closer to their forbearers' philosophies and lifestyle than they may wish, until they eventually resign to the fact that they have become their parents, and for better or worse must grow comfortable walking in the shoes they have long avoided! So, having ended up living with his parents - after losing his money through travels, alcohol and a period of bad busking - Paddy had found himself with little to do when not washing dishes at a local cafe, and had decided to use his time building himself a mortgage free home on wheels. Geri had been delighted to hear this news and hoped that as Paddy was often off wandering somewhere that he could use the caravan for holidays whenever he came back up north from Bedfordshire. In fact, he was so enthusiastic about the plan that he had decided to use his holidays from work to come and help Paddy build. Paddy was glad of the company but unsure as to how beneficial Geris shaking hands, and half-cut coordination would be for the project. Still Geri brought cheer and beer to most things and work was made more pleasant by his friend tipsily whistling old rebel tunes.

Geri's only concern over the project was how they would afford all the building materials they would need. But this minor worry was quickly extinguished when he saw all the reclaimed timber and metal that Paddy's father had lying in his shed, garden and house. Paddy's father hated banks and had never borrowed money in his life, nor worked much either at least not in the conventional sense. He begged, borrowed, swapped, and charmed most of the modest necessities he required. He worked sporadically dismantling garden sheds and fences and building new ones out of the better scrap he had acquired. It was a circular economy based on utilising favours, old materials, and good workmanship. All the old materials that he claimed from jobs, the side of the road or at the tip became either firewood to heat his house, or else were laboriously taken apart and divided into piles depending on use or scrap metal value. Therefore, Paddy had access to limitless reclaimed wood, nails, windowpanes, half used jars of paint, old car wheels and much more. However, the one thing he lacked was long thin planks of green ash, needed to bend and form the structure of the caravan's roof. Good timber is expensive and hard to come by in Scotland, the highlands have long been robbed of the oak forests that once covered them and Sitka spruce - a poor building material - is the widest grown commercial forest. However, in a nearby estate - one perhaps best left unnamed - there had blown down some magnificent ash trees in a storm. These were left on the forest floor to rot and although they were of no doubt great sustenance to the local insects, Paddy felt they had enough wood to gnaw on and could allow him the trunk of just one tree. Moreover, with little regard to the locals who took pleasure and escape in walking through these woods, the estate would soon clear-fell the forest for cash, so the chance was now or never. Paddy wasn't sure if it was possible or indeed wise to steal a tree but the idea had enchanted Geri's imagination so much that he had immediately signed up for helping in any way possible. The thought of wealth redistribution in a forest at night reminded Geri warmly of all the Robin Hood tales he had enjoyed as a child and the songs of The Clash he enjoyed as an adult. It was, he encouragingly told Paddy, 'a most wonderful idea, what could possibly go wrong?'

The eternal optimist in Paddy was inclined to agree with this sentiment but having been caught a couple of times on the wrong side of the law and learnt the hard way that most police put the law of the land before any moral philosophy, he wanted to make sure their plan was flawless. If there was anyone that could help to plan and assist on this venture it was his father, who had got away with 'borrowing' a large amount of 'unused' and 'unwanted' items throughout his lifetime from wealthy estate owners.

Geri and Paddy bought a half bottle of cheap whisky in order to motivate Paddy's father to both plan and help with the deed and sat waiting the man's return in Paddy's half-built caravan A fresh wind blew from the Firth of Forth and cooled the late summer's day considerably. Geri suggested that they could stave off the cold by taking a nip or two from the whisky bottle. Seeing no harm in this Paddy agreed and they passed the bottle back and forth until soon enough they were numbed from the worst of the cold.
'Whisky's the warmest jacket eh?' said Geri jovially as he took a swig.
At that moment Paddy's father and mother arrived back in an old van that appeared to be held together by shoe laces and a great deal of duct tape. It belched out black smoke and rattled its way onto the driveway. As Paddy's parents got out the van Geri leapt out of the caravan with the whisky bottle in hand. Paddy's father jumped back and held his hands up, before squinting in the evening sunlight saying,

'Ah is that you Geri, thank Christ, thought it was somebody from the council about those windaes.'

Geri looked confused, 'eh windae whit windaes?'

Paddy's mother shook her head and walked to the house while his father evaded the question with a congenial smile and a wave of a large weather worn hand.
'Never mind that, is that whisky I see there?'

Geri nodded and passed the remaining dregs of the bottle. Paddy's father savoured them slowly and then cleared his throat and wiped his mouth with a neckerchief.

'Well what's the price for the dram then, I guess use wanted something?'

The boys were taken aback by this intuition but the question seemed to be delivered in good humour.

They told him about the fallen tree and their desire to somehow cut it silently and move it to make planks without being noticed. He nodded attentively and his eyes shone as the prospect of taxing the estate took hold.

When they had finished explaining the conundrum to him he pulled out an incredibly outdated mobile telephone from his back pocket and said,

'We're going to need a battery powered chain saw and a rowing boat, cannae drive a car in there for fear of game keepers. I know just the man.'

Geri was about to say something when whoever was being rung answered and Paddy's father began coaxing them into the adventure.

'Bob! Is that you, been a while, I've still not recovered from that elderberry wine you poisoned me with at New Year! Listen how dae you feel about helping me fell and move a tree on the quiet like?'

The boys strained their ears to try and make out what was being said at the other end of the line but could hear nothing. Paddy's father replied.

'Bob I know ye've a bad back but there's no lifting involved just need you to row and keep watch, listen it's not any old tree, it's no a council tree or a citizens tree it belongs tae yon lairdy who won't let you catch rabbits and tried to claim the shoreline was private property.'

Paddy's father then abruptly hung up the phone without saying another word.

'Wis it a nae then?' cried Geri in dismay.

'Nae? Course no, he said he'll be round in fifteen minutes to plan oor attack, now come and help me lift they windaes I found!'

Paddy winked at Geri and they helped unload the van.

The sun sank lower and lower and the sky was lit up in flames as they worked outside. Geri mused to himself that this kind of task was more pleasure than work and incomparable to the warehouse where he wasted his own days.
They had just finished unpacking the van and were tucking into some tea and biscuits with Paddy's parents when Bob appeared at the gate. He was a man of around seventy with a pointed white beard and a shiny bald pate that seemed to reflect the sunset from his forehead. He seemed to be out of breath and excited, he hopped off the bike and it became visible that a chain saw was slung round his back, tied over his shoulder and to his belt with a piece of string.

'Bleedin' Nora Bob! We didnae think to cut the tree now!' laughed Paddy's father as he welcomed the man in and poured him a mug of tea.

Bob waved a hand derisively and said in a thick Yorkshire accent,

'No time like the present, make hay and all that, ah there's nothing like a freebie from the miser of a lord'

He put down the chain saw and grabbed a handful of biscuits with one hand while reaching out to shake Geris' hand with the other.

'Nice to meet you, I'm Bob and that's me bicycle Sally, she's a post bike from 1952, mind you most of the parts on her are not so old. And that's me electric chainsaw, not that it's up to much now mind you, but I think it'll work, don't you?'

Geri nodded and smiled, amused by the man's way of introduction and eccentricity, he always enjoyed meeting a character and this man appeared to be just that.

'Aye ah dinnae see why no! An ah hear you have a boat for part oh this adventure oh oors? Am a spare time captain maself and hae nae worries aboot me floating sir, I've me pig n me rooster tattoos right here'

Bob looked approvingly at Geri's tattooed hands, and Paddy hid a smirk in his cup of tea.

'Pig and rooster, you reckon? Was a pig and mermaid in my day down south of the border, boy, but that's a few years ago, I dare say you will float aright!'

They chatted of other things, and Bob explained his new technique for poaching rabbits, producing various homemade contraptions from the depths of his jacket to illustrate his discovery.
The last of the sunshine faded from the sky and the biscuits and tea became replaced by homemade elderberry wine both Bob's and Paddy's parents. A friendly competition ensued and Paddy and Geri were forced to decry a winner between the two lethal beverages.

'It's not just about taste' said Bob with great enthusiasm, 'you have to think of the character, the lives of the berries, its only berries with character what goes in ma brew you see'

'Character?' snorted Paddy's mother, 'headaches, that's what those berries bring, it's over fermented, you want a smoother after taste like my wine!'

And on the conversation went until the bottles were emptied and a tie was diplomatically drawn.

'To business!' said Paddy's father as he rose a little unsteadily to his feet.

'Those things will kill you,' he added pointing at Geri's cigarette.

'So will life, its rigged from the start!' retorted Geri with a grin.

'Hmm…A fair point…so anyway, here my suggestion. The gamekeeper is at the other side of the woods between 11pm and 1am, giving us three hours to work unseen'.

'How'd ye ken that?' gasped Paddy surprised.

'It pays to know these things, that's why. Nae mair daft questions! So where was I, ah yes three hours we have. Now the folk down in the village don't care for oor lairdy but they tend to gossip and idle words can lead to long sentences so its best they don't see. By 1am when we return it'll be dark so that shouldnae be any bother. We cut the trunk into two sections using Bob's handy wee battery chainsaw there, it's no too loud. Now last time Bob and I borrowed some firewood in there we put it in a barrow and rolled it back to the village along the path there. But that leaves tracks, takes time and there's always the slim but possible chance of encountering a late-night walker'

'A dogger you mean' laughed Paddy.

'What's a dogger?' said Bob curiously.

'Ach never mind all that! Thing is its gonna be too heavy a load for any backs or wheels to bear long, so we'll roll them down to the sea and float them beside the boat until we get to the village harbour. I happen to know the harbour master is always passed oot drunk by midnight so that's no a problem. We'll take the van with a trailer, load it up and Bob's your uncle, so to speak!'

Bob rubbed his hands together in mischievous glee,

'That just might work boy that just might work! Nice of his almighty grace in that estate to donate to the public for a change. Should be public property anyway by all rights'

Geri raised an empty glass in agreement shouting,

'Mon the revolution and the piracy of estates, gie em' hell!'

The others joined his toast and a date was set for the following Monday evening.

Geri and Paddy passed the weekend through a mixture of carpentry, walking in the woods and hitching to the local village to busk for tonic wine funds. They were greatly excited for their up-and-coming adventure and Geri learnt a couple of new sea shanties, which he promised he would sing in a quiet and discreet manner on Bob's boat. Paddy wasn't sure this was a good idea, but he said nothing and the two of them awaited the adventure impatiently.

Monday eventually arrived and Paddy's mother cooked a large pot of porridge for the boys, telling them they would 'need aw their oats' if they were going to be lifting trees all day.
Bob cycled round after breakfast and together they rehearsed the plan once more. Paddy's father sought reassurances from the boys that there would be no alcohol before or during the boat trip and certainly no singing of songs, to which Geri grudgingly conceded. In payment for their help with the tree, Bob and Paddy's father asked them if could sort through a large pile of rusty metal, before they took it to the local scrap merchants.
'This is gonnae take aw day!' moaned a disgruntled Paddy.

'It had better not coz there's all the burnt porridge pans to wash too!' said his mother.
'And I don't know why your smirking, there's a toilet needing cleaned that someone keeps pissing over' she said pointing at Geri.

Geri began to wonder what kind of holiday this was to be but calmed himself with thoughts of the boat trip and tree piracy up ahead.
The boys stuck to their word and spent the day grafting and drank no more than a single can of Guinness between them.

'Tell ye whit,' said Geri as he finished sorting through a pile of rusty drainpipes, 'we'll be due a drop of the devil's dew after this mission tonight and nae mistake'.

'Aye, yer no wrong there, but I've a feelin' Bob an' the old man will see tae that. There's talk that they've a still between them hidden in Bob's garden shed, so we can ayewis hope fer a night of braw moonlight and moonshine, eh?'

Geri beamed at the thought of this, piracy and illegal liquor ticked all the boxes in his mind for what a joyous eve consisted of.

They stuck on Paddy's parents' Dick Gaughan records as they worked their way through the rusty metal singing Workers' Song together as they grafted.

In the late afternoon Paddy's father pulled into the driveway towing a trailer with a wooden fishing boat upon it. It was an elegant little clinker, a small version of a Shetland sixareen. Bob sat proudly on top of the boat dressed in a faded, yellow Sylvester coat and hat, and he waved instructions wildly at Paddy's father with one hand, while holding tightly to the hull with the other.
Geri stared at the old man in great admiration, he hoped that one day he could look as commanding aboard a sea bound vessel, and he made a mental note to look out for a similar jacket in Bedford's second-hand shops.

The van and its cargo rattled their way onto the drive and Bob nodded approvingly at Paddy's father's parking skills, adding but a few pointers as the man reversed.

'That's it boy, little to the left, eeh there she goes. Lovely now look at that.'

Paddy's mother had come out of the house to see what all the noise was and she laughed to see Bob astride the landlocked boat.
He hopped down with surprising agility for his age and presented a paper bag containing something mysterious to her.

'Pop that in the house will you? It's a little summit for later on you see.'

Geri strained his eyes to see the contents of the bag, but had no contact lenses in. He hoped desperately that it was moonshine or poitin, ready and waiting to greet them upon their triumphant return.
Paddy caught his eye and seemed to affirm Geri's wishes with a confident nod.

Paddy's father came out the van and handed the boys an electric chainsaw.

'Sharpened one of these afore?' he asked.

Paddy and Geri shook their heads causing Bob to look genuinely aghast.

'Thirty something years old and you've never sharpened a saw. You want working on lads, come to garage and I'll show you both how it's done'.

Paddy's father laughed, 'Good for you Bob, every day should be a school day, anyways we cannae leave till it gets dark, so enjoy, I'm away in for ma snooze!'

Geri didn't know whether to be annoyed or pleased. On one hand it sounded quite manly and romantic to learn the art of saw sharpening, yet on the other it was only he who was on holiday and thus if anyone deserved a daytime sleep it should be him. However he had no more time to deliberate as Bob thrust a chainsaw into his hands and pushed him and Paddy towards the workshop.
It was hard work improving the saw blade. Bob explained that every tooth had to be meticulously sharpened at the right angle and with just the right hand movement. He claimed that he had learnt the art whilst working in the Canadian forests.

'I was a lumberjack in Victoria after I jumped ship from her Majesty's Royal Navy. Those old boys working timber could tell you a tale or two, some of them had worked long before the time of chain saws I can tell you, and they knew how to sharpen a blade and fell a tree'

Paddy smiled at him, 'Is this truth or fable then?'

Bob hit him jokingly on the back of the head,

'Never you mind what's true, you just listen to what I'm telling you and sharpen that saw if you want to cut up an ash without getting caught!'

They worked on and sweated away as the rusty metal slowly transformed into a shining set of silvery blue fangs.
Bob inspected their work approvingly, 'that's alchemy that is, pure magic'

'That's hard bloody work is what it is' replied Geri.

'Aint no difference between the two, now take a sip of that for strength and courage and don't tell your father' said Bob producing a long thing hip flask from inside Sylvester.

Geri snatched it before Paddy got the chance.
'Moonshine!' he whispered excitedly.

Eliquatus ipsum is what it is, I'm rather pleased with this batch I am' replied Bob as he watched Geri's face intently to read his reaction to the potent brew.

Geri coughed harshly and shook his head.
'Feck me sir! It's got a kick, tastes of spicy peppermint'

Bob nodded and clapped his hands, 'you guessed it, it's me black pepper and mint triple distilled, you'll not go sleeping on no boat now boy that's for sure!'
'It's fecking wonderful' cried Geri and he savoured another mouthful.

Paddy was about to take the bottle when they heard his father coming and Bob grabbed it and hid it once more in his jacket.

'We can all enjoy that post work' he whispered with a grin.

Paddy's father opened the door and took the saw.

'Great jobs lads, we'll make something of yous yet. Right, its nearly dark enough to take the boat down to the harbour, we'll keep the van engine off mind so long as we can and freewheel it doon the brae to save any noise, I've got all the lifting ropes in the van so I think we're good tae go.'

He stopped and began sniffing.

'Why's it smell oh toothpaste in here?'

'Geri was using mouthwash' Paddy said as quickly as the bizarre excuse formed in his imagination.

Paddy's father looked at Geri with amused curiosity.

'We're stealing a tree, laddie, no rescuing a princess, but fair enough!'

'Well, ye never know, we may meet a mermaid eh!' replied Geri amicably.

'Mermaids eh!' said Bob wistfully, 'Now I met a mermaid once out at sea in 1973…'

'Tell us later Bob' said Paddy's father kindly, 'it's time to get moving noo'.

Bob shrugged and they all shuffled out and jumped into the van. The vehicle only had seats in the front, so Paddy and Geri lay on a mattress in the back, making sure their feet didn't get stuck in the multitude of rusty holes that covered the floor. Paddy's father started the engine to get it out of the driveway and up to the top of the hill and then killed it again as soon as they began rolling down to the harbour. With the clutch down they rolled their way inconspicuously to the water's edge. The van was parked behind a large oak tree and they sat in silence for a few minutes to see if any of the inhabitants of the council flats there had noticed them or peered out a window. Nobody stirred though and the night was silent save for the lapping of waves on the jetty.

'Oh I nearly forgot I brought these' whispered Bob as he reached into a canvas bag and threw some clothes towards them all.

'What are these Bob?' asked Geri, as he struggled to see in the dark.

'Camo boy, in case there's a game keeper around' Bob replied.

'Bob this is desert camouflage it's all yellow, we're going into a forest no the Sahara,' laughed Paddy's father.

'I guess you may be right there lad, just feels natural wearing camo when poaching is all, isn't that so lads?' pleaded Bob.

Paddy and Geri managed to convince him that it was dark enough to be out without the desert gear and Bob finally agreed that they didn't need to wear it, but nevertheless he donned the overalls himself, muttering something about 'old traditions being worth their weight in salt'.

The moon shone bright every time it appeared from behind the clouds, so they waited until it had disappeared behind a giant nebulous haze and then unloaded the boat, carrying it swiftly down to the water.
It was far heavier than it looked and they tripped and nearly fell a few times in their haste. When it was safely floating in the water, Paddy ran back to get the chainsaw and the ropes, and then Bob helped them all on-board with a rough handed grip. Geri and Paddy sat squeezed together at the back of the boat, while Bob rowed and Paddy's father kept a look out at the prow. He rowed gently and without much sound and his technique seemed to be well practiced as they made their way swiftly along the coastline and towards the woods. The never-ending line of trees appeared indecipherable and generic to Geri and Paddy, yet Paddy's father recognised the shape of various rocks poking out the water and told Bob where to pull in. Bob smiled congenially at Paddy's father; he liked the man's efficiency and he loved the thought of theft from those who he claimed had robbed the public of their lands. If he hadn't been holding the oars he would have rubbed his hands in childish joy.

'Prior preparation prevents piss poor performance, take note of that Patrick boy, you could learn a thing or two from your old man!' he said.

The boat came closer and closer to the land until the trees towered above them. No obvious signs could be seen of the

gamekeeper's torch and the night was still silent except for the occasional screeching of an owl in the forest.
They landed the boat on the stony shore and Paddy's father helped the boys off as Bob tucked away the oars. As soon as they entered the undergrowth of the forest Paddy's father turned on his torch and they made their way through the brambles for about ten metres, whereupon they found the fallen ash.

Bob whistled, 'She's a beauty isn't she, make fine wagon boughs and no mistake'
Geri pulled the chainsaw from his shoulder and tried to turn it on.

'Gimmie that laddie!' cried Paddy's father with panic in his voice.

'Ye have tae ken how tae use one of these, and it helps no tae have the jakey shakes in yer hands! The last thing we wants a hand cut aff out here. Nae nae! First we move the trunk it onto another log, then I'll be cutting it, then Bob can get it ready for us tae haste it tae the shore with some of his famed pulley knots. That way if we get caught wi it we can claim its driftwood and that we found it down there.'

Bob was methodical yet quick with his knot tying and each of the men took a rope over their shoulder and slowly lifted and shuffled the great trunk up at an angle over another fallen tree, thus giving the chainsaw space to halve it without hitting the ground. Geri and Paddy were given the task of stopping it from moving by sitting on the bottom of the trunk while Paddy's father would chainsaw from the top down. Before beginning the sawing though he and Bob insisted on spending a full five minutes listening and looking intently for any possible signs of other folk in the forest.

'Seems we're alone except for the Gods of the forest and the green man' said Bob quietly.

Paddy's father nodded and started the little chainsaw up, it was fairly noiseless save for a low hum, but as soon as the blade hit the trunk the volume amplified massively and a mixture of fear and adrenaline filled the boys' stomachs. The sawing went painfully slowly, as the ash was newly fallen and still green and taught with sinewy tension. When the chainsaw had chewed its way about half the way down the trunk Bob instructed the boys to stand back, at that point he felt around on the forest floor until he found an appropriate stone which he jammed into the split trunk to stop it from closing on itself. Paddy's father then continued with the chainsaw and suddenly with great elasticity the trunk sprang apart in two halves which thudded to the ground.
Bob whistled quietly under his breath
'A Canadian clean break they call that, well done boy!' he said slapping Paddy's father on the back.
A crackling sound in the nearby undergrowth put a sudden pause on their elated state. Paddy's father put a finger to his lips beckoning them all to be quiet.
The noise came again and seemed a little closer this time, Paddy's father picked up a pebble and flung it far away into the forest where it clunked as it hit a tree and fell to the ground. As he did so a startled deer raced past them and off into the darkness.
Bob winked comically and gave them all a thumbs up.

'Unless the gamekeepers a shapeshifter then we're alright aint we?' he smiled.

The next part of the job was much harder. The ground was too uneven and there were too many trees to roll the trunks to the shore, instead Bob and Paddy's father took one of the halved trunks between them and Paddy and Geri the other. Despite being more than thirty years younger, Paddy and Geri were the ones who struggled with their load and they cursed and bitched at each other as they tripped their way down to the water's edge. Sticks poked into their faces and brambles tore at their legs, yet despite these hindrances and grumbling they made it to the spot where boat was tied up.

'Jesus! I could use some of that moonshine now Bob!' panted Geri.

'Soon enough boy, but we've got work yet to do, I'll hop in the boat and you float out the timber and hold onto the rope till its floating, then throw them to me and I'll tie them to the boat'

With that the two older men climbed into the boat and Bob rowed them out a metre or two.

Paddy and Geri rolled up their trousers and heaved up the first trunk as they waded with it in the freezing water. They threw Bob the rope and he drew in the log to the back of the boat and fastened it tight. They repeated this process and then beckoned Bob to row in and fetch them.

Bob shook his head and winked at them.

'Did I forget to say, you boys are walking back, well running to be precise as we'll need help at the harbour again. This cargo's heavy enough and I'm damned if I'm rowing two extra bodies! Scarper and earn your moonshine lads!'

Geri was left opening and closing his mouth lost for words to say yet too fatigued to concoct a complaint. He had a searing pain in his shoulders from the heavy lifting and his trainers were soaking. Paddy merely shrugged and shook his head.

'Feck it Geri, when there's hee haw tae be done aboot it then there's hee haw we can dae eh! We'll be warmer if we run, it's an hours walk and we'll freeze tae death if we haver.'

Geri hadn't been jogged since being forced to in school, and began to regret his holiday destination. Nevertheless it seemed he had little choice and before the cold could set in any worse he and Paddy began a rasping and clumsy jog along the stony shore. As they ran and tripped and stubbed their toes they could make out the faint silhouette of the little boat, gliding peacefully along the water and how they longed to be aboard it, warming their bellies with a sip of the fabled moonshine.

After what seemed like a great age they made their way through the village and down to the harbour. They walked as quietly as they could to the jetty, though their sodden shoes seemed to squelch with every step. The older men were waiting in the boat and seemed to be drinking something, but whatever it was swiftly disappeared as they caught sight of the boys.

'Last lap and we're done lads, good effort!' whispered Paddy's father, smirking at their red faces and wheezing breath.

They took the timber ashore first, shuffling with it to the van and loading it in without much noise. It was hard to be silent, the ropes seemed to bite into existing sores but the boys struggled not to groan in pain, not wishing to be outdone by their elders. Finally they lifted the boat over their heads and onto the trailer. Everything was done and nobody in the village seemed to have stirred, all the lights were still out. Bob was about to congratulate them when they caught side of someone making their way towards them. Their hearts froze and they tensed as they waited uselessly for the stranger to arrive.

It was a man pushing a wheelbarrow.

'Duncan is that you?' whispered Paddy's father.

'Aye that's me alright, I'm just out for my nights walk to borrow a wee bit firewood and bring it hame in the barrie….if its ok dinnae mention it tae anyone eh? Whit are use doing oot wi a boat at this time oh night?' The old man inquired.

'Just borrowing a bit of wood too…and don't mention it either boy if you don't mind!' said Bob.

'It's a deal, maybe see you at the dominoes then' replied the man and he continued rapidly down the small high street without another word.

'Phew! Right nae time tae waste afore we meet the next thieving auld codger, lets hop in and get hame, I think we've aw earnt oor dram' said Paddy's father.

They crammed into the van and drove swiftly back up the hill.

Back at the house Paddy's mother had kept the fire going and was up waiting for them, clearly relieved to see them yet irritated at having been made so anxious.

'I started the festivities a wee bit early to calm my nerves,' she said as she ushered them in towards the stove and offered them some soup from a bubbling pot.

The boys pulled off their wet socks and toasted their toes in the crackling warmth. Paddy's mum produced Bob's paper bag and pulled out two unlabelled bottles of moonshine passing them to the congregation. They sunk into their chairs and drank deeply from them, defrosting themselves both out and in.

'Ah that's good stuff! I reckon now it's safe for a bit oh yer famous singin' young sir!' said Paddy's father warmly to Geri.

Needing no further encouragement Geri began to blast out his repressed sea shanties and the audience clapped along.

'To the theft of a tree!' toasted Paddy's mother, 'what strange company I keep!'

Chapter 12 - The Pilgrimage Of Catholic Paul

'Well I'm a rover and seldom sober

I'm a rover o' high degree

It's when I'm drinking, I'm always thinking

How to gain my love's company'

The Corries - I'm a Rover [13]

Linlithgow's son, Paul O'Malley, was affectionately known as Malley. This was because there was an abundance of young men in West Lothian who were Catholic by default and thus, baptised Paul by default too. So great was the count of all these 'Catholic Pauls' that the majority found themselves baptised for a second time by friends in the playground. Similarly to most of the local Catholics, Malley's family were second generation Irish immigrants, a societal group obliged - through culture, guilt and occasionally religious conviction - to baptise their children with a good, papal name and pack them off to Catholic schools and mass. Similarly to Daire Mighton and many others, Malley's attendance at mass came to an abrupt end on the inevitable day when he noticed that his older siblings and father appeared to have taken a long term leave of absence from the proceedings. The tenuous terms of this absence were explained unconvincingly as an unfortunate 'need' to watch the Celtic highlights and engage in jollification with a water more fiery than holy. After this day Malley excused himself from his mother's demands, using the same excuses.

He was a short, scruffy, light-haired man who consistently offered the world a smile and hashish fumes. To the casual observer there was nothing extraordinary to behold about him, but the casual observer lacks any depth of inquiry, being all too lost in the trivialities of their own internal monologues. However, those who studied him more diligently could learn that he was singularly kind and simple in nature. He enjoyed but a few modest extravagances, chiefly; smoking marijuana, drumming, reading fantasy novels and taking care of animals. He excelled at all these pastimes, but, particularly the latter, having an uncanny ability to communicate with animals and read their minds. This skill, combined with a deep lethargy towards financial and academic ambition had led him to his long term position as a stable boy at the local livery. Having spent ten years faecal forking and shit shovelling, he was the longest serving and most consistently, congenial chap to ever have had the role. He lived peacefully in a world of daydreams and fairy tales, travelling through the endless smoke rings of his mind. A school teacher had once commented that, 'Paul abides in a world in his head, but it appears to be a most happy place'.

This being said, while Malley had exhausted the highways and byways of his imagination, he had seen little of the large world outside of it. Thus when invited by Paddy and Ivor to join in a troubadour's trip to Santiago De Compostela, his curiosity was aroused. Moreover, he had a new bongo with which to busk and more importantly, had an unyielding appetite for Spanish hashish. Having mulled over these factors, he concluded that this trip was to be very much within his own province and accepted the proposal. However, along with the pending prospect of unemployment, Paddy and Ivor stumbled upon one other small problem concerning Malley joining the travels. This was that he was paid cash in hand and thus had no bank card to utilise abroad. He could undoubtedly not be trusted to carry large sums of cash, without soon dropping them, having them taken, or giving them away in some generous state of stoned oblivion. After much consideration the trio decided that it would be best if Malley's father paid his son's coinage into Paddy's unused, and empty, 'savings' account which he had once opened in a naive pique of ambition. The pater in question would provide a cash injection on a weekly basis, thus keeping Malley's heedless spending to a manageable budget. Ivor and Paddy were curious as to how calmly Malley's parental units seemed to have taken the news that their boy was about to embark on life as a wandering bum. However, little be-known to his friends, any qualms his forbearers had had about their son's trip had been quashed by his rather surprising explanation that his intent in leaving the labour market was that of a walking a Catholic pilgrimage to the holy bones of St James.

Plans were made and tunes were played and before the boys knew it the day of their departure had arrived.

The unholy trio congregated one mid-summer's morn at Edinburgh Airport armed with kilts, tank tops, and a bizarre collection of instruments. They had agreed to wear nothing but kilts and vests for the unspecified duration of their journey, due to Paddy's notion that kilts might help with the busking, and Ivor's hopes that tank tops might help with the señoritas. The Welsh giant had been confident that to any fair eyes that should behold them, his own bulging biceps would appear but all the more gargantuan when regarded alongside Paddy and Malley's pasty pins. However this assumption somewhat backfired when aghast he saw now Malley's arms, and acknowledged melancholically what a decade of shovelling manure can do to tone a man's muscles.

As their budget was extremely limited - relying on future busking and free accommodation in the style of wild camping - their airport breakfast was decided to be strictly rationed. They would drink there no more than two beers per person, and any food would consist of the mysterious edibles Ivor claimed to have packed for them all in his jacket pockets. Sitting at the airport pub and sipping their overpriced pints of Tenants, Ivor began to fumble within his tattered anorak, before proudly producing from it a carrier bag full of lukewarm sausages. Paddy and Malley abstained, assuring the Welshman that they'd wait and busk for breakfast funds on arrival abroad.
'More for me then, fresh cooked this mornin' at me ma's these were' said Ivor unbothered and then proceeded with great satisfaction to lick a globule of grease off one of the glistening, pork lollypops.

Though the month was August, the Scottish weather held an unseasonable – albeit sadly predictable - chill, and cold mists swept across the runway. This was cursed by the three friends, all of whom had been foolish enough to don their wool skirts, without under garments in place to protect their vitals.

As they queued outside, waiting to board the aircraft, a well spoken English gentleman remarked to Malley that it was, 'cold enough to freeze the balls off a bloody, brass monkey what ho!'

'Nevermind yer brass monkey sir, my baws are long gone, and I fear ma tadger will no be long in joinin' them, poor wee fella's curled up like a frozen prawn!' replied Malley amicably.

The gentleman threw back his head and roared with laughter, promising to buy the boys a whisky on board to warm their frozen 'cockles'.

As the plane took off they soon pierced the swirling mists and entered the deep, blue skies above them. This seemed to Ivor – who was sharply superstitious for a man of science – to be a good omen, one that brought promises of fresh possibilities, pages not yet written and friends soon to meet. Malley and Paddy smiled into the azure and across the aisle Ivor began proudly sorting out his collection of sausages. It was hard to guess where they had come from or when or why they had come to Ivor's possession. They were of various shapes and sizes, some were traditional Scotch square sausages, others were round, some long, and some short and some curled. As he lovingly arranged them on the foldout table, an uneducated eye could be forgiven for mistaking the array as an abstract statement on genitalia likely found at the Tate Modern.

Ivor surveyed his kingdom of pork and then began noisily chomping his way through it with an alarming furiosity.

Sitting to his right was an attractive lady in her late forties. She was dressed like Marks and Spencer's advert for middle class mothers and her look of horror at Ivor's antics soon turned to a glare, which she fixed intensely upon him. Realising he was too lost in his lorne ecstasy to notice her gaze, she began coughing loudly and trying to catch his eye. This too failed to distract the giant from his meal and left her unsure as to her next step. Being a woman of reasonable means and a good education, she had long understood it to be her duty to direct such wayward and lost souls, those long parted from any sense of societal propriety and discipline. That said, she had never seen such an appalling specimen in the empire as this and she made a mental note to fly first class on a proper airline in the future and make time to pamphlet for the Conservative Party during their next campaign to make Britain 'great again'. Gluttonous abominations such as this Welshman were putting at risk the 'Great' in Britain and British manners and she decided that she simply would not stand for it.

'What a disgusting smell of sausages!' she cried, her nose turning up in the air. There came no response save the sound of chomping and finger licking.
Further filled with pious indignation she again attempted to right Ivor's wrongs.

'I did not expect to spend my journey breathing in the obnoxious odour of a strangers sausages' she exclaimed to the heavens.

Ivor glanced around and noticed her for the first time.

'My apologies, madam, where are me manners, what'd me mam say now eh? Tut tut! Would you like some?'

He thrust a handful of sausages towards his irate companion.

'It is not that I would like some' she said, dragging out the word 'some' sarcastically.
'It is that I wish for neither them nor their revolting stench to further intrude upon me'

Ivor chuckled, responding, 'I'm feeling fairly famished so you can have me word they'll be gone fast as the mornin' me lovely, which sadly, I guess may not be true of yer own pervasive perfume? A stench of petunias, so erroneously sweet it may be said to distract a man from his brekkie'.

Silence followed and true to his word Ivor devoured all the problematic pieces of pork with haste and vigour, then belched out the meals conclusion and winked at the woman. Paddy and Malley meanwhile slept blissfully and Ivor soon joined them in their slumbers, waking only on arrival at Paris.

Their time in Paris was lazy and hazy and ultimately of little note to this tall tale. Some good money was earned busking in the metro stations and the Gard du Nord but far more was spent on overpriced snacks and wine. The boys soon decided to carry on and wound their way down to Bayonne in the south westerly part of the country. There they had heard tales about generous pilgrims and wealthy tourists who lined the streets all the way down to Santiago. Moreover, Ivor assured them that they would be well received and never short of a mattress or comradeship from their fellow Celts in the north of Spain.

Bayonne proved to be a worthwhile place for busking, with smiles and pennies appearing at a most agreeable pace. The boys had found a small bridge on which to play, and one that met all the stipule of Ivor's performance prerequisites. Firstly, it boasted a street with little traffic, where passers-by could hear the boys loudly and clearly. Secondly, the pavement was not too wide, meaning that pedestrians were forced to pass close by them and acknowledge their presence. Finally – and of no less importance - it was in a cheerful, sunlit spot, that would bring gaiety and pleasantness to their furious melodies.

The sun streamed down and their legs, once fish belly white, turned lobster pink. The wool kilts were cloying and sweaty but brought the desired attention to them. It was by a fine place to spend an afternoon, seagulls sang, and cool waters gurgled under the bridge in a melodious fashion.
The boys had fairly perfected the art of street performance, and

encouraged children to dance, women to wink and everyone to give generously. It was decided that if a couple approached then Paddy would play romantic ballads, where as if young men approached then Ivor would take over with a fiery fighting or drinking tune, and if families or children came their way then Malley would switch to a comedy number, gracing them all with his grin.

It appeared to be a public holiday this Monday and with so many young families strolling by, it was decided that Malley should do the bulk of the singing. He entertained well and put smiles upon many children's faces with his versions of 'The Dundee Weaver' and the 'Glasgow Cat'. He paused mid verse in his own inimitable style to share a lazy smile and draw upon his hand rolled cigarettes. Youngsters clapped their hands in delight, pleading their parents for coins to drop in the hat. Moreover, the time honoured *'entant-cordialle'* between the French and the Scots appeared to still be valid currency, and several bank notes joined their pile of brass.

The trio retired early due to the warmth of the sun, and sought shade under some plane trees in a park. Nearby a fountain cast liquid diamonds up into the sky, and the boys splashed themselves hastily in its cool, crystal waters before lying down on the parched lawn. Each wore a tweed cap and they pulled these over their faces to avoid the brightness of the afternoon. Malley smoked while the other two chewed silently on stems of dry grass evoking connotations of a 19th century cliché on canvas. One of peasant farmers asleep in the hay, indeed, they would not have looked out of place in one of Millet's most romantic efforts.

Ivor and Paddy sleepily congratulated Malley on his busking prowess, to which the small man gave his thanks and quipped,

'If I couldnae get a smile or two for The Glasgae Cat then I'd no be worth the salt tae ma porridge'

The boys chuckled and then lay in silence again until the spell of the fountain's lullaby sent them to sleep. Bees buzzed around their useless corpses and the locals blushed as they walked by, confronted by all that lay exposed under the sleeping boys' kilts. Unfortunately the local ants had no polite reservations and formed orderly queues to greet the Scotsmen's jewels with their fiery bites. Now, whether one's nether regions hang as low as Napoleon's mighty blade, or as high as a loose brass button makes little difference towards the aversion most men feel to such raw insensitivity. Some things are just not meant to be consumed by insects until long after the soul has left the body. Malley scratched and mumbled in his sleep, while Ivor leapt up with yells and curses fit to make Lucifer blush. He grasped and flapped at his kilt and before long all three were on their feet and rushing to the fountain to splash water on their genitals. So maddened were they by a desperation to drown, crush and remove the audacious invaders, that they exposed themselves more and more. Nearby families who had earlier cast smiles on this tartan army, now covered their children's eyes, and tutted about the behaviour of *'les hommes anglais sans vergogne'*. The distraught friends continued to leap around and eventually took to lifting their kilts and plunging their naked groins into the basin of the fountain. The relief was exquisite, but the local's faces turned black as thunder and outraged eyes pierced the boy's hides. Even the tall plane trees above murmured that it was the vilest behaviour of *'les Anglais'* that they had witnessed in the entirety of their three hundred year long careers as Napoleon's sentries of shade. If looks could kill then our troubadours would have dropped dead in the fountain, but instead they splashed and dunked one another impervious to the world around them. Finally the insects were diminished and the boys began to notice the fickle affections of a once adoring public. They awkwardly removed themselves from the water and decided it would be wise to leave the town.

Without much trouble they thumbed a ride to the nearby town of Anglet and spent the evening dashing backwards and forwards between the burning sands and tumbling surf. There were notices forbidding camping on the beach, and keen to avoid further trouble they laid out their sleeping bags discreetly under some large trampolines that lined the strand. As the sun sank, they crawled under them, saying prayers for an absence of rain and bouncing feet. It would seem that someone paid heed, for their wishes were granted and they slept long and deep despite all the dangers.

The daybreak over the Atlantic would not have looked out of place in the scenery of dreams. Wisps of clouds kissed the heavens and the dazzling blue extended far beyond eyesight and imagination. Fishing vessels dotted the waters, and seabirds greedily surrounded them, squawking an excited chorus in anticipation of their share of the mornings catch. Sand sparkled in the sunlight and a loud snoring could be heard from under the trampolines.
Eventually though, the boys joined the day and broke their fast with a meal of drammach. This was made by mixing oatmeal with cold water, thus creating the tasteless paste that had long filled the bellies of their countrymen whenever they found themselves upon the road and without the means to light a fire. The meal was given a continental twist with canned sardines and a few ripe tomatoes joining the oats. Afterwards, with full bellies and sandy teeth they stretched out on the beach, enjoying the warm sand between their toes and the sound of the ocean. They agreed that while there may be but few beaches that compare to the white bays of Scotland's west coast, it was a rare pleasantry to be able to enjoy a beach without the whistling assault of the north wind or the need for a raincoat and jumper.

Soon enough their meal was deemed to be digested and they found themselves back on the road to Santiago and all the holy promises that awaited them there. From Bayonne they wandered to St Jean Pied De Port, and then for many days through the ragged Pyrenees and along the dusty tracks of northern Spain until they reached San Sebastian.

San Sebastian turned out to be a friendly place and one that was kind to pilgrims in plaids. The town was of rare beauty, and boasted; a graceful bay, buildings carved from warm, golden stone and an artistic mastery of culinary delights. Mouth-watering creations and colourful combinations could be attained for no great expense in all the bars that filled the winding streets. The boys were delighted to learn that it was custom for these tapas to come as an accompaniment for every cerveza purchased. This worked up a blinding greed in the troubadours, and caused them to haemorrhage significantly more cash than they were earning. After a day or two an emergency meeting was called between them and they discussed the details and aims of future busking economics. An agreement was found and for a day or so it was stuck to and functioned, but as is the case with so many great workers' collectives, infighting and mutiny soon broke out. None of the boys minded sharing everything equally, but they each had different interpretations concerning the length and effort of 'a day's work'. Ivor - whose family hailed from the Welsh mining communities - was almost puritanical and Leninist in his proposals. Until the coins met the expressed target he could see no excuse for rest or respite from the hot sun.

Malley on the other-hand had a much more nihilistic and haphazard approach to work, it was the first time he had been without a boss for a decade, and he was keen to relax and spend all they had or didn't have left in their overdrafts, leaving the consequences for another day.

Paddy was however swift to point out that the only overdraft Malley had access to was that of his own borrowed bank card, and that Malley was by no means welcome to that. Paddy instead relied on hazy, utopian dreams, feeling certain that there was a perfect place to busk where they could spend less time and make more money, they just had to find it.

Despite these differences the boys made their way to a cobbled street and again applied an indefatigable assiduity to their art form. The sun burnt and blinded them, and the streets turned out to be paved with an overwhelming amount more dog dirt than gold. The heat baked these canine gifts and it seemed impossible to escape their impecunious odour, which greeted the nasal passages like napalm. Tensions grew after Malley suggested extra breaks, and the boys were on the verge of a schism when out of the blue two prematurely drunk Americans appeared and donated fifty dollars in exchange for 'The Wild Rover'. Euphoria followed and all plans of fiscal austerity were immediately abandoned. Beers were bought and shared with all the beggars and dreadlocked punks on the street. Toasts were made and some elderly locals retired early from a game of dominoes to offer homemade sherry to the fiesta.

As evening came, the plaza filled with yet more people and local gypsies sold cans of cold beer at alarmingly cheap rates. Agreeable smells of grilled fish and garlic and lemons filled the airwaves and caused the boy's bellies to grumble and moan. They decided to rectify this situation and made their way to a taverna where they stood bent under vaulted ceilings and gorged on the tapas which covered a broad oak bar. Each tapa contained a cocktail stick and these were collected and counted as a trusting method to calculate payment. Mouthfuls of roasted peppers, burnt aubergines and delicious manchego were washed down with Spanish ciders. This amrita was poured at height from the wooden barrels that lined the walls. Full of its joyful sparkle, Ivor struck up a conversation with a local lady and was invited to her house for a more private drink, and so left early with a broad smile painted on his beard.

Closing time came, and in good spirits Paddy and Malley tumbled onto the dark streets. A ferocious rain was falling and the pair were soon soaked, without a penny left for a place to stay the night. Malley had no problems with the rain and his tireless grin soon had Paddy chuckling and feeling easier with the thought of a cold night spent on the pavement. They sat a while on a bench and shared old stories but before long both their rucksacks and instruments began to be dangerously saturated. Paddy suggested they take a stroll just to 'see what they may see' and Malley who was happy enough to agree to most things in life, agreed. They rambled up a hill, beyond the west of the bay, and giggled manically at their predicament and the ridiculous nature of their vacation. At the summit they came to a four storey high hostel which, as Malley quickly pointed out, had a bathroom window left wide open on the second floor.

'Naebody would begrudge a man a bathroom flair on a night like this, I'll shimmy up yon drainpipe, you check the coast's clear an' pass me oor bags, we can hop oot early in the morn' said Malley.

With surprising agility for one so inebriated, he leapt at the drainpipe and swiftly made his way up to the window. Once he was inside, Paddy threw up the bags and instruments to him, and then made his own way up with a lot more trepidation and error. The bathroom was dark so Malley sparked his cigarette lighter and they took a look around. It was a good sized room with two toilet stalls and ample space to sling sleeping bags upon the floor. The tiles turned out to be cold and the sleeping bags damp but they quickly reached their dreams regardless.

The next morn the sun got up long before the boys, yet by some stroke of luck nobody else entered the bathroom. When the pair finally stirred, they found themselves somewhat confused by their surroundings and to be encumbered by parched tongues and heavy heads. Upon regaining their whereabouts, Malley assured Paddy that there was nobody in the room the bathroom led to for if it did they would have surely heard them. Not keen on the idea of climbing from the window again, Paddy consented to edge the door ajar and have a peep inside the bedroom. Cautiously, they did so and Malley's speculations were proved to be true, there were two bunk beds which suitcases sat beside but not a soul to be seen.

'Paddy sir, I cannae walk aboot in that sun in this nick. Guaranteed these folk are oot noo for the day. Could we no just sleep half an hour on a soft mattress afore we're back oot in that sun?'

Paddy was still making his mind up as to how to respond, when Malley took the silence to be an affirmation and fell into one of the beds, snoring immediately. His troubled friend scratched his head uneasily but then shrugged and followed suit. This time, however, their sleep was not to be without interruption and after only ten minutes in the land of nod, they were awoken by the door being unlocked and thrown open by a tall bearded man and a short woman with red hair. The man shouted things in an unknown tongue, and flapped his hands theatrically while the woman attempted to placate him. Malley stumbled to his feet apologising with a shy smile, while Paddy hung his head despairingly and waited for incoming blows to fall. However, by some miraculous twist of fate instead of being forced to pay penance for their folly the man and woman began pointing at Malley's kilt and laughing.

'Eh you crazy bastards, are you Scottish? Ow' the hell you get in here, eh? What you do sleeping here?' questioned the girl.

Paddy and Malley confirmed their nationality and began explaining how they had ended up in the room despite a locked door. Meanwhile the man had grabbed his bag and raked through it till he pulled out a cheap tourist kilt of his own.

'We are from the Basque Country, we was living in Scotland six months, we love it there, crazy motherfuckers no?! You like the beer and music!' he exclaimed with a thick accent and a manic grin.

Paddy's internal discomposure dissolved and he gave a silent thanks to the post code lottery of life for having assigned him his country of birth. The Basque couple listened with amusement to the boy's pathetic story, and kept slapping them on their backs and telling them what 'crazy fools' they were and that they must visit their hometown Bilbao if they had the chance. The conversation began to flow and after a while of chatting about the couple's favourite Scottish pubs and islands, the woman suddenly said, 'hey there is a buffet of breakfasts downstairs if you are hungry, I'm sure if you go you can eat free and soon feel a bit better no, just sing us a song first, we love the Scottish music'.

The boys beamed grateful appreciation at her and Malley cried out,
'A've been sent an angel on ma pilgrimage! Whit a fine pair use are! A scran an' a cup coffee would sure start the day a new like! Paddy sing them a song!'

Paddy obliged and sang them a poem he'd been working on called A Hobo's Clothes, which went like this,

I got a hobo's clothes
A broken nose
A deficit that always grows
And all these things I'll gladly give to you

I got sunburnt skin
A loser's grin
A lust for making plenty sins
And all these things I'll gladly give to you

I got a chicken's legs
An unmade bed
An empty belly needing fed
And all these things I'll gladly give to you

I got pointless goals
A tainted soul
A long gone sail that wind can't blow
And all these things I'll gladly give to you

I got lack of style
A vagrant's smile

A groin that's itched for quite a while
And all these things I'll gladly give to you

I got a silver tongue
A crooked thumb
A dream to win what can't be won
And all these things I'll gladly give to you

The couple had expected a more traditional folk number, but they received Paddy's song gratefully and clapped away. After the shaking of hands and a few slaps on the back, the boys made their way downstairs and committed gluttony upon the buffet, all the while lost in feelings of bewilderment and delight.

'That was a rare stroke of luck that' said Paddy upon sating his hunger.

'Luck?!' retorted Malley.

'Ye're a heathen an' a damnable Calvinist oh the spirit if ever there was yin sir! That wis divine intervention, leading a good Catholic boy on a quest'. With that the small man toasted the heavens with a coffee cup and tucked in to his umpteenth slice of well buttered toast.

After breakfast the boys left the hostel via the door and to their relief the receptionist there asked no questions. Outside the morn held the promise of more heat to come and the sky was as clear as could be. They wondered back into town and roamed the narrow streets hunting for Ivor until they heard a furious voice accompanied by a banjo and caught up with their missing comrade. He informed them that his night had also been a success and proudly showed them the violent love bites that covered his neck. Saluting each other's achievements the boys took out their instruments and joined Ivor in some high spirited busking.

After two more days of busking and gorging, the boys left San Sebastian and followed the route of the Camino making good speed towards Santiago.

About a three day walk from their destination they stopped in a village for a busk, and were interrupted by a young girl asking if she could sit with them and sell her homemade wares. She had a roguish manner, and her mischievous green eyes were framed by matted henna hair that tumbled down around her face like a mane. On her head she wore the remains of a blue woolly hat that looked like it had seen the seven seas, and on her feet were battered trainers with more holes than soles. The lads discussed her wish and quickly came to agreement that it would be of no inconvenience to them for her to join them. She gave them an ironic thumbs up and then opened a bag, bringing out a staggering array of rings and necklaces. It was incredulous how much jewellery appeared to be stashed in such a small bag, and was akin to a magician's trick, where a white rabbit hopping out would have come as no surprise. Her collection was then carefully arranged on an array of purple cloths and silk handkerchiefs. Ivor commended her attention to detail and all the boys were glad for new company, especially of company such as this, which promised to bring stories of interest and insight regarding street enterprise. As they began their songs, the friends found they had won a new audience. Indeed, folk who came forward to buy jewellery, tended to cast their change towards Malley's cap. Likewise, the girl noticed that those stopping to hear the music lingered long enough to notice her wares and that she too made a prettier penny. After a couple of hours, each party notified the other of their satisfaction with the arrangement and gave formal introductions of themselves. The girl was called Rebecca Janssen, and turned out to be a penurial, street urchin with artistic capabilities. Vague with her background, she said she was of Dutch and American stock and appeared to be some sort of wandering waif, plucked directly from a Tom Wait's lyric and placed in front of them.

Paddy and Malley introduced themselves and wished their own

histories were more exotic than tales of ex-industrial towns, where excitement was primarily gained through watching the lives of others on television. Ivor, not one to be lightly outdone by men or Gods, presented himself with a string of dubious titles and embellished accolades which he boomed out theatrically in his lilting brogue. With flailing arms and manic brown eyes the rugged giant told tales so fantastical that soon both he and his audience were laughing heartily and he was toasted by all to be capable of 'playing the Dane'. There is no more to say of this merry introduction, except that hands were spat upon and shaken, and a four way working agreement with a split of foods, funds and beers concluded.

True to this agreement they idled their way to Santiago, successfully busking and hawking for the pilgrims that passed them by. In the countryside, they hid their tents under hedgerows or behind the stone dikes lining the lanes, while in towns, they slept out of sight high up on the scaffolding that crept like ivy round most of the crumbling buildings. Here the troubadours slept well enjoying the cleaner air and sunrise views that rewarded their daily ascents. In this manner they travelled many miles and save for an attempted drum theft in Bilbao, the time passed easily and before they knew it, they had arrived at Santiago.

On approaching its industrial suburbs, the gang began to question the Mecca of Malley's imagination, but they soon became pious when he informed them of a rumour of an ancient wine fountain, famed for quenching the thirst of weary pilgrims.

The outer appearance of the town was forgiven, for its centre pulsed life and madness. A cathedral was at its heart, and the streets ran from it like broken arteries, clogged with people and leading to countless dead ends. These crumbling labyrinths were full of curious paradoxes, playing home to a mix of foreign pilgrims, local punks, bong shops, blessed bead stores and everything in between. Malley and Rebecca visited the cathedral, while Paddy and Ivor went to the fountain. Both groups were disappointed by a lack of enlightenment induced through their chosen grails, and sought solace afterwards at a local garage, where empty water bottles could be transformed into full wine bottles for less than a euro. The wine was a vintage of flawed character. A vinegar most vile and perhaps best suited to clean winter windscreens, yet – as with all wines - it improved upon every sip and encouraged energetic busking. The boys screamed and shouted, playing with escalating pace and joy. Their mad ecstasy was reflected back to them by the smiling droves of pilgrims all newly having completing personal odysseys. Pennies were made and soon their bellies were refilled at the bakery and their bottles at the garage.

The group decided to treat themselves to a warm bed, and found affordable lodgings in a pilgrim's alberge. The place backed onto a fine courtyard, and here the eve was spent, enjoying cheap wine and even cheaper humour. The moon rose and the night became cold and clear, with a brilliance of stars piercing the heavens. The Milky Way was visible and time inverted as lights from the past winked provocatively at the present. Eventually Paddy, Ivor and Rebecca made a wobbly retreat to bed, leaving Malley alone on the cobbled terrace. He sat silently, lost in clouds of smoke and the heavenly wonders above.

Hours passed and Paddy was fast asleep, deep in the dreamless coma of a man who has drunk too much, when suddenly he was torn from his rest by someone shaking him and shouting his name.

'Paddy! Paddy! Whit a night I've had, sir.'

Paddy rubbed his eyes and glared at the face of the perpetrator, hovering horribly close above him. Grinning wildly was an exceedingly intoxicated Malley. The small man appeared to have reached the zenith of his good humour and radiated joy from his beaming eyes.

'Paddy sir! I went fir a walk an' found this bar, an' lo and behold it turns out tae be a brothel. So I'm drinking whisky and chatting tae the lassies. An' one of them offers me into her room, and I says I'm too drunk an I'm no intae that kinda scene, but I'll pay to tae craic a while an share a dram. Anyhow it turned oot she wis fae Africa an big intae her dogs, so we're just lyin' on her bed fer hours, lookin' at pictures of all her wee pups and chatting shite.'

Malley then began giggling and roared,

'Sir who'd have thought I'd have the time oh my life with a beautiful hoor in Santiago?'

His loud tenor awoke several others in the dormitory and an irate voice squeaked,

'American Christian ladies do not approve of this kind of language!'

Malley seemed not to notice the extreme impropriety of his conduct, and responded with a chuckle saying,

'I'm sorry, hen, but that was ma pilgrimage, whit a night'.

With that he jumped into Paddy's bed, falling soundly asleep despite his friend's protests.

Morning came all too soon, and despite the unruly hour, the foursome were politely requested to leave the pilgrims lodgings and not return. They trudged to the nearest park, three of them with crushing hangovers, and one of them still giggling contentedly to himself. There they lay in the morning sun and drifted again to a dreamless death. Heat came to the day and

small lizards began to move, their blood defrosted by Rah's affection. The sun tried to share his life giving powers with the comatose gang in the park, but even the magic of his golden gaze could not part them from their slumbers. They slept on, till their faces became rouged and tinted.
When they awoke Malley began his chuckling again,

'Paddy sir, I've gone an' left your bank card at the brothel!'

Paddy who tended to be a placid kind of creature, somewhat lost his composure. This was principally due to the fact that in order to move from couch to couch and cupboard to cupboard without paying council tax, the lanky vagrant had been officially registered as living with his grandmother for the last ten years. Therefore all mail, including bank statements went straight to the old dear's house, where she tended to cast a concerned eye upon them before passing them on.

'Malley ya wee prick! If ma gran reads a bank bill fae a brothel then my days of happy families are gonna be numbered, aside from that I don't want some pimp plunderin' my overdraft, so make haste an' get it back!'

Malley tried to lead the way to the brothel but failed to retrace his steps. He pointed out that perhaps the whole thing was a dream, but it was of little solace to Paddy's twitching nerves. So, after long discussions and heated arguments, the near penniless boys decided to spend the last of their collective cash on wending their way homewards to Scotland once more. Rebecca, who was made of sterner stuff, bid them farewell saying that she would head south for the winter. The boys felt ashamed of their lack of grit, but the notion of Scottish pubs with friendly faces and familiar beers and songs held strong appeal in their broken state.

Some days later the pilgrims took a flight north and returned once more to the green country of their fathers. Malley went straight to his family home to tell his tales of Santiago, though he emitted some of the details as he did so. Later that evening as he sat on his parents' doorstep to watch the sun sinking over the housing scheme, some of his neighbours swore they saw a halo appear above his blonde head. Cynics wrote it off as a smoke ring, but then again, what did cynics ever know of the world's wonders?

Chapter 13 – A Visit to Edinburgh

'Half a capital and half a country town, the whole city leads a double existence; it has long trances of the one and flashes of the other; like the king of the Black Isles, it is half alive and half a monumental marble.'

Robert Louis Stevenson [14].

It was six thirty on a Friday morning. Edinburgh's early commuters walked swiftly through Princes Street Gardens. They hurtled towards Waverley Station, as if in the hope that they could force the day to pass at double speed and reach the relative freedom of the weekend a bit quicker. On such weekends, the charm of doing laundry, buying new socks and visiting family would be treasured pleasures, unsupervised, unregulated and as close to anarchy as suburban Britain would ever come.

Down and outs laid on the park benches, in the Princes Street Gardens, sprawled out over the unforgiving iron and wood, with the all familiarity luckier folk have for their home settee. The steady caravan of commuters paid no heed to them though. The passers-bys' consciences could be easy as long as the dispossessed slept on, keeping their haunting stares and hollow faces to themselves. No looks or coins were cast their way, and the minds of those privileged enough to have options, became firmly focused on busy schedules and choices of coffees. Any fleeting pity granted to the shivering corpses was rarely followed up by any depth of philosophical or political inquiry. At best, a pound occasionally made its way to a charity, ensuring all guilt and responsibility was effectively deferred. At that depressing hour of the morning, it seemed the tabloids had won, and for the bribe of a week's wages, mankind was content enough to forget their brotherhood to their fellow man. As Ivor often said, it was a world made up of 'those that clearly had, those that clearly had not and those that were clearly cunts'.

The morning sun rose a little higher, coaxing life back into the bones of the broken. Perhaps from the suns giddy vantage, all men looked the same, in any case it shone on all alike. As colours flooded into the greyscale of the day, Rah noticed that two of the vagrant slumberers were clearly virginal to the park's bedchambers. Indeed, these two men were undoubtedly novices to the art of picking a perfect cot. They lay crumpled against each other, on the only bench to have a gutter leaking onto it from the roof of a Victorian garden hut. Despite the toxic green of the water dripping down steadily upon them and ruining their clothes, this pair slept heavily, almost defiantly unencumbered it seemed. One of them was long and thin, and filled the contours of the bench like an overcooked piece of overcooked spaghetti. The other had the wild beard and homemade tattoos of a habitual vagrant and made sibilant music as he cackled in his sleep.

Geri was the first of them to wake up.

'Paddy! Wake yersel' man, ye're late for yer work. Where the fecks Ivor?'

Paddy let out a sound that was somewhere between a grumble and a yawn.

'Ivor? Feck knows! Probably dead! Christ, where the hell are we and whit time is it?'

'Time?! How in seven hells would ah ken, fascist feckers clocks, miserable, morose creatures...'

'Alright alright!' Interrupted Paddy.
'Keep yer hair on, if there's something I need afore work it's a warm scran, no a cold dose oh the truth. Naebody needs the truth at this time in the morn, that's why we read newspapers.'

Geri chuckled at that and shook Paddy's hand with a paw so icy that it made Paddy wince and fear for gangrene.

'Yer quite right my man, where's ma manners, fried food afore philosophy less there be foul words an' fights. And whit say ye we buy a warm roll for those two poor feckers lying there? Christ kens that concretes nae carpet!'

Geri thrust his legs out, tightened the duct tape around his flapping sole, cracked his neck and then jumped - with irritating ease thought Paddy - to his feet. Accepting sullenly that the day had begun with or without his invitation, Paddy too stood up and stretched heavenwards and then down towards the ground, staring at the vast lawn that lay before them. A thousand impecunious warriors, baring green blades stared back. Upon every blade were drops of dew, crystal balls that reflected images of the men back to themselves. It seemed to Paddy that each of these mirrors could distort the picture to display a new perspective and countless abstract interpretations of the same scene. He fantasised that these blades of grass stood as straight as they could, but only the toughest of these cloaked, green warriors could stand erect, under the weight of such glistening diamonds. The ones that managed, erected a pearl high upon an emerald spear, and saluted the world with the all silent poetry of the Celtic groves.
Paddy stared a while, lost in these daydreams, but was brought, eventually, back to reality, by the sound of Geri scratching his backside.

'Feckin' itchy arse ye get sleepin' in the rain,' observed Geri with a serious nod that suggested he was imparting Solomon's wisdom upon the world.

'Dinnae look at me wi' that tone ah voice, Paddy! Ayebody gets an itchy arse!'

Paddy shrugged and the two of them trod their shivering way to the Babylon Café for a cheap breakfast.

Inside the café the boys' hunched shoulders relaxed and their aching joints began to defrost in the greasy smoke and steamy warmth that filled the little room. They nursed great mugs of milky tea, and were served a multitude of fried snacks that came in different shades of brown.

'Why's Scottish food ayewis broon?' mused Geri.

'Like whit?!'

'Aw of it. Haggis, tatties, stew, gravy, pizza crunch, battered fish, the list goes on.'

'Chips are kinda yelly are they no?'

'Shite chips maybe! Decent chips are golden broon, wi broon sauce an' broon beer tae wash them doon!'

'Cannae fault ye there sir! Maybe when they banned the tartan they banned colours?!'

'Ye gonnie blame the English for oor pish cuisine noo sir?

'No, but I'll blame the rich an' powerful for whit ah can. Evils the root of all money and the more ye've got...'

'The more of a Tory cunt ye become?'

'Exactly!'

'Well thank feck we have nae mair than twenty pence tae spare after buying brekkie for us an' filled rolls for they ragged boys in the park' said Geri proudly.

Paddy was about to agree when he realised that parting with the last of their coins had left him without the means to pay for a bus to work and he would now have to walk the long road to his work in Corstorphine and hitchhike the even longer road home to West Lothian later. He muttered apologies to Geri, suggested he should look into the health and whereabouts of Ivor, and then marched out into the cold, his face akin to a man set to attend his own funeral.

Geri scraped the uneaten scraps from Paddy's plate onto his own, grateful for extra sustenance yet rueful of his friend's vegetarian ways at the same time. He wiped away steam from the window, creating a viewing hole with a frayed sleeve. The world outside had become overcast and dull. He stared at Nicholson Square where cast iron railings stood like crooked, dead trees, and all the surrounding stone tenements that had shone gold in the sun looked now the lifeless grey of an addict's face. The only colours to be seen were on the blooming cheeks of yummy mummies, who pushed prams, filled with - soon to be - privately schooled offspring. Future prime ministers in waiting, who now spent their days being wheeled between expensive crèches and middle class cafes in Morningside. Geri turned his eye back to the waitresses pale face and prematurely greying hair. Perhaps the rich were indeed robbing the poor of colour?

Putting his hand in his anorak pockets, he checked each one thoroughly to see if he could find some change to leave a tip. A tiny tip such as it was, was a token of acknowledgement from one member of the exploited class to another. Each pocket proved as empty as the last, but in his jacket pocket he found a curious thing. Crumpled but still legible, was a paper cup bearing the name of a local Christian organisation. He considered this discovery slowly. He was fairly certain he hadn't attended mass in over fifteen years, and had had no inclination to alter that. Even more baffling, was the fact that the cup was still moist inside, so it hadn't arrived unseen with his second hand jacket. Glancing furtively round him, less somebody mistook him for a member of a conservative Christian group, he sniffed the cup in the hope of clues. There was a whiff of instant hot chocolate, but one trampled on by the unmistakeable smoke of Ardbeg whisky. Now a memory came back to him. The previous eve, Paddy, annoyed that Geri had not been permitted to enter an establishment, on account of his battered footwear, had entered alone and stolen a bottle of the glorious firewater that is Ardbeg from behind the bar. Drinking it on the street with Ivor and some other buskers they had been approached by well-meaning Christian students and offered hot beverages to stave off the cold. Much to the

despair of these evangelists, they had each topped up their hot chocolates with whisky in a bid for extra warmth.

'God will be annoyed,' one of the concerned young men had told them.

'Damn straight he will!' replied Ivor. 'For it's a heathen crime to contaminate so fine a malt as this, but I hope Odin and all the Gods of old appreciates that its cauld and so a man does what he must!'

They had not been offered any more hot chocolate after that.

The thought of Ivor reminded Geri of the duty Paddy had bestowed upon him - to check if the Welshman still haunted the lands of the living - and so with unsteady fingers he found his friend's number in his phone and called him up. The phone rang a good while before Ivor answered, his booming singsong voice blasting out the speaker and nearly perforating Geris's eardrum.

'HELLOOO!! Geri me lover, is that you boyo?'

'Ivor, ye awful cunt ye, glad tae hear ye're still disgracing this world wi' yer presence!'

'Language son!' squeaked a middle-aged man at a table nearby.

'Sorry, pal, sometimes forget I've left the Tonic Triangle!!

The man looked confused by the response, but was satisfied that he'd been bequeathed an apology, and displayed his manly valour. He gazed longingly into the eyes of the Polish waitress, hoping to have impressed her. She glared back at him, but blushed a little as she made the coffees.

Geri observed all this, all the while listening to Ivor crunching something that sounded like carrots, on the other end of the phone.

'Ivor you still there? Are ye munchin' carrots ya heathen beast? Its rude tae talk wi yet mooth full!'

'Nah, I'm devouring some delicious cauliflower. It's all I could find in me ma's fridge.'

'Yer ma's? But she's aw the way oot at Loanhead, how did ye end up there after night bus hours?!'

Ivor was silent a few seconds, and then answered.

'It's a long and beautiful story, too long for now. I need to go busking today anyways, shall we meet on Rose Street in an hour and I'll tell you then?'

'Grand, aye, where on Rose Street?'

'How should I know matey? You'll hear me, and if you don't then I ain't worth the loverly Welsh blood in me loverly veins.'

Geri laughed and agreed to meet him there. Peering out the window, he sipped the last of Paddy's tea with anticipation and curiosity over what could have happened to Ivor. The man's tales were wonderful things. They had a tendency to be rich in filth and madness and gave their audiences the realisation, that the possibilities of this reality could be as full of unpredictability as its quantum underpinnings.

Paddy, meanwhile, was marching towards Corstorphine. He had managed to sneak on a tram as far as Haymarket and half ran half walked, tripping as he gazed across the road in wonder at the epic stonework and fairy-tale turrets of the Donaldson's deaf school. He wondered if its splendid detailing and grandiose architecture permeated the entire building, or if like other penitences, erected under the Victorian era, such a display of charitable, generosity ran only as deep as the front door, never reaching the objects of charity themselves. He hurried along and tried to focus on getting to work but his mind soon returned to its ceaseless musing and he found himself debating whether charity and the elite celebrating their own good name through public donations of tiny proportions of their enormous wealth, had changed at all in the last hundred years. A passing siren brought him out of his head again and he brushed away such cynicism, chiding himself that anger was a fool's weapon. Instead, he smiled at a passing squirrel, and enjoyed the memory of a rumour he had heard, that although Queen Victoria had demanded the building for her summer palace, the school had refused, reputedly, causing her never to step foot in the area again. There was a light drizzle in the air, but it was good weather to walk fast in, and so with his hands sunk deep into the pockets of his old Adidas hoodie, he marched on. Despite the damp there was plenty joy for the senses to take in. Indeed, the bakers smelt of warm scotch pies, and hurtling busses left rainbow pools of oil drops in puddles. To the south, occasional gaps in the clouds, revealed the curved spine of the Pentland hills and Paddy sighed, imagining a day tramping in the heather, instead of trying to meet the ridiculous demands of the self-righteous customers that pervaded the hotel where he worked. Those that suffered to earn their pay seemed always to be damn keen that everyone else would suffer to earn theirs.

Eventually he made it to the hotel chain where he currently washed dishes. The building was almost remarkable in its complete lack of remarkability. He swung through the glass doors, and up the carpeted stairs, choking on the scent of cheap room fresheners. He passed by the battery farmed, breakfast buffet, and into the kitchen, where he stopped to look at the rota. It was then that he realised his shifts had changed and he wasn't due to start for an hour. He cast furtive looks around him in case he had been noticed, worrying the chef would make use of him early. However, the staff were discussing something in the store room and hadn't noticed his arrival. He tiptoed back out the room, climbed another two floors and walked down a corridor, scanning the guest rooms, until he found one that was vacated. Checking one last time that no one was around, he sneaked inside and lay down on the bed. For all the hotel's charmless flaws, the bed was a delight in comparison to the park bench, and Paddy fell quickly into dreams of wandering in hilltops above the clouds.

Geri dragged himself along Rose Street. His velvet jacket blew in the breeze and his feet tripped one over the other, in soggy mess of untied laces and tape. Hearing Ivor's distinctive banjo thrashing in the distance, he made his way towards the sound. He was not the only one drawn to the noise. Ivor's banjo had a magnetic pull for freaks and vagabonds and a small crowd surrounded him. It was often hard to distinguish whether such folk would begin to clap or attack at his performances, but the Welsh bard's newly shaved head, giant beard and meaty fists, kept the audience cautious of committing violence against him.

'Arighty, Ivor!'

'Hey, Geri!' shouted Ivor, mid song

'I've just worked out The Skids on the banj', listen'

He abruptly changed songs, causing much of his grizzled audience to hiss and walk off in irritation. Geri however, listened with joy and gratitude and sat cross legged on the pavement where he rolled a cigarette. Some nearby pigeons tapped their feet, as they too awkwardly tried to get into the groove.

'Bravo Ivor! Bravo!' shouted Geri, adding, 'Here, have a cigarette.'

'But I don't smoke, Geri.'

'Well, it's all I had tae offer you, but tremendous anyway, outstanding tae hear Into The Valley on a banjo'

Geri's praises were interrupted by three, men in grey tracksuits shouting at Ivor!

'Haw! Upside doon heid! Ye're shite, play some Oli Murs, ya cunt!'

Ivor, who had learnt both boxing and the boxer's stare, in order to survive being the only Welsh communist at a tough Scottish school, gave them a practiced glare. The weasel faced young men, debated challenging him, but then backed down and swaggered off.

Ivor tugged absently at his beard, greatly amused by the idea of having an upside down head, but perplexed by society's uniformed rejection of him.

'Fecks sake! Where do I fit in? The underclass want to thump me, and the middle class think I'm a jobless freak. If I ain't underclass and I ain't middle class then what am I?'

'Your Ivor Ryder-Jones, bro', one of a kind and someday you'll be celebrated for that!'

Ivor's frown softened at that, and he stopped plucking his beard to tousle Geri's hair.

'Jeez Geri! Why you got mouldy moss on yer scalp?'

'Ach! We missed the last bus an' kipped in the park. Boring story. What wis your craic though man, we lost you after the whisky hot chocolates I think?'

With the flair of a seasoned storyteller, Ivor cleared his throat, then gazed into the middle distance and began to tell his tale.

'Well, all that Christian hot chocolate went to my brain. Spiked me sugar levels or something, so I took a brisk stroll to walk it off. So there I was heading down to the green, Hibernian pastures of Leith, my anchovy pizza in hand and mouth...'

'Yer whit?! Feck me, that's vile, dinnae tell me ye actually like anchovies, dae ye?'

'Of course not, and I resent the accusation, but neither does any other fucker. So when every late night drunkard asks for a slice, I simply explain its contents and they back off into the night!'

Geri stroked his beard, his narrowed eyes revealing a lack of convincement over his friend's logic.

'Surely the measure oh yer greed is no worth jettisoning yer digestive tract for is it?'

Ivor gave a sardonic laugh,

'Ah! How sadly you underestimate the power of greed amigo. But anyhow, daylights no time for doomsday prophecies, so back to my tale of my own grubby desires, and pray stop interrupting boyo!'

Again the Welshman cleared his throat and struck a pose, his bearded jaw thrust skyward, as though hoping be eternalised in marble along with the Greek philosophers.

'So homeward bound I was, when a naughty little thought

popped into my head. Now I can only rationally blame the hot chocolate or anchovies, cos it ain't like me to dream like this. See I began thinking, how nice the company of a fine lady would be, and seeing as there wasn't any round, I thought maybe I could find a bordello or a brothel. I had no ill intention be assured but I felt a strong urge to buy a voluptuous lady a drink, a Hemingway daiquiri perhaps, gaze at her bucksome form, and serenade her with Welsh poetry.'

'Welsh poetry? You mean like Dylan Thomas?'

'No! No! No! No! Dylan Thomas is a fine man, but his words were not writ to woo the ears of dames. No I was going to unleash a lovely ocean of old Welsh poems in the tongue of my land and court her ears till we both felt merry and loved'

'Outstanding! And did ye?'

Ivor was silent a minute, staring ahead, and trying to decide whether to recount this section of his tale with shame or pride. He opted for the latter and rubbed his great hands together, blowing life into his cold fingers.

'Well, I'd heard tale there was a gentleman's establishment on the top of Broughton Street. A place where the women are rich in culture and conversation, not merely extravagant of breast. So I found the door, no grim cage down a dismal side street you understand, a large oak door, gracing the facade of a Georgian townhouse.'

'Ivor, ya mad fecker! Ye make a Shakespeare novel oot of pornography!'

'Pornography?! Nonsense boyo, nothing of the sort! So came I did to this great door, and I took the brass ring in hand and I knocked like a clap of thunder. A woman in her sixties answers it eventually. I told her it was a pleasure to meet the madam of such an establishment and shook her hand. It was then it struck me that I had come without coin. I apologised profusely and promised to return immediately after finding a cash machine. 'What for, what for' she implored of me? To pay for the company of one of your fine woman I said. Well she insisted I was at the wrong address, but I called her a sly fox and promised to return imminently with suitable coinage. She replied that she would phone the police, but I knew the old minx was merely testing my resolve. So, off I went to the cash machine, and on my way back I was picked up by two police officers who said they'd had a disturbing call regarding my intentions. I told them there was nothing disturbing about them, explaining I was hoping to pay for a vivacious lady and lavish her ears with Welsh poetry. Well, the coppers laughed at that, told me I'd had too much to drink and offered, or rather demanded, to drive me back to me ma's.'

Geri broke into laughter and shook his head with amused astonishment at his companion.

'Well, I guess at least you got the chance to see yer auld dear when you were back here?'

'I certainly did, I told her how I got my free ride too and she told me it wasn't funny. Oh and I took her old nursing cape from the seventies, I reckon together with the kilt it'll be just the thing for busking attention'

Ivor opened his banjo case and produced a blue cloak with arm holes on either side. He swirled it in the air dramatically before draping it over his huge shoulders.

'Christ on a bike Ivor! You look like a cross-dressing wizard, but you'll grab attention right enough. C'mon, I could do with a pint or a coffee or anything indoors, get busking and I'll pass the hat, everyone thinks I look handicapped when I'm hungover so it may help to raise the funds quickly.'

Ivor picked up his banjo, and pulled on a yellow beret that

looked like part of a school girl's uniform. His cape flapped in the wind and cars roared by on nearby streets, but both wind and traffic were no competition for his sonic boom, and soon enough bemused tourists were filling the hat with coins.

Meanwhile, Paddy lay, snoring on the hotel bed. He could well have slept all day were it not for a cleaner coming in to change the sheets. With a start he asked her the time. She pointed despondently at a clock on the wall. A quick glance told him that he was now an hour and a half late for work. He knew the hotel's policy on lateness, he had heard it and all their other lifeless mottos a thousand times over the three weeks he had worked there. The irritating slogans tore now through his mind, like a banshee ripping open the sky. 'Going to be late? Leave by the front gate'. 'Got time to lean? Time to clean!'

A range of emotions charged in on him. On one hand he hated this job and it was never hard to find another kitchen job, or go and work for food and a bed on a farm. On the other hand, he was brutally penniless after his last busking trip with Ivor and could do with his imminent pay check. He decided to face the music bravely and worry about the consequences when he found out what they were to be. However, erring on the side of caution, lest he lose his job, he used the phone in the bedroom to ring Ivor and Geri and pinpoint their whereabouts, so that at least he could meet them if things went sour. After doing so, he made his way down the stairs and towards a door titled 'management'.

Fifteen minutes later he found himself standing upon the street, unemployed and greatly relieved. Savouring the complementary mints he had purloined from the bedroom, he nodded a farewell to the concrete impasse of the hotel, and silently wished its staff the best of luck.
Having done so, he turned his back forever on the place and took a deep breath. It was time to start busking for money again, and he would soon need another friend's couch to reside

on.

Geri and Ivor stood on Rose Street and busked. Rose Street is a congested, narrow lane, tucked away between the Georgian grandeurs of Princes Street and George Street. Its sense of shadow and gothic unease is heightened by the smoke stained, stone tenements that tower over it from both north and south. As a result, the street functions as a wind tunnel, and a sharp breeze blew from the west. The professional busker could easily be distinguished here from the amateur, as the professional always claimed a pitch to the far west of the street. This is because the wind carries the songs to the ears of the public, long before they have arrived at the busker, thus allowing the public the necessary time to notice the melodies long enough to locate their purses and part with a coin as they pass. Conversely, the amateurs tend to set themselves up to the east of the street, and are quickly drowned out by howling west winds and the rattle of busses making their way up St David's Street.
Ivor - who had unsuccessfully tried to publish manuals on the intricacies of busking – had located himself at the western end of Rose Street. Here he thrashed his banjo, while Geri held out a hat and danced like a pensioner in dire need of a new hip.

They had been serenading the street for around an hour by the time Paddy made it to them and the riches in Geri's hat were beginning to look quite healthy. Whether the coins were due to the public's joy at the innocence and playfulness the pair had evoked, or due to feelings of shame for such public and shameless prostitution, was hard to distinguish. In either case, it was of no concern to the boys, who had been far too busy competing with each other as to who could sing the most plaintive and pretty harmony to city girls walking by. Paddy took out his penny whistle and joined them. It was around midday, a profitable time during which most office staff take their lunch breaks and fill the street. Suited men and women flocked past them and the men simulated joining their female colleagues in smiling at these rogues on the street. However, while the female grins seemed honest and joyful, the men's looked as out of place and unnatural like a scratch down the side of a Porsche.

Some of the men dropped coins to impress their female colleagues, but as their eyes met Ivor's they gave a steely reminder of who the future world leaders would be and who would be the bums. In return, Ivor's own mischievous eyes gave a reminder as to who would be leading the rebellion.

The 'one o'clock' gun bellowed the time over the city and the lunch rush came to an end. Tourists grinned in disbelief at such an antiquated tradition, while office workers glared in disbelief that their break was over before their cappuccinos had even cooled. Rose Street returned to a more manageable amount of overcrowding, and old ladies reappeared shuffling in perpetual droves to Jenners. The local tramps hid cans of Tennants Super behind bits of cardboard for later enjoyment, and the boys took the opportunity to count their coins, acknowledging that sufficient capital had been procured. They had made enough to fill their stomachs and buy bus tickets to West Lothian where their friends and family lived. In light spirits they began to pack away their instruments.
The sky was brighter than it had been, but a wicked wind continued to whistle over the cobbles and bit into the flesh like a leather whip. Warm food was needed to countenance such an inhospitable foe, and now that polite society had eaten, it became the street dweller's time to gorge. Gangs of pigeons huddled around the remains of a pie, waiters ate left over sandwiches, bar-staff stole copious amounts of peanuts and a homeless man devoured crisps purchased for him by Geri. Ivor's stomach rumbled audibly, and the companions promptly made their way to the nearest chain pub, for a budget lunch.

The nameless, featureless establishment they chose, was lit up like a lurid shopping mall and due to a premeditated lack of music playing, it echoed like a swimming pool. Geri complained bitterly about choosing such a woeful establishment, and generally lamented on the state of a world in which pubs became franchises.

'Ah bet this shit hole's run by that kiddy fiddlin' cloon!' he cursed.

'What kiddy fiddlin' cloon?' asked Ivor.

'That feckin' McDonalds cunt, it's got his microwaved fingerprints all over it!'

Ivor snorted,

'What nonsense, this is a far worse conglomerate! McDonalds was the evil empire of the 90s, welcome to the new and improved world order boyo! Commi I may be but it's cheap if not cheerful here eh?'

Despite its dizzying white noise and nauseating neons, the bar franchise boasted the cheapest calories in town and a warm place to sit indoors.

Geri sighed, and shrugged,

'Im a victim oh the feckin' times, but this is a one off boys. Whit a classic Marxist you make Ivor, interpretations oh Communism as malleable as old Stalin's. Yon Marx is probably the only man to be misquoted as much as the messiah…they both hae terrible fan clubs!'

Ivor frowned, puzzled

'I thought you didn't believe in God?'

'I dinnae, nor Marx either, be yer own saviour I say!'

Ivor shrugged and winked,

'Spoken like a true heathen. Get some food in you lads, we're skint, it's cheap. We're hungry, it's greasy. Done deal, it's hard to be ethical in a world of unethical pricks, we'll save pride an' pickiness till after the revolution!'

Despite, fearing that such logic was far from irrefutable, Paddy and Geri's grumbling stomachs got the better of them, and they wandered up to the bar. The boys spilled their pockets upon the counter, and Ivor emptied his sporran. They were pleased to see the amount they had amassed. In front of them lay a great hoard of rusty treasure and a stray femidom from Ivor's sporran.
The barmaid began to laugh at this, profusely apologised and then laughed harder, her face twitching as she tried to contain her mirth. Ivor gave her a mock salute, saying

'A good boy scout is always ready, mam!'

'Whit a creepy thing tae say, tae the poor lassie. Ignore him he's Welsh' said Geri, shaking his head at Ivor and smiling at the barmaid.

'Aw lovely, ma nanna's Welsh, so I've got a bit of Welsh in me, but I could always use some more....! I do like your beret' replied the barmaid, fixing a devious grin upon Ivor.

'Ah, fer feck's sakes. We'll be at the table when use are done, bring the pints wi ye Ivor.' cried Geri and dragged Paddy with him, through the throng of afternoon drinkers.

Ivor continued to talk to the barmaid and made no signs of bringing the boys their beers. Geri tapped his fingers with irritation upon the table and glared in Ivors direction.

'Ah Geri, I ken whit we should dae to this neglectful bastard!' said Paddy suddenly.

'Whit's that them?!'

'On account of gross negligence and an abject failure tae order us fried filth and bring the desired bevy, shall we no leave an open sachet of broon sauce upon his stool? Then when he goes back tae chat again it'l be with dubious stainage on the back end oh his kilt!'

'Paddy, ye're a vile man! I love it!

Without hesitation, three sachets of brown sauce were torn open and left on the vacant stool. The boys hissed with evil laughter and impatiently awaited Ivor.

Eventually the Welshman arrived, humming triumphantly and bouncing over the sticky carpet, three pints in his hands. Geri watched closely, biting his lip in the apprehension of a spill, but Ivor was steady of hand and not a drop fell to the floor.
The boys greedily grabbed their drinks and gulped down half a pint each before returning their concentration to Ivor's choice of seat. However, the man was still standing with an untouched pint in hand, gazing lovingly at the girl behind the bar. Geri gestured in the direction of the stool.

'Pull up a pew, brother, ye've been on yer feet aw day. An cheers for the beverage, nae doot thats the hair of yon hellish hound, that bit me, last night!'

Ivor tore his gaze from the lipsticked distraction and made his way towards the stool. He drew it closer and was about to sit, when he noticed the blood red goo that anointed it. Turning to face Paddy, he wagged a finger, saying.

'Padraic Padraic! I know your work when I sees it. My heart is in bloom yet you sabotage my wonderous wooing with this pestilence of condiments?'

Paddy flung up his hands without protest, countering,

'What's love without a little humiliation and pain?'

Ivor gave this point his consideration, absently wiggling his eyebrows in the process.

'A fine point me luva, albeit a tenuous one designed to distract my thoughts from your malicious intents! Why aye, nothing lasts forever. Perhaps it would be better for me new love to see both the stains on character and would be stains on my kilt now, rather than in six months.'

Sensing that one of the Welshman's insufferable monologues on love was approaching, Geri tried to intervene, and raised the question of how long it would be till their food arrived. However, this only served to broaden the nature of Ivor's contemplations, and he drowned out Geri's interruptions.

'Food eh?! Another fleeting pleasure! Of the same nature as love. Indeed of this fair lady we can dare say that alas, after six phases of the moon, she will inevitably, disband from me for an excess of personality and deficit of cash. Ah, alas a lass like all the others! Truth is a funny old bugger, and love in our crass, commercial lands are but delusions of stability, at best, jean staining eruptions of teenage lust. Tis painful to know the woes of your own future and stumble on anyway, but alas she's a quarter Welsh you see and thus deserves to experience the delights of Ivor Ryder-Jones I think, even if it be but a passing pleasure!'

Paddy and Geri snorted at this, yet raised their glasses to the big man in an amused toast.

'To the gallant and blind foolery of love and lust!' said Paddy.

'To the inevitable death march it demands I dance, and to the sauce staining revenge of some kind that will come your way Paddy!' replied Ivor with a chuckle as he sat down.

The boys established an easy rhythm of drinking and soon replaced their pints with fresh ones. By their third round, the food arrived and with it, came a napkin, graffitied with the barmaid's number. Through a mouthful of chips, Ivor asked his friends if it would be romantic if he left his number back, written in blood.
Geri shook his head, assuring him that, he would not solicit such things, and that regardless of whether the blood came from a banjo wound or not, it was highly unlikely to be deemed pleasing. Ivor looked confused but concentrated on eating. Within minutes the meal had been devoured and Ivor took to licking the other's plates and eating all the sachets of ketchup one by one. Catching Paddy's look of amusement, he loudly contested,

'What?! Free calories innit, boyo! Seems you ain't read the buskers survival handbook eh?!'

Eventually having spent most of their earnings the boys all conceded that it was time to leave, and so bloated and tipsy, they exited the establishment by the George Street entrance.

George Street was its usual self, opulent and glittery, the exclusive playground of the privately schooled, and those that wished that they had been. It housed Edinburgh's most expensive shops, where, for a premium, people with yearnings for 'old money' appearances could purchase Etonian shirts and yacht owning loafers. Its esteemed and expensive nightclubs, were famed for separating the wheat from the chaff, priding themselves on refusing entry to the likes of Geri, on account of their clothing and style.

Paddy let out a whistle as they watched the wealthy walk by with countless shopping bags in hand.

'Phew! This place is for punters on significantly different tax codes to us, eh?!'

Despite having been the one to lead them out onto the street, Ivor glared accusingly at Geri and Paddy, demanding.

'Why did we end up here? You know this place is no good for me ticker! This be the self-satisfied land of idiot Tories, the likes of which can only be dealt with, with guns or patience and I ain't got neither!'

Geri chuckled and lit a cigarette, but Paddy protested.

'I feckin' hate this street too, but you lead the way! And not all Tories are intrinsically evil man, some of them are just....'

Ivor interrupted him,

'You seen their refugee and humanitarian policies my lovely? Cunts the lot of em! Guns or saintly patience is what they require from us good folk, I'm tellin' ya.'

'Well I know some working class Tories, and trust me when your forced tae ken them, you dinnae hate them, ye pity them.'

'Coming from a Welsh mining town, I doubt that, but please tell my why?' queried Ivor.

'Coz, they fall into two categories, stupid, or selfish. The majority are stupid, badly educated and too sheltered from the lives oh others, all too vainly lost in their own concerns tae see oor connection and that's tragic. And the rest are selfish sociopaths who dinnae gie a feck aboot anybody else and that's tragic too.'

'My heart bleeds, but revolutions will be won with guns not words, to quote Mr Che,' mocked Ivor.

'Depends if the desired outcomes to overthrow a regime, or the slow struggle for some long-term peace and understanding'

Paddy countered.

Geri, sensing that the conversation was destined to last for hours and never reach a point of agreement, interrupted them.

'Paddy, ye're a hippy cunt and that's why I love ye, but I've seen you raging at these pricks. Ivor you're a mad Welsh bastard and that's why I love ye, but yer a big softy and ye ken ye'd hug every fucker on this street before ye shot yin. So hows about use both shut the fuck up and we take one last pint, and see if William Douglas is playing at the Royal Oak, afore we part ways for the day?'

The boys perked up at the idea of folk music and a drink, and wandered further down George Street. When they came to the grand steps of The Dome, Ivor paused and rummaged through his sporran.

'Ketchup revenge, motherfucker!' he shouted at Paddy, and whipped out a sauce sachet, throwing it on the ground and jumping hard on it in, causing it to explode in what he hoped to be Paddy's direction.

Geri and Paddy froze, but the tomato contents failed to reach them, and instead sprayed upwards behind Ivor's heel, covering a lady in a beige fur coat.

Seeing the mixture of horror and mirth erupt upon the faces of his friends, Ivor turned slowly to see what he had done.

The lady was too angry for words. From her bust to her knees, she was now decorated by flecks of red. She silently opened and shut her mouth, shaking a matronly fist at Ivor with one hand and trying to rub away the stains from her fur coat with the other.
However, the large, young man, standing beside her, did not share her loss of speech.
He thrust a square jaw so close to Ivor's face, that he could

clearly see the remains of Waitrose spinach between the man's teeth. Casting an eye up and down the Welshman's cape, kilt and beret combination, he gave a disgusted stare, the kind of which is commonly reserved for the finding of human faeces in a favourite mug. Then, using the sharp vowelled, saliva flicking elocution of a Sandhurst officer, he prodded Owen in the chest and shouted,

'What the hell are you playing at, boy? Eh? Eh?'

Giving Ivor no chance to answer, he continued

'You wretched, cross-dressing fool, you have gone too far, have you any idea how much mother's coat cost? I've a good mind to tear you open like a bag of crisps!'

As he spat these words he poked and jabbed at Ivor's forehead with a monstrous index finger. Paddy and Geri were too preoccupied in trying not to urinate upon themselves with mirth, to aid of their friend. They stood behind Ivor, valiantly attempting to contain all vocal expressions of merriment, yet shaking from side to side, and clutching at their aching stomachs.

Ivor, however, looked calm, and appeared to have no fear that he could have traduced himself. He looked the irate man fixedly in the eyes, and said

'I apologise for painting your ma like a period stained polar bear sir! No harm meant and I'm sure you can afford the dry-cleaners. By the way you have spinach in your teeth. Good day.'

He spun around as the man tried to grab him, and marched briskly up the street, his cape flapping regally behind him. The man attempted to chase him, but relented after being warned by his mother about causing a scene. From a safe distance, Ivor turned and shouted back to Paddy and Geri

'What did I say Paddy boy, guns or patience, guns or patience!'

Geri and Paddy could contain their laughter no more and so hurried off for a bus to take them far from the perils of George Street.

Chapter 14 – The Brexit Blues

'For the love of one's country is a terrible thing. It banishes fear with the speed of a flame, And it makes us a part of the patriot game'

Dominic Behan – The Patriot Game 15.

It was a warm June morning, on the day when the result came through that the UK had voted to leave the European Union. The news seemed to Geri to seep in slowly and unexpectedly like urine on a drunk's sheets.

Despite the furore of the press, it appeared to be business as usual in Bedford, with no particular singularities of note. The masses were already at their desks, or hiding in office bathrooms, whilst updating fictitious versions of their lives upon their phones. The High Street was almost empty, save for two or three gossiping pensioners and a Big Issue vendor. There was little noise, apart for the salacious whispers of the pensioners and pre-fab, pop music, which spewed out like budget antidepressants from the guts of a shopping centre. Suddenly, without any warning or so much as a by your leave, a new noise began to assault the morn. It was a strange groaning sound, punctuated with grimacing pleas and curses. These emissions came from the lanky and rather sunburnt form of Daire Mighton, who limped and ran, down the road, all the while clutching his *derrière* as if in great fear it would fall off. On his back was an ill-fitting rucksack and as he ran it rubbed his sunburnt skin, peeling off slices off wafer-thin ham with every movement.

'Christ on a bicycle! Gagh! Hoot toot! Hoot toot! Oot the road!' he cried at the pensioners, as he launched himself past them.

The Big Issue seller tried to hide his mirth when he saw Mighton's frantic waddle coming his way. Mighton glared at him, crying out,

'Hoots, Gordie! This is nae laughin' matter, I'm shitein' through the eye oh a needle here, man!'

Without allowing the vendor any time to question his meaning, Mighton continued to drag himself down the street, his face a twisted contortion of rage and fear.

He hobbled past the bank and the bakers, took a shortcut through the park, where he glanced at the bushes, before hissing dejectedly at the sight of approaching dog walkers. He continued quicker now, down the lane, round the corner and made it to the top of his own street. He traversed the street with a rapid mixture of shuffles and leaps, and sighed upon reaching his door, relieved that his odyssey was now completed. One hand fumbled wildly for his keys, while the other stayed clapped tight upon his skinny rump.
He found the key and stabbed it frantically into the lock, but soon realised there was another key blocking it from the inside. Letting out a blood curdling roar he began screaming,

'Geri! Geri! Open this fuckin' door noo afore I shite oan the street! Arghh! Wake up, ya cunt, ye!'

He continued hammering on the door and roaring, all the while hopping from one foot to the other and shaking.
The old woman next door, leaned her head out the window and told him with smirking pious to consider his language and keep the noise down.

'Haw! Ya auld crone! I'm shitein' through the eye oh a needle here, it's an emergency, ah need a lavvy or I'll be dain' ma business on your doorstep!' Mighton retorted.

The old woman threw a glass of water at him and hissed threats of malediction. Mighton gave up all hope, he would have to break the door down. He took a few steps back mustered his strength and ran at it as hard as he could. Save for a cracking noise and a dull pain in his toe, nothing happened. He tried running at it again. This time, just as he nearly hit the door, it was opened by a sleepy looking Geri. Mighton ran into him at full speed, sending his friend flying to the floor, and hitting his head off a radiator as he fell.

'Whit have ah telt ye bout leavin' keys in the lock?' shouted Mighton as he ran to the bathroom.

The old woman next door banged on the adjacent wall and Geri lay on the floor in a state of concussed confusion. Ed licked his face and was delighted to find food in his beard.

After a lot of groaning and other noises too unpleasant to mention, Mighton left the bathroom and came back through to the hallway.

'Christ, Geri! What are ye dain' still lying aboot on the flair? Up wi ye man ye'll be late tae work'.

Geri informed him that he was off work sick, and stood up unsteadily, making his way into the kitchen to fetch some coffee and cigarettes. He offered Mighton both and they sat down together.

'Im sorry ah knocked ye doon mate' said Mighton earnestly, 'ah wis just dyin' on a shite!'

Geri shrugged with irritation and rubbed a lump now growing on the back of his head.

'Dinnae be a baw bag man, here, a've got ye loads eh duty free baccy an a new harmonica fae ma holiday' responded Mighton, and pulled out several pouches of rolling tobacco from his nearby rucksack.

Geri's face palpably changed and he smiled forgivingly at his friend, inquiring kindly how his holiday had been.
Mighton explained that it had been wretchedly hot and that on the second day, whilst nursing fried freckles and a duty free hangover, he had been both mugged by locals and dumped by his girlfriend. Mildly depressed and mightily broke, he had spent the rest of the trip lifting his spirits through indulging in a diet exclusively of Parma ham, mothers-pride bread and cheap wine. Whilst these delectables had been a great source of solace, they had come at the price of a two week absence of his defaecation abilities. He had begun to look like a piece of red string, with a broad knot tied in the middle.

Having a lack of language skills and medical insurance he had waited to return to Old Blighty to deal with this situation. On landing in the UK he had made his way to Bedford's emergency doctors who had been quick and efficient in pumping him full of laxatives before sending him on his way. Unfortunately, though Mighton's journey from the doctor's front door took an hour, while the laxatives' effect upon his back door had taken a mere ten minutes, creating a panic and a pace of movement hitherto unknown to him.
The experience of such a travesty caused him to assert,

'Never trust a quack, Geri ma man, they'll leave ye wi shite comin' oot oh yer creek wi nae a paddle, nor a pan for a hundred mile'.

Geri hissed a giggle at this and forgot the growing lump on his head as he opened a duty-free cigarette packet.

The housemates spent the rest of the afternoon in different ways. Geri enjoyed his foreign tobacco and suppressed endless fits of giggles over his friend's misfortune. While Mighton cursed loudly in the bathroom and parted ways with the remains of his holiday diet. Ed meanwhile dug up the old lady next doors plants and urinated on her lawn. The day was pleasant and boasted a concerto of humming bees and cooing doves. Tarmac roads began to soften in the sun, long lines of liquorice, melting their way through the township and bringing back old summer memories to those who walked along them.

In this manner, the afternoon disappeared, and eventually evening fell.

Ed was by now satisfied with the art of his destruction, Geri was bored of changing channels to avoid Brexit updates and Mighton felt he knew the landscape of the bathroom too well after six hours of surveying it from the toilet seat.
Geri stretched out, and yawned, suggesting a pint and a game of cards at the pub. Mighton, now fairly confident that he had given the bathroom all that he could give, agreed.

They wandered their way through the park and down the lane. The sun was slowly sinking and swallows swooped and dived in the last of the light. In the high street they stopped to talk to Geordie, the Big Issue vendor, who was packing up for the day.

'Alrighty, Geordie sir, how's the day been?' inquired Geri.

'Been alright innit, apart from that bleedin' pop music blastin' on repeat from the mall' replied Geordie.

Geri glared in the direction of the mall, and cried out,

'Aye! It's a bleedin' travesty so it is, polluting respectable ears wi crass, commercial filth!'

Geordie nodded glumly, and added, 'The worst of it is even if you hate it gets in your head, so I hear it all over again on mental repeat when I'm back at the hostel.'

Geri ruefully scratched his groin and shook his head, saying,

'Aye its catchy right enough, as catchy and unwelcome as a feckin' STD!'

'The gift that keeps gieing eh Geri?! Come oan, let's get tae the pub' laughed Mighton.

The boys offered to buy Geordie a pint, but he declined and in truth they were glad, for they were on the wrong side of their overdrafts again. Just outside the pub, Mighton muttered something about 'round two' and cast his half smoked cigarette to the ground, dashing as quickly as he could, through the door and to the lavatory. Geri, who felt it to be most ungentlemanly and un-leisurely to rush or interrupt a cigarette, finished smoking with slow dignity, before picking up Mighton's butt and smoking it too. He stood in the doorway in a trance, enjoying every long inhale and the watching the wisps that danced from his lips as he breathed out. Finally, he finished, and fully sated, he too made his way inside the pub.

It was a dimly lit hole, a rotten place with the smell of stale tobacco which still clung to the walls stubbornly despite the decade that had passed since the smoking ban. The mottled brown and red walls and stained décor added to the feeling that one had entered a tumour rather than a wine bar, but the prices were low and that was all that mattered.

Mighton was nowhere to be seen, but there were however two girls animatedly conversing in what Geri guessed to be Polish. Both were striking women, with high, regal cheekbones, and electrifying eyes. Geri lifted his cap to them and gave a clumsy kind of bow. The girls returned his attentions by giving cold looks, and disparaging sighs, before going back to their chatter, and ignoring him completely. Geri shrugged and made his way to the bar, where the only other customer was sitting. The customer was a broad shouldered, angry looking specimen, with a face the complexion of boiled ham. One thunderous look from him was enough to stall Geri's attempts at conversation, so instead he drank in silence and awaited Mightons return from the bathroom. The barman turned on the television and it blared out its usual blend of emotional porn and numbing dullities. More news of Brexit was announced and the large, red-faced man began to whistle 'Oh Happy Days' and stare malevolently at the Polish girls. Apparently annoyed that they ignored him, he shouted in their direction,

'Soon you'll be speaking fuckin' English, or on a boat home, lazy, fuckin' job thieves!'

The girls shifted in their seats and looked annoyed but said nothing, staring uncomfortably at the floor.

Geri was infuriated, crying out, 'Ignore this eejit, lassies, he's a fool and a bigot'.

The big man turned towards him, shouting, 'What did you call me you jock bastard?'

Geri was somewhat remiss in apologising and answered,
'I called ye a fool sir, and now it seems ah must call ye a deaf one at that.'

Any likeness the man's complexion had had to a boiled ham now evolved into a shade of uncanny similarity to the cremated gammon steaks that Geri periodically found forgotten in his oven. The girls watched nervously and whispered to each other. Raising a thirty kilo fist, the man screamed in Geri's face,

'Have you no patriotic pride for your Queen or country, you ginger cunt! It's time to make Britain great again!'

Geri calmly wiped away the man's spittle which had evenly covered his face, and replied,

'If by 'again' ye mean repeats oh slavery, apartheid and theft, then no, I'm no really intae it! This worlds a small feckin' rock floatin' roond space mate, patriotisms for pawns an' fools, an' I'll take ma chances as neither or!'

The man swore with turbulence and fluency, and then grabbed Geri by the neck of his T-shirt, shouting,

'Let's settle this outside like men, if you are one you tartan skirt wearing faggot!'

'If it makes ye feel like a man tae knock aboot ma thick skull then on we go, but I'll no be hittin' ye back ya radge clown'

Geri managed to down his pint before the man dragged him into the beer garden and head-butted him before punching him square on the jaw. The barman, who had been up until then trying to ignore the whole fiasco, and concentrate on polishing glasses, was now begrudgingly coerced by the screaming girls to phone the police.

Geri had meanwhile hit the ground but in a pique of stubborn insolence he struggled to his feet for the third time before

receiving yet another blow. His lip was torn and his eye swollen, but he seemed more irritated than afraid.
He faced his attacker, spat out a mouthful of blood and asked,

'Well, ya muckle great oaf, do ye feel like a man noo? Findin' happiness wi' every hit?'

The man was black with rage and made all the angrier by what he saw as Geri's unsporting and assumed homosexual refusal to hit him back. Any hopes of mollifying him with non-violence appeared unlikely and he grunted and roared as he smashed another fist into Geri's mouth. Geri staggered back, wiped the blood from his beard and began manically cackling, 'Would ye no feel mair like a man if ye tried again a bit harder ya big Jessie, ye?'

The big man roared and head-butted him on the nose, after which Geri fell once again to the ground in a mess of mud, and blood and beer.

How long this would have continued, or how it would have ended is impossible to say, but fortunately, Mighton, having left the toilet and hearing the commotion came hobbling into the beer garden. Seeing Geri lying bleeding on the ground, Mighton sneaked up behind the big man quietly. With one hand he tapped him on his shoulder while with the other he continued to clutch worriedly at his own leaking rump. The man turned round, and with great éclat and all the finesse of a champion fencer, Mighton lunged at him with his long and bony small finger and prodded the man's eye. The big man howled and leapt back, rubbing furiously at his face with great concern for his ocular capacity.

'That's fer punchin' ma brother an' interruptin' ma shite, coz o' which, ah had nae time tae wash ma haunds, so that's a stinky pinkie you got ya baw!' cried Mighton.

He helped Geri to his feet and supported him back inside the pub. By this time the police were arriving and they were directed to the big man, who was still rubbing his eye and muttering about suing. They wrote down everyone's names and after hearing the girl's accounts they took the man away in handcuffs.

'The back o' a black marias just the place fer a swine like that! That'll teach yon Goliath tae be mair wary o' David's dirty fingernails' smirked Mighton, as he smiled proudly at his murderous phalanges. Deciding to wash away the day's malice, the boys searched their pockets for enough pennies to share a pint. As they fumbled past fluff and receipts in their pursuit of brass, the two girls sidled over to them. They smiled coyly at the lads, with a flutter of eyelashes and a display of snow-white teeth behind their painted lips.

One of them stroked Geri's battered forehead and said, 'We just wanted to thanks you that was so brave.'

Geri blushed from his feet to his ears and felt immediately remedied.

'Here, it was ma fingernail that saved the day hen,' spluttered Mighton jealously.

'Yes! Yes! You were brave too. We want to invite you both back to our home, we clean you up and then share some vodkas and beers if you like?' said the other girl, patting Mighton's arm gratefully.

Geri and Mighton looked at each other and then both broke

into grins and nodded in mutual consent. The girls linked arms with the bearded rogues and they left all the pub together. On their way up the road they bickered in good humour with their new friends over the superiority of whisky versus vodka, and the night became one to remember, causing Geri to comment, that, 'fortunes change too fast in this life tae bother frownin' at much for long'.

Chapter 15 – The Surprise Tattoo

"I, wisdom, dwell with prudence'

Proverbs 8:12 [16.]

Geri was annoyed. He harboured an irritation that cloyed at his brain and robbed him of his habitual nonchalance. The cause of his vexation was the realisation that his affection for his friends and his penchant for whisky had perhaps began to counterbalance his prudence, and the throbbing pain in his leg was a painful reminder of this fact.

Paddy and Ivor had visited Geri the day before, and the afternoon had naturally become a night of riotous festivities. Now, late the following morn, he had found himself to be lying on the living room floor, overwhelmed by a series of overwhelming aches and pains. Some of these he was well used to and were clearly the work of whisky. Indeed the twitching nerves in his chest and dull ache in his head presented no troubling curiosity as to their cause. However, the excruciating throbbing that came from his leg were a hitherto unknown experience and could not be so easily attributed to booze. He became suspicious that such aches could well be the doing of other humans, dastardly scumbags of the sort he called friends. Lying prostate he surveyed the room with his blood shot eyes for clues of such culprits. He could see an unconscious Mighton, an unhinged Ed and an undeniably guilty looking Paddy, who lay gazing at the ceiling, trying to avoid all eye contact.

Geri gave up on catching Paddy's attention and was too tired to shout at him. Instead, he racked his brain and tried to puzzle together his memories of the past night. There had been value price whisky, yes and some saccharine sweet, synthetic high had done the rounds, but while these could explain his rumbling guts they offered not a bit of insight as to the pain in his leg.

He attempted to sit up and examine his ankle but the arduous nature of such work was too overwhelming and he quickly gave up. A vague memory now circulated in his mind and he recalled an eBay purchased tattoo gun being passed around. Panic shot through him as he remembered his insistence that his companions should feel free to 'colour him in' with it. Even more worrying was the fact that any memories after this point had melted into the syrupy dreams of a comatose drunk and were thus completely inaccessible to him. The fear engulfed him and pumped adrenaline through his body to such an extent that he vomited up bile. He wiped his burning lips and glared at the green goo on his jeans. Still though the eve's antics evaded his mind, and he was forced to sit up and make a first-hand examination of his leg. He rolled up his trousers and was affronted by a word etched upon his aching leg. Indeed, badly scrawled in his swollen and bruised flesh was the word YES. It was so poorly scribed, that from a distance one would mistake it as merely a violent varicose vein yet regarded closely - and through the remnants of the previous day's contact lenses - Geri recognised the scrawl for what it was. A homemade tattoo and a Scottish political statement.

Now Geri had no quarrel with bad tattoos, he collected amateur memories made of ink just as naturally as a diary does. The handwriting of the tattoo was also of little irk, he made little distinction between foul cacography and fine calligraphy. But the quarrel with which he most certainly had with the thing was that he had become permanently endowed with political affirmations.

He was a firm follower of Dylan's lyrical philosophy, 'don't follow leaders and watch the parking meters', condemning nearly all political movements, as fools wasting hope in hierarchies and false heroes. It thus vexed his very constitution, to find himself indelibly inked in this way. Seeking to identify the culprit and their motives, he wrestled again with his fatigued mind, commanding it to use logic and deduction in order to solve the mystery. Despite dehydration, a lack of rest and perversely poor grooming, his mind cranked slowly into gear and it deduced the following.

1. 'YES' was almost certainly meant in the context of the Scottish independence movement, where it had become the prominent slogan.

2. Whoever had written it had clearly never tattooed anybody before.

3. Whoever tattooed it had poor handwriting skills.

While this wave of insight was informative, it offered no immediate illumination. Indeed, most of those who had enjoyed the night's jollity would be happy to watch the last bastion of the British Empire crumble into a pool of Conservative tears. Additionally, none of them were known for their handwriting or tattooing abilities.

However – he mused - while most of the attendees perhaps liked the idea of the end of the United Kingdom, they were ironically, quintessentially 'British', in that they preferred political grumbling to political action. This no doubt meant it must have been someone wildly optimistic or ferociously political.

Now Ivor Ryder-Jones met the latter, but he had disbanded early from the previous eve for a kebab and had never returned, so was clearly not the culprit.

In terms of 'wild optimism', Paddy certainly met the bill. Geri cast a suspicious eye across the room at Paddy. The skinny poet lay under a woollen blanket, with only his prominent nose and unruly curls greeting the day. Despite being clearly awake, he continued to guiltily reject all eye contact, apparently fascinated by something on the ceiling. The guilty face aroused suspicion but the man lead a colourful life and it could indicate a multitude of other sins. On the other hand, his buskers cap which lay next to him was compelling evidence of the crime. Pinned onto the faded tweed was nothing less than an LGBT YES badge and a CND saltire.

Geri congratulated himself on his detective skills, and concluded his case to be over, and the miscreant to be caught.

'Paddy, you damnable swine ye! Did you scribble this appalling nonsense oan my leg?'

Paddy gave up on staring at the ceiling and nodded in sheepish admission.

'Ye did say tae tattoo whitever we wanted, man'

Geri, beginning to enjoy the role of the vindicated accuser, and wagged a finger and retorting,

'Fine and well tae say that noo, but ye've sense enough tae ken I've nought but a bad taste in ma mooth for yer political pish! I trusted ye man.'

Paddy looked a little downcast and gazed ruefully at the floor. Seeing a can of Stella still half full, he slid it to his friend by way of apology. Geri's frown softened and he snatched the tin, relieving the aridity of his mouth with a monstrous gulp. Relief, however, was not to be had and he coughed and projected the stagnant liquid over Paddy's face, roaring,

'That wis a feckin' ashtray, ya feckin' eejit!'

Paddy rubbed the black globules from his face, torn between outrage and amusement. He settled on the latter and burst into laughter so contagious that Geri found himself sniggering, despite the taste of charcoal that lingered in his throat. Paddy attempted to take advantage of his comrade's improvement in humour saying.

'I'm sorry, man, I thought ye'd be aw for the breakup oh Britain, proportional, local power instead?'

This irked Geri and he shook his head, did some more finger wagging and tut-tutted.

'What change will that make? The problem remains that we cannae be arsed tae fix shite oorselves, we're aw tae busy being greedy cunts! So we aw vote some new leader tae dae it for us, an then we bitch an moan when they cannae be arsed tae dae feck all either!'

Paddy pondered this a while and then conceded, saying,

'Theres a ring oh truth in that, I guess tae varying degrees we're aw just slaves tae our ain excesses. Maybe true freedoms tae ken oor ain immoral impulses an' indulgences an' choose ourselves how we act upon them. An' in that case you'll be soon quitting the meat an' milk eh Geri boy?!'

Geri took offence to this and cried,

'Will ah aye?! Noo if its savin' the planet we're oan aboot then ye'll be quitting the cheap flights tae third world beaches ah take it? And that swine Mighton'll have tae cast his eyes away fae endless porn if he's tae keep playin' punk songs aboot human rights abuses! Aye, in a world full oh lazy hypocrites whit goods a new government?'

Paddy laughed and said, 'Well, my merry nihilist, you've fallen in yer ain trap! For according tae yersel, its of nae good for anyone tae vote until we commit tae some self-improvement, so whit'll ye improve the day ma man?'

Geri half smiled and half glared at his curious friend, and pondered over the question for a while. He mentally conceded that despite him being a foul hippy, Paddy often raised fair points, and ones which he would find himself pondering over for vexing lengths of time. It troubled him to consider arguments against nihilism, it had successfully fuelled his escape from a conservative world bent on dull ambitions. However, if nihilism was meant to help him live carefree, then it had not been functioning of late. Try as he liked, he was not immune to the age of mass anxiety. Snippets of endless terrifying news sneaked unwanted into his periphery. This gave rise to a gnawing sense of concern and impotence over the complexities of the world. Moreover, hangovers were intensifying with age and alcohol no longer delivered the promise of freedom it had made in his youth. Still, it wouldn't do give voice to such thoughts and give Paddy the satisfaction of thinking he had won a debate. No, his insufferable grin would last for days. It was easiest to vaguely agree to some mild self-improvement and later re-examine these thoughts at his own leisurely speed.

'Paddy, ye'll be delighted tae ken I've already taken tae yer so called 'self-improvement', by means oh exercise.'

Silencing Paddy's sceptical splutter with a dismissive wave, Geri continued,

'I've discovered a dip in the council baths is a fair tonic fae recuperating from hangovers, and being parched as paper I think I'll away there the noo'

Ignoring Paddy's snorts, Geri struggled to his feet and grabbed a pair of damp and festering swimming shorts and an oily looking towel from the kitchen. With a blasé shake of a hand, he rebuked Paddy's concerns - that the pool's notorious urine content, would most likely infect his tattooed limb - and limped out the front door, a proud athlete off to meet his destiny.

It was now approaching midday, yet morning mists still floated through the streets, in an army of ghosts, shrouding the world with their raw embrace. Old men with tobacco-stained beards, stood hunched outside the early house, counting the minutes until it opened and they could buy their first drink of the day.

They wheezed on cheap cigarettes and spat tar upon the ground, cursing the weather with a series of mumbles and rattling coughs. Geri shuddered in apprehension of the likelihood of this being his own future, but then remembered that he was voluntarily taking exercise today and would thus no doubt live a long and healthy life. A smug smile spread over his face and he tipped his hat to the older gentlemen.

On reaching Bedford Pool, he peered through its steamy windows and noticed that it was occupied almost exclusively by young families teaching their children to swim. He felt a tad uncomfortable and made a mental note to swim in the evening next time so as not to be mistaken for some kind of solitary pervert. Inside the building the steam and chlorine made his hangover insufferable, and he made haste to get to the changing rooms. Despite being packed full of screaming children, the warm water looked appealing and he undressed quickly, keen to be submerged as soon as possible. While taking off his trousers, he surveyed his abstract gallery of a leg, glaring again at Paddy's contribution.

Suddenly, to his horror he caught a glimpse of yet more new ink, hitherto hidden to him behind his thigh. He strained his neck to try and read it, but could only make out the words 'I AM'. It looked awfully like Mighton's writing, and the thought of this caused Geri some premature palpitations. Fumbling through his pockets he found his phone and using its cracked screen as a mirror. Glancing at the reflection he could clearly make out the words 'I AM A RAPIST!' written on his leg. The horrifying slur was made even worse by a suffix in the style of a smiley face lexicon.

Geri's face turned a curious blend of purple and white, of precisely the shades that local farmers sought after in Bedford's prize radishes. His fists clenched and he sucked in air through his teeth with a hissing sound, as he violently pulled his trousers on again. He grabbed his towel and marched out the swimming pool. This time he was too angry to notice the pungent chlorine, and any steam now appeared to be coming from him rather than the pool.

When he returned to the house, Paddy had left and Mighton was still unconscious and heard neither the slamming of the door, nor the stamping feet that came his way. However, his slumber was to be short-lived, and he was rudely awoken by a penny whistle being cracked across his forehead. Leaping to his feet, he glared at Geri through eyes that he found hard to focus due to blood dripping into them. His mouth snapped open and he was about to eject a torrent of furious indignation, when Geri cut him short, shouting,

'The merits oh your companionship ah have noo drunk tae the dregs!'

'Christ oan a bicycle whit shite are ye talking noo! Whit the feck are you oan aboot? Quit fannyin' aboot wi' ma whistle afore ye hae ma eyes oot'

Geri raised the whistle again and swung it deftly upon Mighton's nose, causing the lanky Scot to jump unsteadily to his feet, and raise his fists like a Victorian boxer. Blood now escaped both his nose and brow and he raised a hand to quell its flow, only for Geri to crack his knuckles with the deadly flute. Mighton squealed and fell back upon the couch, attempting to kick Geri in the process.

'Did you tattoo that filth oan me last night, ya devil's hoor ye?!'

Mighton looked momentarily confused, but then the light of

elucidation could be seen to gleam in his bloody eyes.

'Well aye, maybe, but who wis it that said tattoo, whit ye like? If ye will act like a fish's tit an' make a daft request and whit de ye expect? If ah kent you'd get so arsey I wouldnae hae bothered, took ages wi you squirming'

Geri swung the whistle yet again, and roared,

'An' how the fuck am ah meant tae go swimmin' noo? Ah just came back fae the pool, an' am lucky no tae be arrested!'

Mighton erupted in laughter, 'You're no sayin' ye went tae the pool wi that tattoo are ye?! Christ had legs! I'm gonnie pish maself laughin'!'

Seeing Geri menacingly pick up his prized guitar, Mighton flung up his hands and shouted,

'Calm it Janet! I'll pay for ye tae get a cover up job, you've been on aboot wanting a ship done professional for ages eh?'

This caught Geri's attention and caused his humour to improve markedly. For though his love for fine tattoos was large, his lust for whisky was larger, and tended to diminish the financial possibilities for well done tattoos. Moreover, being the proud owner of a 'ship', Geri considered every nautical tattoo to be a badge of honour, undoubtedly noted by his fellow 'seamen' on Bedford River. Perhaps, he mused, this foul slander upon his leg had come with a silver lining; free ink and further authentication of his captainship. Keen to strike a deal while Mighton was still in a state of pain and remorse, he said,

'Alright, I forgive ye. Buy me an' aw day breakfast on the way tae the tattoo parlour and we'll call it quits. I guess it was kinda funny, even if it ruined ma new keep fit regime.'

Mighton snorted,

'You? Exercise! Geri, sittin' in yon steam room, starin' at lassies and sweatin' oot a hangover isnae gonnie turn that flabby keg o' yours intae a six pack!'

It was Geri's turn to laugh and as quickly as night turns to day, anger turned to comradeship and the old friends were on good terms again. They decided to drink the last of Ivor's whisky before leaving the house and did so while spoiling Ed with some cans of tuna and speculating on the possibility of Shane MacGowan outliving the Queen.

It was three in the afternoon by the time they finally tripped out the front door and made their way to The Tavistock for an all-day breakfast. There they sat in good fettle, consuming mountains of miscellaneous meats, fried eggs and beans on toast. Mighton enjoyed a long grumble between mouthfuls of food, about the scandalous indecency of calling a breakfast 'full', when it contained no haggis. Geri nodded absentmindedly, trying his best not to let memories of Paddy's vegetarian arguments spoil his appetite for sausages. He concluded that Rome wasn't built in a day, and thus, neither can a man's habits be improved in one. Like all moralists, instead of living up to convictions for improvement he shifted the responsibility to those nearby.

'Mighton, ye eat a damnable amount o' meat for a man that sings punk songs aboot the environment?'

Mighton choked on a handful of bacon and stared at him in bewilderment and suspicion.

'Aye?' he said warningly.

'Ach nothing, forget it. Shall we sink a jar for Dutch courage afore we head to the tattoo place?'

Mighton agreed and wandered up to the bar, carefully unfolding his crumpled, Scottish banknote to pay with. Geri sighed,

'Mighton, why dae ye save them? Ye try this every time we're here! Ye ken fine and well they dinnae take Scottish notes doon here.'

'And you ken fine and well ah enjoy the argument and that its legal tender!'

With that Mighton and the waiter embarked on a long and furious discussion, each as keen for a quarrel as the other. Geri gave up and waited outside for him, passing the time with a cigarette. The mists had worsened now, and the dampness seemed to bit him to his marrow. It filled the streets and diffused the light, creating an eerie sense of timelessness that could have been anywhere between dusk and dawn. A local cat came prowling and Geri beckoned for it to come to him, stroking it and and enjoying the warmth of its fur. Eventually Mighton burst out, apparently quite sated with his argument and in high spirits.

'A couple more jars on me Geri sir, an' then we'll aff an' get yer tattoo'.

The boys disappeared through the mists together, like spirits moving from one world to the next and the cat chased after them, keen to prolong their affection and find a place out of the cold.

The Bear was full, so the boys tried a new pub on the High Street. It turned out to be yet another generic coffin of glass and steel, with a prosaic interior that offered all the originality of an Ikea showroom. People in fashionable overcoats and cashmere jumpers stared, as the two shivering redheads – clad without jackets and accompanied by a cat - strolled in.

Nonplussed, the boys ordered a pair of pints and devoured them quickly at the bar. Silently and simultaneously, they acknowledged that it would be foolish to brace the cold air again without first warming themselves with another ale, and so Mighton bought a second round. The cat curled up by Geri's feet and fell asleep on his battered shoes. The barmaid was unsure as to the regulations surrounding the presence of felines in the premises but being a little nervous that the boys might be deranged, she allowed its presence to pass without altercation.

The thought of the cold awaiting them outside still haunted the boys, and so more beers were bought and then more besides, until eventually they forgot all about the tattoo parlour.

Coming to their senses when the time bell rang, Mighton was forced to admit that he'd spent the budget for the tattoo and had a mere five pounds left to his name. Geri, now more than tipsy, swung an arm round him and suggested they buy a bottle of 'gut-rot' and worry about it tomorrow.

Mighton agreed, and back at the house, the taste of spirits and the sound of The Corries was the last thing Geri was aware of.

Waking again in the afternoon, Geri became convinced he was experiencing some kind of time-loop continuum. Again, he found himself on the floor, and again his leg throbbed and again Mighton lay unconscious on the couch. He sighed with relief when he noticed that Paddy was not there, and it was in fact a new day. Mighton stirred and woke,

'Christ had legs! I'm hangin' oot ma arse! Jeez, go an' grab us a glass oh water Geri? Still happy wi' yer new tattoo?'

Geri's face froze and his heart beat like a marching drum.

'Ye miserable swine ye, whit did ye tattoo this time?!'

He rolled up his trouser leg and using his phone to glance at the back of his thigh, saw an enormous blue shark there. It looked more like a cartoon sardine than a mighty predator, yet with its squint fin and irregular teeth, it had undeniable character.

Mighton hesitated.

'Well? Dae ye still like it?'

'Aye! You ken whit, I do. It looks like the kind o' thing a sailor awakes wi', after a lost night in Bermuda. Mighton my man, you've outdone yersel!'

Geri smiled at his friend and hobbled into the kitchen to fetch a glass of water. He picked up the tattoo gun en-route and slung it into the bin. Speaking out loud to himself, he muttered,

'Enough noo! Perhaps Paddy's right, if ye cannae see the pattern ah yer ain cause and effect, then you're nae better than the swine in parliament.'

Chapter 16 – The White Sands of Morar

'We feel free because we lack the very language to articulate our unfreedom'

Slavoj Žižek - Welcome to the Desert of the Real [17].

Morar beach lies on the west coast of Scotland, somewhere between Mallaig and Arsaig. It consists of a stretch of sand that runs along an estuary to the sea. Green hills roll down to this beach, and from the tops of these, one can clearly see the island of Eigg and the preternaturally, sharp, black peaks of the Cuillin mountains in Skye. The icing sugar sands of Morar are white, beyond the ambit of description. Yet poets, musicians and other hopeless romantics have been trying to do just that for centuries. Paddy likened them to fresh snow, Geri to cut cocaine, and Mighton to cunts as they had made his fish and chips crunchy.

The three friends found themselves at Morar whilst on their way to the isle of Eigg, and they were joined by Joe, Jill, Malley, Paddy's girlfriend Magda, and Donovan McLaughlan.

Donovan was an age old companion of the lads from West Lothian and a heavens-taught artist of many disciplines. Despite irregular practice and no formal training, he was an accomplished harmonica player, a talented painter and the director of many wondrous, and surreal films. Like all great artists, he was completely unknown and shared his work with virtually nobody. Occasionally, when too drunk to be embarrassed, he would air his films, in his bedroom to a few lucky residents from the local housing estate. Here they were gratefully inhaled and always received standing ovations from all the idlers and day drinkers of Buckfast wine, who saw their lives artistically parodied in Donovan's dreamscapes. The wider majority of the local populace knew only of Donovan as the unemployed man with the wild hair and mad collie, who wondered the canal at night, lost in thought. Even if they had seen his films, it is unlikely they would have hailed their local bard differently, or paid homage to his work. When it concerned cinema, the town of Linlithgow tended to stick to prescribed pretension from Edinburgh's high art establishments, or prosaic, popular culture from the multi-screen complex in Livingston. Donovan was therefore unknown and free to roam his canal as an unsung genius.

Reclusive in nature, and obsessively attentive to endless, film making, his empire was only as expansive as his room and the banks of the old canal. However, fate - or his sister, depending on how one views such things - had brought a new girl into his house and life. Jill was as madly creative as he, but to the joy of his friends, gently encouraged him to expand his territories. So, it had been, much to everyone else's surprise and delight, that Donovan and Jill had also joined the trip to the isle of Eigg.

The green, craggy isle was a favoured holiday location for all the group, for differing sentiments. For Joe there was Scottish history, for Donovan and Jill haunted caves, for Paddy and Magda, community land ownership, for Mighton and Geri, a local brewery and as for Malley, he was happy to go anywhere as long as he could smoke and wasn't expected to help organise anything.

Mighton had chartered one car - containing Geri and Joe - all the way from Bedford, and after a long, arduous voyage to the north, he was aching to reach the ferry terminal in Mallaig. He flew down country lanes at alarming speed, slowing only to yell obscenities at the sheep and tourists that clogged the Highland's narrow arteries. Malley captained the other car, and having given up on keeping Mighton's deadly pace, he now rolled along, with a speed that saw him overtaken by cows and cyclists alike. His tiny car was filled with elbows, knees and an endless array of unconventional camping snacks. Despite his slovenly progress and the cramped conditions, the passengers were relaxed by his smoke, his smiles and his Charlie Musslewhite records that howled from the speakers.
A convoy of cars and camper vans followed Malley through the

hills and valleys, but their beeping horns were barely audible over the wail of old Charlie's harmonica, and so Malley's trundled along, slow and unperturbed.

Mighton reached Mallaig by the late afternoon and had half an hour to look around until the ferry was due to depart. The weatherman had promised the hottest weekend of the year and his sooth saying skills were confirmed by Mallaig's melting streets. Children dipped their feet in the cool waters of the harbour and lovers shared sundaes by the quayside. The township was a picture of serene tranquillity, framed by purple, heather hills at one side and an expanse of green sea at the other.

Every atom that made up the summer's afternoon was calm and glad, except for those buzzing particles that made up the furious mirage of Mighton. He had worked overtime for the last two months and had counted down the days to his trip to Eigg's remote brewery and now due to Malley's herbal indulgences and late arrival, it was becoming more and more possible that they could miss the ferry. He hopped from one foot to the other shaking his fists with histrionic outbursts, and cursing Malley for having the tents. He lamented poetically and profanely the surety of missing the boat. Whether Mighton's fury fulfilled his prophecies, or his prophecies fulfilled his fury, is hard to know, but it is known that the ferry did indeed come and go while he, Geri and Joe watched helplessly and waited for Malley to arrive. As their fading hope and the ferry disappeared into the emerald shimmer, Mighton flung his hands skywards and glared up at the God he didn't believe in. Geri and Joe tried their best to console him, cajoling him towards the chip shop, with the promise of fresh fish and Stornoway black pudding.

Their timing was auspicious, for the chip shop was empty, dozing in a lull between its lunch and dinner service and void of its usual queues. The boys placed an order and watched with ever abating greed as the food was fried. The molten meals were ineffectively wrapped in newspaper, and they juggled these scolding packages down to the harbour for immediate consumption. As they sat and gorged on the delights - known to be responsible for both great levels of joy and great levels of fat in the hearts of their countrymen - Mighton regained his spirits and burped up his Irn Bru cheerfully.

'Feck it, it's no a bad place to spend a night anyhoo, we could camp doon the road at Morar beach, eh?'

Joe and Geri, who were still enjoying the act of belly expansion, gesticulated their agreement. Mighton was appeased and leaned back on the bench, rubbing his stomach and laughing at the clamorous seagulls that menaced the boats.

Geri finished his extravagance of fried foods and patted his heart apologetically.

'Mighton, I'll away and check the timetable for boats for the morra, a'm sure there'll be plenty.'

'Aye, maybe, but make sure there's yin coming back the next day, they're no so often. An' make sure it's a direct yin, ye ken ah get unco seasick!'

Geri gave a theatrical bow and wondered to the harbour's little office.

Malley meanwhile had finally reached Glencoe and the caravan of angry traffic behind him could no longer be ignored. He decided to pull in and admire the epic glen first hand. He bumped the vehicle up onto the grassy verge and began rolling a smoke in honour of the place. As if releasing a cork from a bottle full of wasps, countless angry cars behind him now swarmed past, many shouting insults or raising a finger out the window. Malley looked as untroubled as a new morning, and turned to his passengers, lighting a spliff and saying,

'Funny feckers, tourists, stressed to get tae the next place aw the time and soon enough the next place is hame again afore they ken it!'

As soon as Malley had removed himself from the car, Paddy, Magda, Donovan and Jill pushed forward the driving seat and came tumbling out into the fresh air. They all stood at the side of the road, stretching their crushed limbs and cursing the length of their legs. Malley nodded sympathetically, but all his attention was given to sculpting a tulip shaped joint. It was the only thing he ever did, with exactitude and care, combining an engineer's precision with artistic flare. He then managed to puff away at the monster whilst holding it only in his lips, requiring a sound knowledge of angles and gravity. Moreover, he skilfully spilled no ash at all upon his stubble or jeans.

Everyone stopped their grumbling and became transfixed with Malley's mastery and the majestic backdrop of the glen dwarfing them. It was an eerie place, battered, baron and soaked in the blood of a grim and murderous history. Yet at the same time it was wondrous and profoundly empty, save for the thin road that ran through the bottom of it. Cars, voices, and human accomplishments, all seemed inconsequential compared to this giant and austere cathedral. The silence and stillness was deafening. It forced one to become acutely aware of the noise of unwanted thoughts and fears normally drowned out by the noise of cities, coffee machines and idle chat. Their presence now crashed noisily into their minds like drunken exes entering a wedding.

The companions sat and absorbed the silence for a while. Some of them were used to meditation and the mind, while the others were at least comforted by the second-hand fumes of Malley's smoke. Glencoe's emptiness commanded respect and it was dually given.

Malley finished his smoke, and without uttering a word

everyone squeezed back into the car, where they were glad to soon hear the lively sounds of Charlie Musslewhite again. Their collective spirits lifted as they reached the gentler terrain of Glenfinnan and by the time they passed the sprawling oaks of Arsaig and reached Mallaig they were once again ecstatic with holiday jubilation.

By now the sun had passed its zenith but it was still a fine, warm day. Malley pulled up next to Mighton's car at the harbour and his cargo of crushed souls escaped from their confines and stretched their limbs. Donovan spotted Mighton and the boys sitting by the water's edge, and they all went down to meet them.

Seeing Malley approaching, Mighton leapt to his feet.

'Malley, sir! Are ye smoking smack wi' that grass oh yours these days? Whit feckin' time dae ye call this? Ye've missed the ferry by two hours!'

Malley attempted to glance at his watch in surprise but was reminded by the sight of a naked wrist, that he had misplaced it some years before.

'Sorry, Mighton! Got a wee bit lost in the view in the tunes ken! There'll be another boat but?'

The very mild look of stress that appeared on Malley was foreign and unsettling, and Joe quickly said,

'Yeah! It's no worries mate. There's one tomorrow mornin', innit. Geri checked already'

The hint of stress disappeared from Malley's face as quickly as it had arrived, and he relaxed back into his smile, lighting another large smoke. In the lamplight of his beaming grin everyone became helpless to do anything other than to grin back, and soon even Mighton felt forgiving.

'Ach, forget aboot it. We're aw here noo, and it's crackin' weather for a guid holiday. Ah ken a braw spot tae camp at, at Morar beach if you's are game?'

The prospect of enjoying a Scottish beach - without a raincoat and umbrella - appealed to all present, and so – despite not wishing to enter a cramped car again, they did just that – and to the white sands of Morar they soon arrived.

It was an ideal spot for wild camping, there was clear water to swim in, woods full of kindling for the fire, and best of all they were out of sight from the nearest road. There are no trespassing laws in Scotland, and in theory - if no damage is caused – then one can camp wherever one wishes. However, the friends knew that the owners of estates and second homes liked these laws little, and liked state-educated plebiscites like themselves even less. Therefore, to be well hidden from the tweed clad 'City of London' gentry was always wise.

When the tents were concealed, they strolled down to the white sands and the cold, greasy remains of the fish and chips were resurrected and washed down with purple cans of Tenants Super. The famed and feared Scot's midges were relatively few, but everyone had suffered enough camping trips as children, to know it to be prudent to light a preventative fire. A small pyramid of twigs soon crackled as flames leapt into life and Malley tried to cook some of his camping snacks on it.

'Why the hell hae ye brought a bag o' raw beetroots and five rolls o' pastry, camping?' asked an irritated Mighton.

'Ah fired intae ma dads hoose on route tae scrounge a scran, coz I'm no paid till next week. But ye ken whit he's like, only ever buys in bulk whit's goin' oot at the end oh the night for a few pence. Sometimes its braw, maist oh the time its shite. But he can ayeways make a magic curry fae it!' replied Malley proudly.

'Aye fair enough, but probably wi utensils, we've no even a pot fit fer stew or stovies, just a shitey wee fire.'

Donovan, who'd sculpted the twig pyramid, before committing arsine to it, tutted at Mighton.

'It's a fine fire, man, braw enough for a warm night and no attracting attention fae toffs.'

Joe laughed, 'It's an artwork Donovan! But you'd be as well cookin' that beetroot over a cigarette, Malley!'

Malley shook his head at all the fatalism, and continued to grill his beetroot, placing a mouldy turnip by the fireside to 'cook'. Magda and Paddy went in search of more sticks to keep the fire burning through the night, and everyone else tucked in thirstily to a large bottle of gin Jill had brought.

When the stick collectors returned in half an hour, the gin was already finished and the instruments were out and being put to good use. One song quickly blended into another and then another. Everyone sang along, and it was only when Mighton began the plangent chorus of 'The Ghosts of Glencoe' that the merriment morphed into recollection of the ghostly valley, and the tragedies that had befallen the place.

However, such blues were soon brushed away by Joe playing a few raucous jazz numbers, fingerpicking on Paddy's tiny, travel guitar. He plucked vivacious melodies and unique harmonies at lightning speed, and the beatnik renditions he performed seemed to become fertilised by the sweat and alcohol than ran from his fingers down unto the little guitar. Malley beat his bongo, Geri roared and stomped and Donovan and Jill tried to film the scene with unsteady hands. The sun winked farewell and as the night swept in she blew kisses of glittering stars through the cosmos. The fire grew in size and the songs in volume, until eventually both died away and bodies stumbled into tents and dreams. The only creatures, left to stare at the stars, were Malley's army of vegetable outcasts. These creatures lay silently in the ashes of the flames, still as raw under their charred exteriors as when they'd first arrived.

A rosebud dawn swept her way gracefully over the inland peaks and slowly ignited the beach. She gave her pink smile freely, asking nothing in return from the sleeping world, like the ever-patient kindness of the mother of a devious child. In the cities, multi-storey declarations of progress, blocked her embrace, and people were too busy to glance upwards anyways. But here by the sea, there were no distractions, and one was touched by the majesty of the moment and the lapping of the waves. Here it was easier to shake loose the chains of culture and re-join one's own essence as nature, surrendering to all our ever-changing mysteries. There were not many people here to witness this, but there still remained handfuls of crofters, who had evaded eviction and persecution, and carved a living from the earth, treading directly in the footsteps of their forbearers. It seemed that such folk were indistinguishable from the land they toiled, generations melting one into another, like the changing of the seasons. They understood their environment and could not run the risk of living 'separately' from it. They knew that if the rivers became poisoned by pesticides that you could not eat money, and they knew that man relied on nature far more than nature relied on man.

Peat smoke rose in acrid coils from their small white cottages, and a recently awoken Geri blinked at them, filled with envy and intrigue.

A monumental hangover had caused him to be the first one up and he had decided to climb one of the nearby hills, to watch the daybreak over Skye. It was a tranquil start to the day and helped to rid the petrol fumes and piss liquor of the journey from his mind. When first he rose, the Cuillin Mountains had looked dangerously tame, softened by the morning light, but now as the sun rose higher, they regained their ebon menace, jutting up like razorblades in the distance.

As he climbed higher and glanced down, he could see that the rest were now up, and appeared to be making tea over the rekindled fire. Geri plucked absentmindedly at the small flowers peppering the grass, and stared at the deep, blue sea.

'Tis a fine auld day tae be a sea fairing man' he muttered happily under his breath.

After a time a thirst came over him and being equipped with neither water nor wine, he decided to return to the beach below. The descent from the hill was noticeably harder than the ascent had been. Soft moss and dew drops, in combination with his tread-less trainers, made for a few falls and curses. Finally, though he returned to his fellow campers, and Donovan greeted him passing a hot cup of milky tea. Everyone was sitting round the fire, watching Malley attempt to eat – and pretend to enjoy - a raw turnip while listening to Joe playing some Burt Jansch tunes. Malley howled suddenly, as the rock-hard turnip broken loose a piece of one of his back teeth.

'Oh ya fucker! That wis sair! Feck you turnip, ye can gang tae the gulls.'

He rubbed his mouth in shock and pain but upon recalling his mission to prove the edibility of the root fruit he quickly added, 'Tellin' yous though, it'd have made a braw curry if we'd only had a pot.'

Mighton, always torn between his two inherent dispositions of cynicism and compassion, weighed them up and decided on the latter.

'Fuckin' hell Malley sir. That's a fair chunk oh tooth ye've lost, dae ye need a ride tae a dentist?'

'A dentist? Nae way man. Always on aboot fillings and brushin' an' pish like that! Av no been tae those sadistic bastards in over ten year.'

Placated by knowing that he'd given niceness a try Mighton now returned to his more regular role of cynicism.

'Aye ah can see that, an have ye brushed yer teeth in thae ten years?'

'Well, ye ken hoo it is, sometimes after a wee smoke in bed wi a good book, these things kinda bypass yer attention, and ye end up asleep wi a mooth half full oh rich teas…'

Malley trailed off sheepishly at the end, and Geri interjected.

'Feck Malley's teeth, the man will live, I've seen him break thae powdery pearls on milk porridge. Its aboot time tae take that boat ride roond aw the islands, so let's get goin'.'

Mighton stared at Geri intently, scrutinising his friend with a penetrating frown.

'Geri, you says we were going tae just one island, no a bunch o' them, a'm returnin' early the morra so I can get tae ma work oan time. Ah only hope the brewery there's worth it, ye ken ah get seasick, an' if ye're up tae yer tricks I'll be spewin' at you!'

'Tricks! Y'ere as whiny as an auld sweetie wifie! C'mon lets away, ah've a new captain's hat tae wear for the voyage!'

With panache and a lack of self-consciousness, Geri whipped out a grubby white sailor's hat from his back pocket, placing it firmly on his head. His ears stuck out from under it, and with his magnificent, pointed beard, he bore more resemblance to a gnome clad in fetish gear, than a seasoned sailor. Nevertheless, he was happy with the effect and his face broke into a wide grin. Donovan was encouraged by such nautical lunacy and rolled up a sleeve to reveal a new jolly Rodger tattoo. Mighton shook his head morosely,

'Christ! Theres two of use! Alritey then Captain Ugly and Seaman Stains, lets away and catch that boat'.

Everyone gave a hungover cheer, and began the job of taking the tents down. Soon they were squeezed into the cars, sand between their toes and cheeks, and making their way again to Mallaig harbour.

Cars were not allowed on Eigg, so the vehicles were left at the harbour. Nobody had thought to bring any large bags or rucksacks, so all the camping gear, food and instruments were draped across their shoulders and strung around their waists. Geri volunteered to carry the beer crate, and his desire to drink them caused him to loosen his grip on a purple sleeping bag, which slid down his back, billowing behind him like a regal cape.

'Cunt looks like Bonnie Prince Charlie!' laughed Malley.

'Feckin' acts like a royal too, stridin' off sippin' ale while ah battle wi his campin' stove an' tent' snorted Mighton.

Other than a few things being dropped and Geri's sailor hat blowing away to commit a salt water suicide, the fifty metre journey went well, and the friends soon reached the ferry terminal. Geri mysteriously announced that he would buy the tickets now, to save everyone waiting in the queue, and they could pay him back later. After fifteen minutes he returned triumphant, and they boarded the awaiting boat.

The vessel smelt of salt, fish and rotting seaweed, and the

friends took it all in gladly from their seat on the top deck. The ferry housed a restaurant serving local produce and a shop full of tartan, tourist tat. Perhaps because it is only now that most Scottish people are rediscovering their banned and eroded culture, or because the highlands are only available for the most Scots to holiday in, as opposed to make their homes in, Scots make incredibly earnest and dedicated tourists in their own land.

Tangible examples of this could be seen aboard the boat, as Glaswegians and Dundonians, lovingly bought the postcards, shortbread tins and tartan teddies, which had been designed for undiscerning Americans. The friends at first resisted the temptation to join in, but soon found themselves delighting over soft toy Nessie's and Edinburgh snow globes. Furthering their delight, they found that the restaurant served fish and chips and local ales, and soon they were all spending money they didn't have and enjoying a hair of all the previous night dogs.

Over the sea, the sun kept the weatherman's promise and the wake of the boat sparkled in the sunlight. They passed the south of Skye and soon the clipped peak of Eigg came into sight. Everyone looked delighted, but Geri sat twitching his thumbs nervously, before eventually cleared his throat, and saying.

'Eh, Mighton, I've just realised fae checkin' on ma phone the noo like, that ah misread the timetable. Turns oot there's nae boat back fae Eigg for three days, so we cannae get off the ferry there and stay or we'll be late back. But on the bright side we can sit here for the next few hours as the ferry pulls in and oot eh o' the wee islands?'

Mighton struck a fist hard on the formica table.

'Geri! Ya wee prick! I knew ye were up tae something! Ye kenned aw this fine an' well a long while, but ye kent ah wouldnae go on a ship wi nae reason, coz I hate the sea...'

Suddenly, Mighton stopped speaking, distracted by something in the water. 'There's feckin' dolphin things cuttin' aboot, look that way, noo!'

Everybody turned their heads in disbelief and then rushed to the other side of the deck. Leaping high from the sea and performing a sequence of phocoenidae acrobatics, was a pod of young porpoises. They cartwheeled and dived, slicing through the water and shining in the sun.

In the delirium of the moment, Mighton forgot to be angry, and looking down, realised he had his arm round Geri's shoulder. He tried to frown at his friend but found that his grin would not cooperate. Geri took this opportunity to strike the proverbial hammer and said.

'I'm sorry if ah press ganged ye, but ah kenned ye'd love it oot here on the open waters, and ye cannae deny it now. At least we got to see Eigg a bit closer and we'll come back.'

'Hmm, well ah guess it's no so bad oot here, am no so disimpressed after aw and...oh ya dancer! They're jumpin' again Geri!'

Geri let the grammatical flaw slide and pirouetted round. Mighton slapped him on the back in a forgiving manner as they watched the next display together.

Half an hour later, the boat landed at Eigg, but its singing sands and glens of rowans passed by unobserved by the group of friends. Indeed, they were sound asleep, exhausted by exhilaration, beers and a lack of sleep. With contended minds, and bellies they slept long and deep, resting in the assurance that nothing they would miss could compete with the oceanic Olympians they had seen.

Geri, was again the first to wake. He had had trouble sleeping of late, but this time it gave him an opportunity to acquaint himself with the ship's female passengers, without the others' mockery. He crept away quietly, keen not to have any unwanted truth tellers, spoiling the scope of his nautical, tall tales.
Tiptoeing backwards, with an eye on his friends, he tripped over someone's foot and fell with a loud bang, his head hitting the deck. Beginning an accusatory flurry of insults, Geri turned to face his assailant. He was immediately silenced. Standing in front of him and apologising profusely was a beautiful girl, with olive skin and a lilting Italian inflection to her speech.

'I'm so, so, so, so, so sorry. Are you ok? Please let me take you to the cafe and buy you a little coffee? What is it your name?' said the girl.

Geri was a little shaken by his fall, and very taken by the look of concern, radiating from the girls large, chestnut eyes. He became lost in them, utterly transfixed by these deep, well springs of compassion. Finally, he became aware of her question and replied, 'My name's Geri...or well actually it's no, ah just get called that coz I had ginger hair like the Spice Girl when ah wis in school, but well I guess it may as well be ma name noo, only my ma that calls me otherwise and there's nae need for you tae dae that.'

The girl nodded and looked a little confused. Taking his apparent lack of interest in going to the cafe together to be out of anger, she gave an apologetic shrug and said,

'If you change your mind I'll be in the cafe'

She walked slowly away with the impeccable posture of a dancer, her ashen ringlets bouncing off her long back. Geri stood silently, his concussed eyes squinting after her. Everyone else had awakened with the commotion, and they too stared silently, their confused gaze resting upon Geri. Donovan was the first to utter a word.

'Ah might be wrang Geri, but as unlikely as it seems, that lassie just offered ye a coffee an' her time, and yet ye dinnae seem tae be obliging?'

Jill joined in, 'Yeah Geri, she's gorgeous, what the hell are you still doing here?!'

The others followed in thunderous agreement, and whatever soporific spell had hindered Geri's movement, vanished. As fast as he could he hobbled after the girl as she vanished downstairs into the cafe.

'Make your coffee Irish, for good luck!' shouted Joe, and flung an enormous, hip-flask full of whisky towards Geri. It came close to hitting his head, but Geri had good reflexes when it came to alcohol, and he caught it neatly, sliding it inside his back pocket and behind his T-shirt. The gang debated going straight to the cafe window to witness his progress but were persuaded by Magda to give him at least ten minutes privacy first. They sat and counted the seconds on their phones, and Mighton groaned as the waves began to pick up and rock the boat in their swell. Dark clouds appeared on the horizon and bruised the beautiful afternoon. It is said that the gods mock predictions of fine futures, and it seemed the weatherman's claims would not be the exception.

Downstairs, in the bowels of the boat, the girl brought two cups of coffee over to the table where Geri waited. She introduced herself as Roberta and apologised again for tripping him up. She was, she said, so happy to meet a real Scottish man, for she had only met other tourists on her trip so far, and not even red headed ones. Geri gave an internal thanks for the mysterious survival of the recessive ginger genes and did his best to impersonate Sean Connery when addressing her.

'Shay, would ye like shum cheeky whisky in your coffee, it's very Shcottish?'

She laughed delighted, and he poured a drop into both their cups. They talked a while and the conversation flowed as easily as Geri's whisky. Every time Geri he topped up his cup with the malt, Roberta would give an exquisite little giggle, so he did so with increasing regularity.

Whether due to the whisky or his fall, his head thumped with a dizzying ache, and he was glad of the seat.

'Phew! Itsh good tae shit doon here.' He said, still in Connery character.

Roberta looked a bit concerned and raised a quizzical eyebrow.

'Naw, I meant its good tae sit doon here' Geri rapidly clarified. She giggled and he relaxed and poured another slug of whisky into the cup.

Upstairs, the friends had escaped from the rain and huddled into a lounge area, all except Mighton who had begun vomiting over the side of the ferry. A few Canadians watched him from a distance, both disgusted and delighted by the litany of curses that he ejected through mouthfuls of sick. Suddenly Paddy noticed that three quarters of an hour had passed since Geri's disappearance, and he had still not been ejected from the fine company he was keeping. Intrigued the comrades rushed off to spy in the cafe. Mighton was left alone to face the waves, and he growled at them, shaking his fist and howling down to Neptune. Japanese tourists gathered round and took photos of him in his vomit covered kilt, while he greeted their presence with words that they, fortunately, did not understand.

Down the stairs, the gang peered excitedly through the café door, and were dismayed to see what appeared to be Geri, alone either asleep or dead, with his head rolled back and his mouth wide open. They ran in and looked around, but Roberta was nowhere to be seen.

'She's poisoned him!' Paddy cried dramatically.

'He's poisoned himself, dickheads gone an' drunk all my whisky, innit!' said Joe.

They decided to get him into the fresh air and out of sight as quickly as possible, and propped him up on Donovan and Paddy's shoulders, dragging him outside. Geri's face was meanwhile turning as green as his football team, so he was taken to the rails beside Mighton for the safe passage of vomitus. Sure enough, he was sick and the smell caused Mighton to again project his guts into the sea. After a few moments Geri regained some colour and composure, and turned to face Mighton, saying 'Itsh very Shcottish to be shick you know.'

'Geri! I dont know why yer lisping like a deid cat, but ah do ken it's your fault I've spewed aw over ma new gutties!'

Mighton pointed furiously at his bile stained trainers, with an angry finger. But was interrupted by the clouds erupting over the deck.

'Itsh aw washin' off noo, Mish Moneypenny,' said Geri with a drunken wink, and then fell into an unconscious sleep in Paddy's arms.

Geri dreamt long of white sands, blue skies and leaping porpoises. He saw the colour of lullabies and caught bubbles of weightless beer as they floated by. He dreamt of an Italian girl, of whispering in her ear to tell her that she tasted like the end of his life, and then he kissed her. A loud bump awoke him and he found himself to be crushed in some damp, dark box. He wondered if he was having a nightmare or had awoken in his own coffin, but his senses soon streamed back to him and he realised it was no box that he lay in. He was packed into the boot of a car, with a wet tent on top of him. He pushed it away but it was still dark. The only lights came from headlamps racing by and burning his retinas.

'Where the hell am I and whit time is it?' he cried out as he pushed a protruding tent pole from his ear.

He heard the sound of Joe's laughter and Mighton replied, 'Ye're two hours fae Bedford. You've slept the last six ya beast!'

'Whit?!'

'Aye! The rains blew and and all our gear we wis carrying got drenched, an' besides it wisnae a night fer camping, so its homeward bound'

'Oi Geri boy,' said Joe, 'remember that Italian girl?!'

Geri groaned and lay back down. The boys chuckled and Joe passed back a cigarette and can of Irn Bru to him. Geri gave a grunt of thanks and then said, 'Tell me yon dolphins were'nae just a dream, eh?'

'Ah man, they were fucking marvellous, as real as Thatcher's iron dick in your forefather's rings!"' replied Joe.

'Thank feck for that, coz I'm decided that one day I'm gonna get a croft on yon headland and enjoy watchin' thae dolphins and Eigg stead' oh sitting roond in Bedford waiting tae die!'

Mighton cackled,

'Mate the closest you'll get tae Eigg is that ugly egg lump on yer heid after yer trip! A muckle big egg it is too. You'll as likely change yer postcode as yer tax band!'

Geri groaned again and rubbed the protruding bruise on his forehead, pushing aside all snippets of memories from his time in the café with his latest, failed love. The Irn Bru and cigarette soon settled his nerves though and the syrupy, nicotine-rich high caused his heart to regain a normal rhythm and his thoughts a calmer tempus.

Soon enough they were back in Bedford, and the short lived holiday became nothing more than a foggy, hungover memory. However every one of them brought with them some of Morar's white sands in both their souls, socks and shoes from that day forth.

Chapter 17 – The End of the New Beginning

'A human being is part of a whole, called by us the 'Universe' —a part limited in time and space. He experiences himself, his thoughts, and feelings, as something separated from the rest—a kind of optical delusion of his consciousness. This delusion is a kind of prison for us, restricting us to our personal desires and to affection for a few persons nearest us. Our task must be to free ourselves from this prison by widening our circles of compassion to embrace all living creatures and the whole of nature in its beauty'

Albert Einstein [18].

Geri and Mighton had just got back from Benidorm. The sands had been impossibly golden, the sky a blanket of sun and the water a myriad of floating diamonds. All had gone as smoothly and as well as anyone could dare to expect of a budget break surrounded by drunken Brits. At the all-inclusive hotel, they had lived as **Bacchus and Dionysus**, consuming immortal quantities of iced whiskies and Hemingway daiquiris, yet encountered no liver failure or fistfights. At the little diners that lined the beach, they had eaten ungodly amounts of cheap seafood, yet suffered no gastric repercussions or gut aches, and on the sands at night, they had avoided all sexually transmitted diseases, or at least those with obvious symptoms.

For Geri this was due to an inviolable rule of chastity, which though not chosen by himself, seemed to be a law of nature, vexing his entire holiday. A disease would have been as miraculous for him as a child was for Mary. Conversely, Mighton's miracle was to escape with nothing worse than an infected love bite and a, congealed eye, the cause of which, even he found too embarrassing to discuss with a doctor.

However, despite these minor miracles, and the much welcomed weather and respite from work, both boys returned to Old Blighty, feeling curiously disappointed with the excursion. The travel agent had sold them a promise of utopia, but the sands had soon turned too hot, and beach life became as boring as work's mundanity. It had been curious to be in such a beautiful place, and yet be joined by the familiar aches and anxieties of home. Such uninvited feelings, appeared to sneak into one's suitcase, just waiting to hop out in paradise, full of unsolicited intent like a rogue, mother-in-law with a hairbrush.

Upon arriving home, Mighton had no time to reflect on the possible whys and wherefores of this conundrum. Austerity measures had badly affected the care home he worked at, and he was called into a shift within an hour of arriving in Bedford. He spent a few minutes playing with the idea of refusing it and enjoying the last day of his agreed holiday leave, but he was too fond of those he cared for and his conscience soon got the better of him. Cursing the unpropitious February weather, he left the house, slamming the door behind him.

Geri was left alone with Ed and the two sat silently in the living room, lost in thought. Geri was confused and curious as to how a place as light-hearted as Benidorm could fail to lift his spirits. His age-old remedies for joy appeared to be failing him, and this terrifying possibility seemed to necessitate some heavy pondering. Forcing his mind to focus he began audibly to hum and haw. Within seconds he realised that this was a complex matter, and it would thus be prudent to prioritise these reflections over all other commitments. So, filled with conviction, he picked up the phone and - again - rang in sick to the warehouse, and - again - blamed bad prawns for his indisposition. To his relief the call went straight to voicemail, and upon leaving a message, he quickly turned off his phone, lest some jobsworth should try and return contact. Keen not to slip from investigations into sleep, he settled with crossed legs and an upright back upon the couch. Inspired by a Sherlock Holmes book he had read on holiday, he was excited by the idea of embarking upon indefatigable contemplations, and readied himself for a long day by pulling a thick blanket around his shoulders and lighting a duty free cigarette.

He sat there a while blowing ribbons of smoke, coaxing his

internal monologue to calm and cease, and slowly creating space for his mind to examine itself.

He recalled that the last time he had deployed this method of enquiry had been more than a decade ago. During this period, an unfortunate blip in sanity had allowed him to succumb to the dreary dreams of West Lothian schooling, and he had woken up one morning to find that he had been working at a bank call centre for a year. The rationale for this eluded him, but somehow, he had become lured into this mundanity by the promise of promotions and pay rises somewhere on the dull road to death.

On this day, ten years ago, he had also taken sick leave, and spent it considering what trajectory had led to his anaesthetised half-life. He had sat rigid for an hour or two, with his eyes squinting and his mouth contorted in concentration, establishing the cause of his lamentable path. This- he had discovered - was that he inhabited no job-related sense of ambition, so had allowed others to prescribe him their own ambition of 'freedom'. 'Freedom' for most in West Lothian, was simply financial success, which was seen as a method of providing one with the means to do as one wished, a 'freedom to do'. Whether spurned by family memories of poverty down the pits, or just motivated by nouveau riche ambition, wealth was indisputably the symbol of success and the key to freedom there.

Converse to this outlook Geri had reasoned that there was another very different kind of freedom. This was the 'freedom from'. In his case he hoped this would be to create a life free from the idiotic demands of society. Somewhat serendipitously, he had just heard Bob Dylan's quip that, 'a man is a success if he gets up in the morning and goes to bed at night, and in between he does what he wants.'

This struck a chord with him, as it seemed to describe a richer freedom than the financial one he had unwittingly laboured towards. Moreover, it was distinctly less troublesome to attain. Indeed, his private wishes for his days were simple and inexpensive, consisting mainly of, good company, cheap wine and loud music. None of them in moderation.

At this stage in his deliberations, he had begun to look forward immensely, to finding freedom from outdated societal conventions, especially those that frowned upon the consumption of alcohol, between Mondays and Fridays. He laughed now, remembering how alcohol had still been a relatively unknown acquaintance to him then. Undeniably he had already had a pleasant introduction to it, but their relationship hadn't yet grown to be the close one that it now was. That had taken further acquaintance to develop into the tight partnership they now had. Yet if truth be told, it seemed recently, alcohol and he had somewhat outgrown one another, sticking together out of habit, not love, in an ever more abusive relationship.

Alcohol's caprices were though very much a recent realisation to Geri. Ten long years ago, debaucherous nihilism had offered a delightful escape, and freedom from dull expectations. At that time, to die for insanity had seemed the obvious choice compared to living for mundanity. So, in the chase of wild company, large whiskies and all the mad joys that could be found, he had decided to throw caution to the winds, and followed Mighton to Bedford. Most Brits dream of starting again upon the French Riviera or in a lofty Manhattan Apartment, yet it was in the brick lanes of Bedford that Geri had dreamed of finding freedom. In these pastures new, he had enjoyed a decade of indulgence, and had chosen only sporadic jobs that held no promise of progress with which to trap a soul.

'T'was fun, there's nae denying that' cried Geri spontaneously to the tobacco-stained wall that judged him with its silence. Yet, as he now admitted to himself, his lifestyle no longer brought purely, unadulterated joy. Instead, it increasingly brought liver aches, mood swings and existential vexations. At the age of twenty, death had seemed a trivial matter, one of little relevance best left for a later day. But that was changing. Whether invited to or not, death and the questions it posed, now walked a little closer. Its cold hands had greeted a companion or two of late and Geri began to worry if what he had once called freedom had become the very chains than fettered him.

His head ached from all this thinking, so he raised himself from the couch and strolled to the kitchen for a moment of respite. The dingy room smelt of stale cooking fat and old cat food. Fumbling through the pile of unwashed crockery, he gave a triumphant exclamation upon finding a mug devoid of mould. In the time-honoured British tradition, he eased his stresses by boiling some water and preparing a large mug of milky tea.

The day outside looked as grim and grey as it had in the morning, and Geri soon gratefully returned to the comfort of the couch. He swaddled himself in woollen blankets and enjoyed blowing hot steam from his tea onto his face. Upon hitting his golden beard, the vapours transformed back into liquid, becoming fronded there like copper, dew drops. He sipped the scolding liquid cautiously and found it to grant his desires for a calm and comfort. It was, he thought, a quintessentially, British sort of satisfaction, that could be granted by a grey, insipid, beverage. The sort of which, brings confusion to the refined green tea drinkers of continental Europe. He smiled wryly at the thought of feeling an affinity to any kind of 'Britishness', albeit only in regard to tea.

Always keen to spill tea on Geri's lap, Ed jumped upon him and curled up a drooling ball of fur. Between the wonders of tea and the warmth of his feline friend, Geri was soon rejuvenated and ready to face the maze of his own mind again.

It occurred to him that, his notions of freedom were somewhat limited, if they were to be based within the binary of being 'free to do something' or 'free from something'. Certainly, they were luxurious states to achieve, but in themselves, they didn't lead to a deeper sense of freedom and concerned only his relationship to the physical world. He didn't believe in a soul, but nonetheless it felt like some greater essence of his being was left unfulfilled.

Indeed, achieving one desire did nothing to quench the thirst for the next desire. It was a self-perpetuating cycle, leading to nowhere, greed or death.

Death was nothing Geri fancied for the time being, and he shivered to think of the string of his own existence being cut too short. Once he had thought a fast life and a young death would be his middle-fingered farewell to society's leaders. But now he found himself cackling out loud at his own foolishness, musing that, if the elite noticed his passing with regret, it would be solely for the decrease in alcohol and tobacco revenue. Sadly, an indisposed drunkard posed no threat to them.

Then there was the nature of greed, it occurred to him with horror that chasing one drink and thrill after the next, in the name of freedom, was little different from the elite chasing personal profit from one unethical deal to the next.

Geri was stirred from his thoughts by Ed wriggling in his sleep. He realised he had forgotten to drink most of his tea, and that it had grown a skin on top. His head now throbbed uncontrollably, and he let thinking slide for a moment, concentrating instead on the gentle lullaby of Ed's snores.

In this calmness he was hit with an epiphany. This came in the form of a recollection of a book he had read on Da Vinci from which he had been astonished to learn that the artist's inspirations were not calculated by thought but were instead the spontaneous fruits of moments of mental stillness. Moreover, most of the artistic bums and musicians he knew in Bedford, also claimed that their greatest creative creations came from some place of inner stillness rather than their own thoughts.

Exhausted by the agonies and fruitless labour of his own thinking, he gave the technique a try. He remembered some of the instructions from Paddy's failed attempts to teach him to meditate, and concentrated on finding spaces between the relentless monologues in his mind.

He sat a while, watching thoughts arise and letting them depart, all the time keeping a loose concentration on the flow of Ed's purrs. At first the process was deeply relaxing, but he soon became restless and irritable. Where was the lightning flash of elucidation? Where was Paddy's promise of a direct encounter with a greater reality beyond the linguistic symbols and grammatical conventions of thought?

'Feckin' hippies!' he snorted out loud.

'Ayewis promising paths tae paradise, but too stoned tae gie the right directions!'

He gave up on any hope of an answer, cast Ed from his lap, and began hunting in Mighton's jacket for enough change to purchase a pint at The Bear. His humour soured as he found none, and he vented his irritation towards Paddy for his stupidity and towards himself for having such overwhelming emotions.

It was during this pique of agitation, that a new understanding of freedom spontaneously appeared before him, blessing his aching mind with a much-needed moment of clarity.

'Ya feckin' dancer!' he cried.

'Ah ken whit real freedom is! Its tae notice aw whit's going on aroond ye, and inside ye, and tae choose how tae respond tae it.

No just believe in, an' act on yer ain stupit, cunty thoughts. A'm fair mad at Paddy, and oan impulse ah could pick up yon phone an' call the lad a fanny. Or a can calm doon, let the thoughts go, and mind myself he's good an' bad like the rest o' us.'

'Ed, ya furry bawbag! Here's the deelio! Freedom's being aware o' yer thoughts and feelings, no a slave tae them!' he called to the cat.

'Real freedom's nae from something or tae do something! No at a deeper level anyways. Its tae ken yer ain manky mind, an deal wi reality in a way ye wish, 'sted oh believing yer thoughts an actin' oan blind impulse. I'll see the world first hand, 'sted o' being lost in ma bias wee heid!'

'Don'tcha see this is the truth o' it all, Eddy baby?! That ye cannae change most things, but ye can change how ye relate tae them. Ye can choose tae forgive or hate, tae write yer ain reality! It's no aboot yes tae that thing, an no tae that thing, abstinence or overindulgence, black or white. It's aboot balance, choices based oan kennin' the truth o' yer ain mind and madness.'

Deeply triumphant with these conclusions, he rang Paddy, towards whom his mood had since changed drastically. He shared his revelations with Paddy, but received only the irritating suggestion, that if he wanted to know his own mind and learn how to respond to reality, then he should perhaps start training it through some meditation or yoga.

Hoping for a response to his illumination – that came with less hippy demands - Geri rang Mighton.
To his surprise, Mighton answered immediately despite being at work.

'Whit is it Geri? A'm comin' up tae the end oh ma break, and dinnae want it ruined hearing you've burnt the hoose doon?'

Geri began to respond but Mighton interrupted, 'And see if yer locked oot again, ah swear tae Christ, if ye smash that windae, I'll..'

'Calm doon Mighton. A'm ringing tae tell ye, I've discovered whit freedom really means and it's no whit we've been thinking.'

'Geri! Hae you been eatin' thae funny mushrooms fae the park again? Whit the fuck are ye interrupting ma break tae tell me this for?'

'Mighton, listen sir. It's like that thing Satre, said, aboot the true voyage of discovery not being in travelling far to see new places, but in having new eyes to see with. A've got new eyes an' ah can choose the legacy ah leave behind!'

'Keep yer poncy quotes tae yersel! Legacy aye? Very good hen. Whit the hell dae ye mean? An' whit ye oan aboot new eyes for, has yer Da paid for laser eye surgery?'

'Eye surgery?! Whit the feck dae you mean man?! I mean it's all aboot how ye see things and being aware, no just being confined tae yer thoughts an' impulses. Am gonna take a walk doon the Bedford back streets an' ah promise ye, I'll notice mair beauty an' life there noo than we did in a week in Benidorm!'

Mighton snorted, 'Aye? You'll see nought but a deid cat an' auld shopping trolleys. But if yer oot an aboot go an pick up some chilli noodles and keep them for when I get hame?'

Feeling generous in his new found freedom, Geri instantly agreed, prompting Mighton to ask, 'Are ye sure yer feeling alright?'

'Never better, Mighton, never better! Like Scrooge waking up on time tae make Christmas jolly!'

Mighton paused, 'Well in that case will ye pick me up some smokes and ice cream for the freezer?'

'Nae bawhair at aw! I'll notice every goddamn second as I'm dain it tae and every second will be a miracle of a life lived wi intention an' attention!'

Mighton laughed, 'Geri, yer a strange creature, and ye sound like you've joined a cult, but ye've fair improved ma break! Enjoy yer alleyways an' deid cats and I'll catch ye later! Oh, and dinnae go getting any saintly ambitions, coz yer too ugly to be painted on the Vatican walls!'

Geri hung up the phone in high spirits, pulled on his boots, and swaggered out the door. Standing in the cold mists, of the late afternoon Geri thought the world had never looked more beautiful.

'Who needs a holiday, when you learn tae put new contact lenses in,' he thought, and walked down the gloomy street with a grin.

Chapter 18 – A Walk by Blackness Bay

'Time to shut this book, coz our tale it has been told
Time to start another coz sweet Miss Fortune favours the bold
My ripped tonic stained trowsers like me are growing old
And summer dont last forever, lets move on before the cold'

The Romany Rogues - Outro (Sweet Life) [19].

Deep in the woods near Blackness Bay, beads of dew were clinging to the branches in suspended clusters of pure white light. Autumn had dressed the woods in splendid, golden clothing and planted a lingering death kiss of frost upon the leaves. Wisps of mist hung ethereal in the air, punctured by gentle sunbeams, which made their way lazily through the colourful canopy. It was a still and noiseless place, save the creaking of a tree and the occasional chirp of a bird.

Suddenly, a noise broke the silence. A ruby-bearded man was relieving himself against an oak, whilst staring up at the sky and gibbering loudly. Unfortunately, like most men, his ability to do two things simultaneously was somewhat limited and the urination process appeared to water his boots as much as the tree.

'Paddy! Look at that!' he cried, thrusting a finger upwards at small bird. 'Whit truths it wordlessly proclaims! Nature dissnae lies, dissnae shroud itsel' in dogma an' manifestos! Ah whit we could learn if we had time tae blink an eye ootside, a chance tae live in the woods and be a part ah whit we are, tae piss in a world o' beauty, no in some vile chemical contraption!'

'Or on a shoe!' remarked Paddy with a toothy grin.

'Whit? Oh aye' said Geri glancing downwards unperturbed. 'They're only work boots an' were needin' a cleaning,' he said

with a shrug.
After giving his boots a quick rub on the muddy grass he then proceeded to saunter onwards with his friend, his fly down, his chin up, and eyes squinting jealously at the feathered creature overhead.

Geri and Paddy ambled aimlessly, crossing the brown burns of peat, and shuffling lazily through moulding mounds of beech leaves. The russet skeletons of which clung to the boys' shoes, temerarious and reckless, glory bound upon one last ride to God knows where. The wild abandon of the leaves reminded Paddy of a story he had read, of a dying woman, who had become so infected by the 'mad' joy of a last-minute understanding of her own impermanence and inherent interconnectedness, that she had escaped from a geriatric home, and attempted to hitch hike to Afghanistan. When asked why she had replied, to bless the world with a smile of humble acceptance. Perhaps 'madness' is the key to liberation, thought Paddy and winked a green eye at the leaves.

The woodland world was rich with the smell of decomposing fauna. It was a deep earthy aroma, that subsumed the beauty of both life and death and the continuum of their symbiosis.
Geri pointed at the sky.

'That wee birdie, I bet it inhabits a rare auld nest and it didnae pay for it wi' thirty five years o' its life. Oh no! It dissnae pretend tae own it fer eternity, disnae fight against bureaucracy or a rich cunt for its humble right tae be there. 'Stead it goes tae the woods, builds a cosy hame, and uses it as long as it needs tae use it. That's real civilisation man, why the fuck can we no dae that!' he said seriously.
Paddy released a chuckle which leaped up and down several octaves, like a pubescent boy hiccupping. He gave Geri a friendly hit on the back, and cried, 'Your impassioned today, me auld mucker! But I dinnae deny a word you've said. One of these days we'll build a cabin deep in the woods wi' the rest o'

our mates, an' what a merry little gang we'll be. A goat fer milkin', some tatties for eatin', soil in oor fingers and space made fer dreamin' and singing'.

Geri smiled and sighed, lost in a silent utopia in his head. He combed his fingers through his flaming beard and said slowly, 'We're livin' far fae our real hame brother. I dinnae know whit the solution is but I'd rather try an' be part of it than be perpetually part o' the problem, trapped in a pointless job that's nought but a poison to this planet an' my soul. Aw I needs a simple life, an' good company, I can live by nature's rules and instability.'

Paddy laughed again, his manic eyes shining while the fat, black caterpillars that framed them danced up and down with enthusiasm.

'And I'll tell ye somethin', else man, we need nature more than it needs us an' nae mistake! Christ, we cuid be like stewards of the woods an' hills brother! Workin' wi God's green earth, no against it. Scotland's nae good though, there's nigh on nae woods left, just gridlocked phonies and burnt heather deserts for toffs tae shoot in. An' dinnae get me started oan England! It's as wild as the shopping mall in Livi. Hmmm, we must think where the forests remain and assemble the troops!'

Geri laughed, saying, 'There's plenty ah wild beasts in Livi, that's fer sure!'

Paddy punched him jokingly and they ran and stumbled through the trees, hitting each other with sticks and throwing piles of leaves into the sky.

That evening they were joined by Mighton, who was also on a home visit to the old country. A quiet spot with a fine view was found and they camped in there in the woods near South

Queensferry. Mighton erected his tent and was agitated to find it to be peppered with cigarette holes and missing a pole.

'Geri, I lent ye this tent brand new last summer ya clown! Whit the fuck happened tae it man, were ye campin' durin' a bad day in Baghdad?' Mighton grumbled.

'You ken how it is, a man stumbles after a jar or two an' wi' no intent o' evil happenstance occurs,' replied Geri. 'An' besides, now we'll see the sunrise fae bed'.

Mighton snorted, saying, 'Sunrise! Aye, nae wonder we'll notice it, we may as well be sleeping under a hanky for aw that's left o' ma tent!'

Nonetheless the three friends enjoyed an evening round a campfire, telling tales, singing songs and burning their fingers in an attempt to cook a can of beans. As the sun sank the stars came out to play and the friends lapsed into a wistful silence. All of them became lost in the distant lapping of the Forth and the crackling fire.

Over breakfast a pact was made not to return to Bedford but to find a way to live a life less ordinary amidst the trees and lakes. To dare to experience nature unrefined and to find the conditions required to notice this fleeting and bizarre thing called life and the companions made throughout its winding roads. Such moments of enlightenment appear in many folk's lives, when one sees that a Friday night can no longer be called freedom nor a bulging wallet success, and these friends had their moment of clarity and decided to act upon it while they were young enough and foolish enough to dare. They would they hoped, at least attempt, to walk upon a simpler path, one less trodden, the middle way that often lies unseen somewhere between the standardised and sanitised and the bad livered and blood-shot eyed. They would search for that quiet place both inside and out. A place that I hold hope that someday more may learn to call home.

Whether the collection of misfits migrated to the great forests of Romania or Sweden remains a mystery, but it is known that after that unassuming morning by the sea, Geri never returned to work at the warehouse again.

As the sun sinks on this story and on the deeds of these rare creatures I have the honour to call my friends, it feels poignant and fitting to quote the eternal words of the Welsh barbarian and bard Ivor Ryder-Jones.

'If you feel yer born in the wrong place, at the wrong time, then you're right where you're meant to be! See all those boring cunts who fit right in, an' smugly seem to have it all sorted, what are they gonna question, what are they gonna change, what reason have they got to spend their lives singing with the freaks on the street, or howling poetry at the moon? If modern society rejects you - for gorging on bin food or sleeping on strangers couches in order to escape mortgages and permanent contracts - well then you're living with eyes wide open. If Marx and Jesus and Buddha had felt at home in this insane slaughterhouse, we call civilisation and just consumed themselves numb, then what pale and feeble words would they have given us instead of love and truth? None of our heroes fitted the fabric of this place. So, if you feel your born in the wrong place and time my lovers then live proud and loud wi' a smile on yer filthy faces, 'coz ye're right where ye're meant to be!'

Quotations Reference List

In order of appearance.

1. Leonard Cohen (2019) *Listen To The Hummingbird.* Columbia Records and Legacy records

2. William Butler Yeats (1919 & rev. 1920). *Later Poems.* London. Macmillan Publishers

3. Donovan (1965) *Try and Catch the Wind.* Pye Records

4. *Tintern Abbey by William Wordsworth.* The BBC, viewed 07 December 2020, http://www.bbc.co.uk/poetryseason/poems/tintern_abbey.shtml

5. Robert Sencourt (1971). *T.S. Elliot: A Memoir.* New York. Garnstone Press

6. Hailey Lind & Juliet Blackwell (2007). *Brush With Death: An Art Lover's Mystery.* New York. Penguin Group

7. Gary Taylor & John Jowett (2016). *The New Oxford Shakespeare: The Complete Works.* Oxford. Oxford University Press

8. Emily Dickinson (1986). *Selected Letters.* London. The Bellknap Press of Harvard University Press

9. Screechinth C (2016). *Oscar Wilde and his wildest quotations.* Kindle Edition

10. Betina. J. Wittels & Robert Hermesch (2008). A*bsinthe, Sip of Seduction: A Contemporary Guide.* Colerado. Speck Press

11. Virginia Woolf (1989). *The Essays of Virginia Woolf - Volume 1.* San Diego. Harcount Brace Jovanovic

12. Woody Guthrie (1945). *This Land Is Your Land.* Folkways Recording Company

13. The Corries (1996). *Those Wild Corries / Kishmul's Gallery.* BGO Records

14. Robert Louis Stevenson (2019). *Edinburgh: Picturesque Note.* London. Throne Classics

15. Dominic Behan (1957). *The Patriot Game.*

16. John Gill (2009). *Book of Wisdom.* Xulon Press

17. Slavoj Žižek (2002). *Welcome To The Dessert Of The Real!: Five Essays on September 11 and Related Dates.* London. Verso

18. Walter Sullivan (1972) *The Einstein Papers: A Man Of Many Parts.* The New York Times, viewed 07 December 2020, https://www.nytimes.com/1972/03/29/archives/the-einstein-papers-a-man-of-many-parts-the-einstein-papers-man-of.html

19. The Romany Rogues (2019). *Outro (Sweet Life)*